To Bubbles
lots of love Kirbs

WHAT A COUNTRY

A tale of every day life in a suburban pub...
or maybe not!

PAUL KIRBY

ISBN: 978-1-09838-463-0 (Print)

ISBN: 978-1-09838-464-7 (eBook)

To my good friend Kevin, who persuaded me to persevere
with this story.

CHAPTER 1

On his release, having served three years of a five-year sentence, Joey Dell was determined he would never spend another day in prison. This one had felt like a ten stretch. What had really got to him this time was the ease with which Islamic extremists seemed able to convert cons to their ideology.

Dell was fifty-two and about five foot ten. He had dark brown hair with a very slight hint of grey and a scar to the side of his left eye that carried along down the side of his nose. He also had a scar in the middle of his forehead where he had been gashed with a broken bottle. He was well built, not fat, and menacing in appearance.

Waiting as Dell walked out of the prison gates was his longtime friend and local bookmaker Albert Kinsley, on hand to give Dell a ride home as he had done so many times before. Albert was a good few years older than Dell at sixty-nine, with grey hair. He had a big Chelsea smile of a scar that ran more or less from ear to ear and a big beer belly to match. But most people probably knew him by his distinguishable rough, gruff, booming voice.

Everyone knew when Albert was in the building. He and Dell had been friends since Dell was a youngster visiting one of Albert's shops. Albert had a betting shop on the High Street just down the road from the pub the boys now frequented, which was owned by Dell's old school pal, "Mucky" Mickey Staines. The pub was a favourite with Dell's villainous mates and Albert's punters alike, so it sat well with both men. However, for whatever reason, while Dell was inside Mickey had gotten a business partner named Bill Winters and that was going to complicate things in the future.

Dell had left a large amount of cash with Mickey, which had been kept in the safe. This was not uncommon, as Mickey was "safe as houses" and one of Joey's most trusted pals. He had been looking after the gang's money on and off for years.

After exchanging the usual pleasantries and greetings, Dell explained to Albert about the radicalisation going on in jail and how he had no intention of making any return visits of any kind. He was actually thinking of getting a real job and going completely straight. Albert didn't believe a word of it and responded by telling Dell all about Mickey's new partner and how he loved a punt on the nags and how much money he generally lost. Dell's answer to that was, "Well, let's drop into Mickey's and have a couple and catch up with the news."

"Also," replied Albert, "there's a right pair of idiots just started using the pub, Dick and Bart Durley."

"Are they brothers?" asked Dell.

"No, worse! They're a father and son double act. A right win double, You'll spot 'em quick enough, Joey, my son. You'll smell the bullshit straight away."

"No! No! I've had a bellyful of that over the last few years. So just make sure you keep the cunts away from me."

"They'll be all over you," Albert laughed.

"Durley, eh? That name rings a bell. Well, are we having a few today, Big Burt?" Albert was commonly referred to as Burt, after his shop, Big Burt the Bookmaker's (not to be mixed up with Bart).

"'Course we are. Got Baz and Tel coming to meet us in the pub about one-ish with my son and whoever else decides to show their face," said Albert with a big grin on his big scarred-up face.

"Good, 'cause I need to go back to my flat and get cleaned up and get the horrible smell of prison off me for the last time," Dell replied.

Back at his flat Dell quickly showered and got a fresh change of clothes and then off they headed toward Mickey's for a meet-up with the "boys" for a beer or two and a quick catch-up— also to arrange a proper business meeting with his partners in crime, Barry Ronald Richards, known as "Ice Cold" and that's not just because his initials were BRR, and Terry "Torrial" Funnel. Dell also wanted to make sure his money was still safe with Mickey and to start making plans to get it back out earning. Albert informed Dell he was also holding money in his safe at Big Burt's for the boys, which he understood Dell also had a share of.

Waiting at the bar when they arrived were Ice Cold and Torrial with a greeting of "Flowery, how are ya?"

"Flowery" was a slang term for cell, a friendly reminder of Dell's time spent in one. Handshakes, back slapping, smiles, jokes, stories, and everything else were in abundance that day as the boys were reunited. The whole mob filed in over the course of the afternoon and when he got the chance, "Flowery" mentioned the money in the safe. Mickey assured him that it was safe and well and that he hadn't laid a finger on it. Happy days!

The Durleys were standing on their own at the other end of the bar and could see that a bit of a gangland gathering had emerged in their new local. They wanted to be a part of it. They had heard loads of stories from others about this little firm and Dell in particular and were chomping at the bit to get acquainted with him. "Yeah, this could be a life-changer for me and my son," Dick muttered to himself.

Age sixty-five, Dick was nearly bald with darkish greying hair that was very thin and wispy. He had a medium build with a proper beer gut and a vacant look about his slightly pockmarked face. He also had a distinct, annoyingly high-pitched voice that had earned him the name "Squeaky" and had contributed to his unpopularity with just about everyone who had ever met him.

"You what?" Bart asked his dad.

"Ah, nothing, just thinking to myself. Another drink, son."

"'Another drink, son?' Thought we were going."

"Well, see that lot over there? I think we should hang about a bit and see what happens. 'Cause if we play our cards right, we could be on a nice little earner," Dick stated in his most irritating voice. He meant well, but just couldn't put it into effect. In reality, he was a no-good, cheating, lying nonce who had spent his whole life trying to pull the wool over everybody's eyes!

Dick and Bart moved along the bar and tried to listen in on what was being said, partly to see if there might be a business opportunity, and partly to see if they might get to find out something incriminating that they could use to their own advantage should such an occasion arise.

Bart was slimly built with thinning wispy ginger hair very similar to his father's. He was also slightly pockmarked around his nose, a result of mild acne as a teenager. Along his left eyebrow ran a small scar caused by a friend with a golf club in an innocent accident during secondary school, although Bart liked to brag that he got it in a fight during the football violence years. He was soft-spoken with a face that had thinned due to drug abuse. He was six feet tall.

As the Durleys manoeuvred themselves into a good position, in walked Gerry Funnel, the twin brother of Terry. He joined the Durleys at the bar.

Gerry used to work for Dell and company, but Dell wasn't keen on him at all and had never trusted him in the slightest. Flowery was a bit of a homophobe, to say the least, and as Gerry was a regular crack cocaine user and a user of every other narcotic for that matter, Dell felt he was neither reliable nor to be trusted in stressful situations. He also talked too much. This was probably why he had gotten friendly with Bart Durley recently as Bart was also a regular user and very convincing with his bullshit stories. They seemed a good match. When Dell spotted Gerry, he was not pleased to see him. He leaned over to whisper into Big Burt's ear: "What's that cunt doing here? And who are those smarmy-looking twats with him?"

Albert looked along the bar and said, "Fucking hell, Joe, that's them Durley pricks I was telling you about this morning and they were at the other end of the bar twenty minutes ago."

"So what are they doing with that batty boy?" asked Dell.

"Dunno. Didn't even know they knew each other. Best watch what we say from now on—that's a win treble there that is of no effing good to us at all."

Now seemed a perfect opportunity for Dell to say he was looking to get back into work. Dick Durley's ears pricked up when he heard Dell say he was looking for a job, although Dick didn't know at that precise moment the man who had said it was the infamous Joey "Flowery" Dell. Dick paused and thought to himself that when the opportunity arose, he would introduce himself to the man. The Durleys had heard the odd story and rumour here and there, but neither one of them knew who Dell was. That was until Gerry told them. Now both were even more eager to introduce themselves and to offer Dell some work, perhaps cleaning people's homes, offices, or even windows.

For the rest of the day, Dell managed to avoid the dreaded Durleys, who eventually both sloped off home, thinking there was always tomorrow. As they exited the pub, in walked a very stressed-looking Bill Winters, Mickey's new partner. He was a wiry individual with big ears, a long nose, a sallow complexion, and drawn cheekbones. He seemed to have a permanent downtrodden look about him that said, "Nobody loves me." Bill and Mickey had worked together a few years before in a Soho sex shop, hence the name "Mucky" Mickey.

Back then Irishman Bill had always had a little bet on the horses and kept it very simple and under control, but his gambling habit had spiralled out of control and he was in well over his head. He'd been placing extremely large bets on a far too regular basis and as the betting shop was just up the road from the pub, the glad recipient of Bill's huge losses just happened to be Big Burt. Drinking plus gambling is a lethal mixture and as both were Bill's favourite pastimes, he was now in serious debt.

When Bill learned Joey Dell was out of prison and drinking at the pub he had a financial stake in, his chin hit the floor and he turned white. What was he going to do now? He knew he was in serious trouble as he'd been helping himself to the money in the safe. He had been replacing it with old newspapers that he'd cut to size so no one would notice.

CHAPTER 2

A couple of miles away at the Islamic Centre, even more trouble was brewing and the man banging the loudest on the war drums was an extremist known only as "The Ayatollah." He spread hate like most people spread jam. His ideas involved death, destruction, and terror for the unsuspecting British public. He was a great manipulator and had had no trouble, in a very short time, getting together a would-be terror cell, which oddly included a British woman.

Karen White was an unusual recruit, about five foot six, Caucasian and extraordinarily pretty with proud cheekbones, brown eyes, black hair, pronounced lips, firm breasts, and a body to match. She had been married to a British soldier who was killed while fighting the Taliban in Afghanistan. This had had an incredible effect on her, as she and her husband had been planning to start a family on his return. Now at the age of just twenty-eight, she was a widow and her dreams of becoming a mum had shattered. Her anger and bitterness had been vented on the army and instead of feeling contempt and hatred toward the organisation that killed her husband, her hatred had turned toward the establishment and against the British people in general. Karen had turned to Islam for comfort. This was a very mixed-up woman and pure evil and hatred now bubbled in her veins like some kind of witch's potion.

For Karen, it wasn't a religious thing—this would be her revenge. Revenge for the loss of the life she wanted and the life she could have had. But life doesn't always go as planned and even during her blackest moments, this wasn't in any way what she had thought her life would become. She now had no doubt about her future path. She even came to despise her name, Karen, as she thought it sounded too much like Koran, the book she was now obsessed with. So she started to call herself Cairo. This was a name The Ayatollah approved of and it put a smile on his face whenever he heard it.

Not too much was known about The Ayatollah, just that he came from Iran. As he was on a fake passport, nobody even knew his real name. He was tall, a good six feet four, a sinister-looking man with a long oblong head, long grey beard, large pronounced nose, and deep-set cheeks. He spoke with a deep melodious voice. He had penetrating black eyes and those who saw him could easily imagine he had an evil past. But he had a presence and when he spoke, people listened.

Two other men had started using the Islamic Centre on their recent return from fighting for ISIS in Syria—Imran Badini and Hussain Dasti. They were lifelong friends and had learned many terror-related skills in Syria. They were both London born and bred and in their late twenties. They were known to the British authorities and were suspected of very horrific crimes, including beheadings, although they were not thought to be part of the infamous "Beatles," as other ISIS fighters had come to call them. This little band of brothers (and sister) had all met originally at the infamous Finsbury Park Mosque and now they all frequented the Islamic Centre, which just happened to be smack bang in the middle of Joey Dell and his little firm's "Manor." This was a surefire recipe for disaster.

The friendly neighbourhood terrorists considered the local Islamic Centre a low-profile venue that was not as well known as Finsbury Park, and therefore the Centre became their headquarters. They didn't bother to try to recruit any more would-be terrorists for their cell as The Ayatollah wanted to keep well under the radar. Besides, his three new recruits would be more than capable of doing the job he was planning on their own. Now firmly rooted on Joey Dell's turf, they set about trying to mingle as best as possible without drawing too much attention to themselves. However, they didn't know they were in fact very much on the radar as they were being closely monitored by MI5 and the Anti-Terror Squad.

Badini and Dasti were in charge of fundraising for any mission that lay ahead and had gotten friendly with an Asian man by the name of Ifty Khan who happened to be the owner of a local taxi cab company. Ifty was very well known in that part of London as he had been operating in the area for quite some years. Amongst the local Pakistani community, Khan was a bit of a legend, one of the first and one of the very few Pakistani men to mix in English and Asian circles and to get on equally well with both. The English people he knew all called him "Shifty" Ifty and he loved it. Ifty wasn't exactly a straight flier and had a reputation for being able to get his hands on both bent and honest gear. What ever you wanted generally Ifty could get it. When he wasn't driving his cab, he spent a lot of his time drinking down at Mickey's pub. He got on well with the boys there, including Dell. Dell didn't mind him as he had known him for years through the pubs and his cab company, but he did throw a few funny glances in his direction sometimes. He didn't fully trust Ifty and certainly would never do any sort of business with him.

Gerry Funnel, however, was a low-level drug operator who wasn't that bothered about who he did business with, and he did trade with Ifty. Gerry was thirty-eight with a fair, curly mop of hair. He had a much thinner face than his twin due to years of drug abuse; it was almost drawn in appearance with a rough and rugged complexion. He was broad shouldered and around six feet tall. Ifty had decided to introduce him to Badini and Dasti, as they had mentioned they were looking for a trustworthy drug supplier who could keep them supplied on a regular basis with whatever narcotics they needed.

Gerry was not only Terry's twin, he happened to be homosexual, though you wouldn't really think that on meeting him. This didn't sit too well with Terry, who was far too macho to want to even try to understand his twin brother's sexuality. It was also almost certain that this information would not have been well received by the two Asians Gerry was about to do business with.

Ifty had done narcotics business with Gerry before, so his introduction to Badini and Dasti was regarded as a safe one for all parties involved. As the ISIS recruits set about their fundraising campaign, The Ayatollah went scouting for a suitable site for what he hoped would be his first act of terror on British soil. He moved swiftly about town from site to site with the evil tenacity of an Arabian falcon, his eyes shifting from side to side, hardly even blinking until he would stop to visualise the destruction he might cause. He didn't stand out too much either as hundreds dressed like him walked the multicultural streets of London. He wasn't aware, however, that his every move was being very closely monitored by MI5, as were the actions of all the members of the group. He was a determined man, but to pull off his plan, he was probably going to need some help from above.

With the treasury department of the cell now earning some money, thanks to their introduction to the feminine one of the Funnel brothers, and The Ayatollah scouring the streets for a perfect target, the scene was set for a battle of strangers and opposites.

CHAPTER 3

Dell woke up the next morning at the usual prison hour of around six, only this morning he was feeling the effects of yesterday's drink and drug binge that had taken place in the Country Life pub in celebration of his release. He was a free man and he intended to stay that way. He lay back on his bed and thought. He'd grown used to being alone after a couple of fair-sized stretches in the nick, but this time he was considering a life free of crime and everything that went with that.

Where was his ex-partner, who'd left with their young son, Harry? More importantly, how was young Harry? His ex had left him because he couldn't stop doing the things he was doing and keeping the company he always kept. He was in more than a little doubt over his future. After all, it was his first morning of freedom and he wasn't too sure about the way forward—he certainly didn't know the way back. He was chomping at the bit to get back to business. This part of Dell's persona had no reservations at all. He would do anything to get what he wanted.

After a few hours of nursing his hangover and watching daytime TV, he decided to ring the pub to see about getting some of his money out of the safe.

"Hello. The Country Life pub," said the Irish voice at the other end of the phone.

"Alright, Bill, it's Joe. Is Mickey about?"

"Err, err, sorry, who is it?" stammered Bill.

"Joe, Joey Dell."

"Ooh! Joey, sorry, I didn't recognise your voice there. I'm sorry, Joe, no, no, Mick's not about at the minute. Can I take a message?" He had a very good idea what Dell was ringing about.

"Just get him to ring me when he gets back, please, Bill?" said Dell.

"Yeah, yeah, mate, 'course, leave it with me Joe, mate," stammered Bill once more.

"Thanks, see ya later." Dell hung up the phone. *Fucking hope not*, Bill thought to himself. Bloody hell, what was he going to do? He had lost over half of Dell's money in Big Burt's shop and as things stood, he had no way of paying it back. He knew full well what Dell and his boys were capable of and he didn't fancy any of it.

Dell thought no more of the conversation and returned to the sofa.

When Mickey returned about twenty minutes later, Bill shot off a bit lively without telling him Dell had rung. Poor old Bill, he'd only gotten involved with Mickey and the pub as a way of keeping himself out of mischief after getting out of the porn shop game. Keeping out of mischief, eh? That was a laugh. He'd gotten himself into more trouble than he'd ever been in in his entire life. Bloody gambling! It had started out as a bit of fun to pass the time, a few quid here and there, and then as often happens, the stakes got higher and higher until it looked like he might have staked his life.

Bill sat in the park pondering his future, saying a few Hail Marys here and there and praying to God for a miracle. He could always go to Ireland and hide out somewhere. Then, as he sat there in despair, his mobile rang. He looked at the number, fearing the worst, and saw that it was his brother-in-law over in Ireland.

"Hello, Fergus. How are you?" inquired Bill in a slightly miserable tone.

"Hello, Bill. It's Fergus."

"Yes, I know. That's why I said, 'Hello, Fergus.'"

"Oh, sorry, Bill. How are you?"

"Ooh, not bad, thanks, Fergus."

"How's ya luck, Bill?"

"Rubbish. How's yours?"

"Not bad, not bad. Now, listen to me, Bill, I have something for ya."

"Good, 'cause I need something. Is it a gun, Ferg?"

"No, no, don't be fucking stupid will ya? I have some horses for ya, but you gotta keep them to yourself."

"Horses? Now where am I going to keep em?"

"Shut up, Bill, and listen. You know I have good connections in the racing game over here in Ireland. Well, there's a big scam being pulled this afternoon. Do you have a paper there?"

"Ah, hell, Fergus, I'm in enough trouble because of the nags as it is."

"Bill, listen to me. This is your big chance to earn a good few quid. It'll get you right back on top."

"Ok, Ferg, go on then. What is it?" asked Bill, thinking he'd got F-all to lose.

"Right, Bill, there's a gambling syndicate over here and you know the man but I won't say his name. Well, they've pulled it off before and my man tells me they're doing it again today. This very afternoon, Bill. Now, do you have a *Racing Post* there, Bill?"

"No, Ferg, I don't."

"Well, go and get one and call me straight back."

Bill sat there for a second shaking his head in disbelief. *This can't be happening to me*, he thought. He hurried off to get a *Racing Post*, thanking the good Lord as he went. His prayers may just be about to be answered. Bill was not normally of a nervous disposition, but the release of the notorious Joey Dell and the gambling away of the man's money had all of a sudden turned him that way. Bill purchased his *Racing Post* and then got back on the phone to Fergus, his potential great saviour.

"Hello, Ferg, it's Bill here."

"Ah, Bill, do you have the *Post* now?"

"I do, Ferg, I do."

"Well, turn to Leopardstown, will you?"

"Right, got it, Ferg, but could I just ask, does the man in Ireland, does he have the initials BC?"

"That's right, Bill, he does."

"Bee Jeessuss. Thank Christ for that."

"Okay, Bill, they've been planning this for a couple of years now, so make sure you keep it to yourself. If it gets out, they'll shoot me for certain, so they will."

"Don't worry, Fergus. I won't, I won't. I need this right now more than you do."

Fergus gave Bill the names of four horses running that afternoon, two at different courses in Ireland and two in England. None of the four had run for at least a year. They were all at small meetings, so they had a far greater chance of winning while not creating great betting interest. They were all big prices and all guaranteed to win. Game on.

"Thank you, Fergus, what sort of bet should I do then?" asked Bill.

"Well, Bill, don't go placing big bets now; we don't want alarm bells ringing."

"I can't be doing big bets anymore, Fergus. What are you having on?"

"Just before the first one goes off, Bill, I'm having a hundred (e/w) on the Acca."[1]

"Is that all, Ferg? You're not going to get rich on that, are ya?"

"Don't be so daft, Bill. Have you seen the prices of those things? If the first one wins, you've got almost two grand going on to the next one, man. What's wrong with you, man?"

"Okay, I'll do the same then. What do ya think the chances are, Ferg?"

"Pretty fucking good, Bill. Like I said, this has been two years in the planning and you know yourself how good these boys are."

"I do, Ferg, I do," said Bill with a feeling of utter elation and relief. "Thanks, Ferg, I'll go and have a look now."

"Be sure to keep it under your hat, Bill, for Christ's sake, and good luck. I'll speak to you later."

Bill looked at his watch and saw he had two and a half hours before the first race. What was he going to do with his time? He didn't want to go back to the pub just in case Dell had gone there to pick up his money. If he found out, Bill knew he was a dead man, or at least a very injured one.

Joey was making a speedy recovery from his hangover and decided to give the pub a ring again to see if Mickey had returned. He had and he answered the phone when Dell called.

"Hello, the Country Life Public House." He made the place sound very posh and upmarket.

"Mickey, is that you?" asked Dell.

---

1   An accumulator in which all four horses have to win or be placed, and the money builds up if they win or are placed. (The e/w is place money.)

"Yeah, it's me. Is that you, Joey?"

"Yeah. Am I alright to come over and grab a bit of scratch, please, Mick?"

"'Course you are, Joe. How you feeling today, mate? Good little drink yesterday and good to see you out and looking well."

"Thanks, Mickey. Yeah, it was and good to see you too. Not feeling too bad now to be honest, but I felt pretty s**t this morning."

"Well, you're entitled to, mate. A lot of people turned up in the end, didn't they?"

"Yeah, they did. Are you there all day, Mick?"

"I am, mate. Bill's out, it's his day off, and the bird that's on today doesn't start until three."

"Tell you what, Mick, I'll come over about three-ish then, if that's alright with you?"

"No worries. See you then," said Mickey, putting the phone down.

CHAPTER 4

By the time Dell got himself together, it was probably about half past three, which was the same time Bill was sitting in Big Burt's watching his investment. He was already one horse to the good with the next one about to go off. Bill was understandably very anxious and worried that something was going to go wrong. Why hadn't he just lumped on each horse with a single bet and been done with it, rather than doing an accumulator as well? He was reliant on the next three horses winning to get him out of trouble. If they all came in, then happy days, but that scenario seemed a long way off right now.

As Joey sat in one of Ifty's cabs, Mickey didn't feel any of Bill's anxiety. In fact, he felt quite relaxed and had another pint while he waited. When Dell finally walked in all smiles and happiness, he and Mickey greeted each other like long-lost friends for the second time in as many days. Mickey poured Dell a pint and after a bit of a conversation led him upstairs to the safe. They had taken that journey together plenty of times before, but what they saw when the safe was opened this time changed the mood completely. Dell's stash of cash had diminished since his time away, and it certainly wasn't mice. Both men looked at each other in astonishment as piles of newspaper cuttings were pulled from the bag.

"What the fuck?" both men said in unison, staring at each other.

* * *

Meanwhile over at Big Burt's, Bill Winters had just landed his second winner in the Acca and he'd just got his second single up too. Not fortunes in front, but in front and still with the potential to be much richer by the end of the day. Knowing the score with the Irish, Bill was starting to count his winnings, if not also his lucky stars. Well, they had got two up, why couldn't they pull off two more?

* * *

After asking a few questions, Dell took what was left of the cash, which by now was less than ten grand, and asked Mickey to ring Big Burt. He needed the advice and guidance of his older, wiser, and trusted friend.

Mickey rang the shop, but Albert wasn't there. It was a young girl who answered, and she'd only been there for a couple of weeks. Normally, Albert would have been there poking his nose in to make sure everything was going alright, but as it was only small meetings in England and Ireland, he felt it was alright to take his wife, Janice, for a bit of shopping at Westfields in Shepherds Bush. Why not? He thought if it got too painful, he could leave her with some dough and get himself over the Country for a couple. Dell might come in for one or two as well.

By now of course this kind of thought was getting painful, as Burt wandered from shop to shop, dragged behind Janice. He kept looking at his watch. If he heard "Do I look fat in this?" one more time, he was off. They'd been there all this time and she hadn't bought anything yet. Another shop visited and still nothing.

"Janice, love, I've had enough of this now," he bravely said, looking at his watch yet again. Janice looked at him with that look women give you when they're disappointed with you and replied, "Well, it didn't take you long, did it?" He sighed.

"That's the last time you come shopping with me, Albert bloody Kinsley. You always do this to me, you do."

"Do what?" he asked.

"Make me go home when we've only just got here," Janice replied.

"Only just got here. Only just got here three hours ago, you mean," said Albert with an irritated expression.

"Well, just give me some bloody money and I'll meet you in the pub later," Janice said, giving another one of those looks.

"Ah, love, are you sure? I can't leave you here by yourself, can I?" he said with a fake pained expression.

"'Course you bloody can. Now give me some money, and I'll get a cab and call you when I'm on my way."

"Are you really sure? Okay then," said Albert, digging in his trouser pocket for money, feeling very relieved. He pulled out a nice big wad of crisp lobsters (£50 notes) and asked, "How much do you want?"

"Erm, you might as well give me ten of them then," said Janice with a completely straight face.

"Ten?" Burt said in a rather loud voice. "You'll be here until Christmas. You ain't spent F-all all day and now you want a monkey" (£500), said Albert, irritated.

"Oh shut up, Burt, you know I can't shop with you huffing and puffing in my ear. Just give me the money and go to the pub," she encouraged in an "I've now got the hump" tone. Burt counted out ten 50s and passed them over, gave his wife a peck on the cheek, said goodbye, and headed toward the car park as quickly as he could.

Once he'd found his motor, he opened the door, then the glove box. He pulled out his mobile phone and turned it on. There were no text messages or answerphone messages, which was just how he liked it. Burt made a call to the Country and spoke to Mickey. "Where are you, Burt?" asked Mickey.

"Just about to leave Westfields and come over to you. You sound a bit agitated. Everything alright, Mick?"

"Well, not really, Burt. Something's happened."

"Nothing serious, I hope."

"Serious enough. Dell is doing his nut."

"Ah no, why, what's happened?"

"I'll tell you when you get here."

"I'll be as quick as I can, mate," said Burt, putting the phone down. If Dell was doing his nut, something had happened, and Burt didn't like it. His mind raced during his drive over to the pub. Who the hell had gone and upset his old mate. Surely not the Durleys. Surely not even they could be that stupid. He parked the car behind his shop but didn't bother to pop in. He just hurried down to the pub.

Inside by now, Bill Winter was in a far more relaxed and happy mood having gotten the treble up. There seemed no reason to think the fourth wouldn't oblige. The girl on the till had no idea a bet of this size was three quarters in and that she should have alerted Burt when the second one came in. Then Burt could have started to lay off money elsewhere to minimise his losses. But, as hardly anyone was in the shop that day, she had become bored and was on her mobile most of the time, texting her boyfriend, checking Facebook, and doing all the modern things youngsters do when they should be working, which in her case meant checking the shop's computer to see if any big bets were going to be landed, and if they were, letting Burt know so he could deal with the problem. But in this case, Burt was just as guilty as she as he'd left the phone turned off in the car. She wouldn't have been able to reach him anyway, but neither of them knew that.

Bill sat quietly and nervously in the shop by himself waiting for his last horse, in what was going to be more than just a life-changing bet. Just half an hour to go before the off. Bill couldn't wait. This was it, he told himself. He was either going to be out of the mire or much deeper in it. Bill was confident and nervous at the same time.

While Bill was quietly contemplating life, Burt walked into the pub to find Mickey at the bar, together with an extremely angry-looking Dell.

"Alright, boys?" asked Burt, knowing they weren't.

"Let me get you a drink," said Mick, "then we'll go out the back and explain what's happened." Mick got Burt a pint of his usual and the three of them walked out the back to the kitchen. Mick locked the door behind them.

"Must be serious serious," said Burt.

"Burt, remember the morning you picked me up from the shovel and you told me about Bill's gambling?" asked Dell.

"Yeah, yeah, 'course I do."

"What sort of money was he putting on, do you reckon?"

"Well, pretty big stakes to be honest, Joe. Sometimes a few hundred at a time, sometimes a few grand. Why?" asked Burt a little nervously.

"Well, we went to the safe earlier to get some of my money, and most of it has gone, replaced by newspaper cuttings. And only Mickey and Bill have the combination and it definitely weren't Mick, so that leaves Bill," Dell said through gritted teeth.

"Fuckin' 'ell," replied Burt. "The betting has been going on for a good few months now, maybe longer. You reckon he nicked your dough then?" asked Burt.

"Sure looks like it. And now I'm gonna make the thieving cunt pay, Burt," Dell's voice took on a more sinister tone. Burt had seen this before with Dell and he didn't like it.

"No, don't be too hasty, Joe. Let's think it out."

"I have, Burt. I've got a nice bit of handiwork put away. I'm gonna blow his thick paddy brains out," replied Dell.

"You can't do that. They haven't shut your cell door yet, for fuck's sake."

"You watch me, Burt. He's a dead man. He's gotta go. I can't have this. No way, no fucking way."

"Mickey, talk some sense into him, please. He's only been out five minutes. They'll throw the key away, for Christ's sake."

"Yeah, he's right, Joe. I know you're angry, but killing him ain't gonna get ya money back, mate, is it?" said Mickey in a calming sort of way.

"You know he's right, Joe," Burt reassured. "Come on, let's go back into the bar, have a beer and a think and consider our options, and whatever happens, don't let on to anyone what's happened. This has to stay between us three for the moment. Just try and act normal." This was why Dell always sought Big Burt's advice. He had a fatherly influence on him and the seventeen-year age difference made Dell respect Burt all the more.

Over at Big Burt's, the fourth horse romped home, leaving Bill an extremely relieved and happy man, although he wasn't going to show it in the shop. He just sloped out, clutching his betting slip, and headed back to the park. This was a life-changer for Bill. He would be free of the infamous Flowery Dell forever. Well, that's what he thought anyway. Bill got his mobile out of his pocket as he neared the park bench he was on earlier and phoned his brother-in-law.

"Fergus, you little beaut, ya," he bellowed down the phone when Fergus answered.

"I know, Bill, I know. Wasn't that fricking great? I told ya, didn't I, Bill, I fucking told ya!"

"Yeah, you did, Ferg. Jeessuss, the bookies must have lost some serious dough there, Ferg," said Bill with the biggest smile on his face possible.

"Fuck me, have they, Bill, millions I would say because those boys don't bet small, do they?" replied Fergus.

"No, they don't, Ferg, that's for sure. Oh, thank you, Ferg, thank you. You just saved my life, so you have."

"Well, I'm glad about that, Bill. I'm now off down the pub to celebrate."

"Okay, Ferg, and be sure to say hello to my big sister and tell her I love her dearly and I'll be over to see her very soon."

"Will do, Bill, now you go and enjoy yourself, mate," said Ferg, hanging up.

Bill walked away more than just a happy man. He felt alive again. As he bounced through the park like a spring lamb, he suddenly had a bad thought. *I should have put that bet on with one of the large bookmakers like Corals or Ladbrokes. Why did I do it with Big Burt? He is a small independent book-maker. I might have ruined him and he is a big pal of Dell's too. This could turn out terribly after all if it ever gets out.* He paused. But this was an Irish sting he'd gotten wind of. What the hell, hopefully no one would realise. He could've just gotten lucky and picked the horses himself. Doubtful, but he could have, couldn't he? Looking at the situation now, Bill thought it best he just went home and had a little celebratory drink indoors by himself. He would then go to Burt's in the morning to hand over his betting slip when the dust had settled. Looking on the bright side, he could pay Dell back and just say he'd borrowed the money. He just hoped news of the betting sting didn't get out. And as Burt's shop had taken the bet, it had no option but to pay out.

CHAPTER 5

Back in the pub, Burt, Dell, and Mickey were having a drink, having calmed Dell down a bit and gotten him to consider his options. As it stood, the plan for the moment was to act as if nothing had happened and to carry on as normal.

Burt was telling the boys how he'd also been a victim of crime that day, having been robbed by the missus at Westfields. Of course he had no idea he'd just been taken to the cleaners by Bill as well. The girl in the shop, Sharon, would lock the place up if Burt wasn't there, so he had no need to go back that day. He could enjoy a few pints and go home once Janice had arrived. It was a pretty normal day for Burt, really, nothing out of the ordinary, except for Dell's missing money. He was sure that could be resolved. All was normal in the pub too. Then the Durleys walked in, all squeaky voices and bullshit.

"Look out," Burt said to the other two as he heard that really annoying voice that belonged to Dick.

"Alright, lads?" he squeaked.

"Yeah," they said together in the same bored, uninterested tone. The Durleys must have gotten the message—they didn't try and join in. They stayed at the bar while the other three sat at a table talking very quietly amongst themselves.

Not so the Durleys, though. They were both talking loudly, making sure everyone could hear and desperately trying to impress anyone who would bother to listen. The poor barmaid had to listen to it all while appearing interested. Bart started banging on about a boat he'd gotten that he kept moored up at Poole Harbour, a forty-five-foot motor cruiser that slept six people, that cost him a fortune, and that he intended to use more now the weather was picking up a bit. He asked the barmaid if she fancied a day out on it with him, but she politely claimed seasickness.

Mickey just happened to overhear this conversation. He listened in as it all sounded very believable and very convincing, but it was Bart Durley telling the story. Nonetheless, Mickey took it all in, thinking to himself, *Those boys love to spin a yarn, don't they?* Then he thought, *Supposing Di had taken him up on his offer, what the hell would he have done then?* That really would have been funny, watching him trying to wriggle out of it. Probably all bullshit as usual, but what if it wasn't? *Hmm*, Mickey thought for a moment. *I'll store that*.

At that moment Janice walked in, armed to the teeth with bags of shopping. "Well, you certainly got something then!" said Burt, greeting her with a hug.

"Yeah, and you owe me another hundred and fifty quid."

Spitting out a mouthful of beer, Burt said, "*What*?!" then looked across the table to Dell. "Bloody 'ell mate, and you think you've been hard done by. I've got this for the rest of my life."

Dell smiled for the first time that afternoon and then got up and kissed Janice on both cheeks. "Nice to see you again, Janice. How are you? What would you like to drink, love?"

"Ah, Joey, good to see you too. You are looking very well, my love, all things considered, and thank you, I'll have a large dry white wine, please, if you don't mind."

"My pleasure," replied Dell as he got up and ordered more drinks all around. Now, with Janice joining them at the table, the conversation took a turn for the better and they were able to take their minds off the money incident—for now, anyway. And to make things even better, Gerry Funnel turned up and joined the Durleys at the bar, keeping them away from Dell's little crowd. They were still itching to get acquainted with Dell, but at the moment, it just wasn't happening for them.

After a while, Mickey leaned back in his chair and couldn't resist asking Gerry in a loud tone if he'd ever been on Bart's boat. "Nah, but he's told me all about it, Mick. Why?"

"Well, I was thinking of organising a sea fishing trip and wondered if he would take a few of us out for the day, that's all," said Mick sarcastically.

"No problem," Bart chipped in. "Just let me know and I'll sort it."

"Okay, then. I will." Mick turned back to talk to the others.

The reason Gerry had come in to see Bart wasn't to have a drink with him, although he stayed for a couple; it was to supply him with drugs, cocaine, in fact, which he would take home to the missus. They'd be up half the night talking shit and watching porn and all the rest of it.

The time was getting on a little bit now and Dell announced he was going home after a final one. Burt and Janice agreed. They'd had a long day and were quite happy to do the same.

"Give Shifty a bell for us, could you please, Mickey?" Dell asked.

"Yeah, no worries, mate," and he did just that. "Ten minutes."

"Lovely. Thanks, mate," replied Dell. They agreed to meet up again the next morning to discuss the day's events. Little did any of them know the day had been more eventful than anyone could have imagined.

CHAPTER 6

Burt was the first to rise the next morning, even beating Dell's early morning prison routine. He had to open the shop himself and be there before the staff arrived.

He jumped in the shower and washed his big frame. Once out of the shower, he dried himself, then wrapped a towel around his waist and ran hot water for a shave, going extra carefully around the cheek-to-cheek scar he had sported for over thirty years. Now that Burt was in his late sixties, the Chelsea smile he was so well known for hadn't faded any since he had first received it during a fight with a man of Arabic descent on the Edgware Road.

Burt had thought long and hard as he shaved about the missing money Bill Winters had quite obviously stolen. Bill would be a very lucky man if he was to get away with a scar just twice the size of his. Anyway, he certainly didn't want his friend Dell killing Bill, and he certainly didn't want Dell going back to prison. Burt finished his bathroom routine, dried his face, put on his dressing gown, and made for the kitchen. After a nice cup of tea, he went to the door, got his newspaper, and sat down for a read before making his way to the shop.

The headlines screamed of yet another terror attack. This time, in Paris, yet another vehicle had been used to mow down innocent people going about their everyday lives. "Fucking wankers, cowardly no-good bastards," Burt muttered to himself. He turned to the financial section, checked his shares, and had a quick read before heading to his betting office. As he strolled the mile and a half to work, he kept turning around when he heard a car approaching—he was starting to feel a little unsafe walking the streets of London these days, as were many other people. Who knew when these extremists might strike again?

Burt reached the shop in one piece. As he walked through the door, he bent down and picked up all the day's broadsheets and the two copies of the *Racing Post* delivered each day to the shop, supposedly giving punters all the information they needed to make some easy money. Burt put one copy of the *Racing Post* on a table in the shop and kept the other copy to read himself. He looked at his watch. It was only seven thirty and the shop didn't open until eight. He had plenty of time to have a good read and see what was happening in the world of racing. He looked around the shop, smiled, and thought to himself that Sharon was a good girl. She always left the shop nice and tidy and did everything he asked her. *I think I'll keep her on*, he thought.

Burt's eyes lit up as he saw the headline that dominated the front page of the *Post*, which was very different to that of the national papers. "IRISH BETTING SCAM COSTS BOOKIES MILLIONS." Burt chuckled to himself. This sounded interesting. As he read on and turned to the inside page, he shook his head in disbelief. *Well, I never. They've got some cheek, these boys*, he thought, and kept on chuckling.

Having read the story about the Irish mob, Burt had a quick look at the day's meetings to see if there was anything he fancied as he didn't mind the occasional flutter himself, but not in his own shop, obviously. Burt switched on the screens and his computer at the front desk. He saw a notification flash up on his screen. "CAUTION, BIG WINNER." Burt wasn't overly worried as he'd seen these warnings many times before, and they would only amount to a few hundred pounds. But to his shock, this one was very different. This one amounted to a few hundred grand. *What the fuck?* thought Burt. *Who the hell has pulled this on me? Why didn't Sharon let me know this was happening? I could have laid a lot of this off. I'm finished. What am I going to do? I can't pay this sort of money out. This will ruin me.* Poor Burt couldn't think straight. He was lightheaded and also very, very angry, upset, you name it, he felt it. Every emotion you don't want, Burt had. What was he going to do?

He sat down with his hand over his forehead and thought long and hard about the situation he found himself in. He hadn't opened the shop up to the public yet and already he was the best part of three quarters of a million out of pocket. Was it worth opening up? He would have to sell his house in Cornwall to pay for this, and if that wasn't enough, he'd have to sell the apartment he lived in with Janice. Janice—Christ, what was he going to tell her? This was one great big mess that needed to be sorted and quickly, before he had a heart attack. Burt was stressed out to the maximum, but he needed to find out who was in the shop yesterday. He would have to ring Sharon and get her out of bed. He needed to get to the bottom of this fast. But there was no bloody answer. *That's great*, he thought. She wasn't due in until 1 o'clock and Burt certainly couldn't wait until then. He needed to know who the punter was with the contact in Ireland that had pulled a stroke on him. "Ireland, Ireland," Burt thought, then a certain name flashed into his brain: Bill Winters.

Bill was already up and about, feeling really pleased with himself on this bright and sunny morning. All his feelings of apprehension had now left him, and before he went down to Big Burt's, he thought he should get himself a copy of the *Racing Post* from the corner shop and just have a look to see if there was any mention of the scam pulled yesterday. Bill didn't think there would be. He'd be alright handing over his winning slip. Bill got the shock of his life when he saw the scam had made headline news. "Shite. No," Bill said out loud as he handed over the correct money while reading the report, without bothering to look up at the bloke behind the counter. He hurried out of the shop and went back to the same park bench he was on the day before. As he read the story, just like Big Burt, Bill chuckled to himself, but of course Bill was on the right side of the scam and Burt wasn't. What a difference a day makes. Burt couldn't prove Bill hadn't picked those horses himself, and fuck him anyway. The shop took the bet and Burt paid up the stake. Bill was owed a nice few quid and that was that.

Burt wasn't feeling quite the same way, but he desperately needed to get hold of Sharon. He continued ringing until she finally answered.

"Hello, Burt. What's up?"

"What's up? What's up?" said Burt angrily. Then he composed himself. It wasn't her fault. She was only doing her job and she was a good girl really, just had a lot to learn. "Sorry, Sharon, I didn't mean to talk to you like that. Were there many punters in yesterday?"

"No, not really. What's this all about? I haven't been nicking out of the till or anything, you know," said Sharon with a bit of attitude in her voice.

"I know that, and I'm not ringing about that. Did you recognise any of the punters in here yesterday?" Burt inquired.

"Not really, Burt. Only that bloke from the pub, the Irish one, you know, the one you said keeps losing his money, he couldn't pick his arse."

"Ah, right, yeah, that one," said Burt. "Did he have a four-horse Acca with a hundred pounds each way on it?"

"Yeah, something like that. I didn't really take that much notice. Why? Did it win?"

"Yes, it bloody well did."

"Cor, lucky git," said Sharon with an element of surprise in her tone.

"Yeah, well, he might be, but I'm in a spot of bother now," Burt said.

"Ah, no. Have I still got my job? 'Cause I like working for you, Burt, I do," she said, creeping now.

"Yeah, 'course you have, Sharon, but I need a favour. Could you come in early, please? I'll look after you, my love, don't worry."

"Yeah, alright, Burt. Give me an hour and I'll be there for ya."

"Good girl, Sharon. Thanks very much. See ya soon then," said Burt, hanging up the phone. Apart from his intimidating exterior, Burt was really a nice, soft-hearted bloke, although he wasn't feeling like it right now.

When Sharon arrived as promised an hour later, Burt shoved a fifty-pound note straight in her hand as a thank you for coming in early.

"Ahh, thanks, Burt. That's well nice of you," she said, grinning like a Cheshire cat.

"Make the most of it. There might not be too many of them flying about soon," replied Burt. He didn't have any sort of smile on his face, apart from the Chelsea smile the Arab had given him.

Next on Burt's agenda was a call to his old mate Dell, asking him to rally the troops in order to decide how to get on top of this thing. Before Burt knew it, Flowery, Ice Cold, and Torrial were at the shop ready and waiting to hear what Burt needed. This must be pretty serious the others agreed, for Burt to ask for all of them. He also wanted Mickey there.

Sharon would man the tills and if Bill came in with *that* ticket, she would have to put him off and tell him he would have to deal with Burt in person. Burt needed time, lots of it, and this was just the start of the stalling process.

Once all the boys were settled in the office, Burt took off his jacket, loosened his tie, and cleared his throat. "Thanks for coming at such short notice, boys," began Burt in his deep, rough London accent. "Now there's been an eruption, a diabolical liberty has been taken, not just on Joey here and on

Mickey for that matter, but I am also a victim of that sneaky little Irish cunt. Read this." Burt threw the morning's *Post* on the desktop so all the lads could read it. There was a couple of deep breaths and a "Jessuss" here and there as Burt began to explain how the Irishman must have gotten wind of the scam from somewhere and then had the nerve to place the bet in that very shop. Sharon had taken the bet while Burt and his missus had gone out shopping, and his phone was off for the best part of the day. Anyway, it wasn't her fault.

Now the big question was, what were they going to do about it? Burt felt exactly the same way Dell had felt the day before. "He's gotta go, Burt," Dell said with an evil snarl on his face. "I told you that yesterday, mate."

"Yeah, I know, I know, and now I've decided to call a rule four," said Burt. Dell now smiled and nodded in agreement, for he knew only too well what a rule four meant. This wasn't the first time a rule four had been called, and this wasn't the first time Dell had been asked to deal with it. He was licking his lips in anticipation. The snidely little Irishman had asked for it, and now he was going to get it.

"What the hell's a rule four? asked Ice Cold Richards.

Burt and Dell looked at each other. Richards wasn't much into horse racing and certainly didn't know the terminology of the game. "Tell him, Joe," instructed Burt.

"When Burt calls a rule four, this is what it means. A rule four is when money is deducted from your winnings when a horse is withdrawn from the race at the starting line. The amount of money deducted depends on the price of the withdrawn horse. In this case, Burt is suggesting we take a very large percentage from Bill because he has pulled a right dirty stroke, or we remove him from the race altogether."

"What race?" asked Richards.

"The human race," replied Dell, his irritation showing.

"You mean kill him?"

"Yeah," said Big Burt as he raised his eyebrows and looked around the room to see what the lads' reactions were. They were all nodding in agreement, which pleased Dell the most because that was what he had wanted to do all along.

"Right, then. How are we going to do this?" asked Dell.

"Well, what about the old motorbike, passenger, gun job?" suggested Terry.

"No, no, we can't shoot him. The Old Bill will be all over us like a rash. It would be too obvious. 'Big winner at Big Burt's gets mysteriously gunned down by a passenger on a motorbike.' No way. We need to make it look like an accident," said Burt with an air of authority in his voice.

Then a smile came to Mickey's face, "Aha! I think I've got it!" He told them how he had listened to Bart Durley the night before bragging to one of the girls behind the bar about the boat he had down on the coast and that had given him an idea. Big Burt was right. They couldn't use a shooter on Bill; it would be far too obvious, and as he felt responsible for the mess Bill had caused, Mickey thought it only fair that he should make a contribution to the solution. After all, it was going to be the outcome that really mattered he.

"So I said to your brother, Tel," Mickey turned to Terry. "Have you ever heard him saying anything about a boat before Gerry? Gerry said he had. Well, there may be some truth in it or there may not, but if he can get access to a boat and we can get him to drive it, well, we might have the perfect scene for an accident," said Mickey, looking around the room at the very serious faces that now stared back at him.

"How does this help us out then, Mick?" asked a rather puzzled-looking Terry Funnel.

"Well, I happen to know that Bill loves a bit of sea fishing. I've never seen him turn down an opportunity," explained Mickey.

"So, what are you suggesting? That we kill him on a boat in front of Bart Durley, then lose his body in the sea?" asked Dell.

"No. I happen to know the Irish twat can't swim, can he?" said Mickey, looking very pleased with himself. "And I'm sure you boys can arrange for him to accidentally go overboard, can't you?"

"Too right we can," chipped in Richards.

"I tell you what, Mickey, my ol' son, I think you might well be on to something here," said a rather impressed-looking Dell.

"Yeah, but you lot seem to forget that prick Bart and his dad are full of it and that he probably doesn't own a boat any more than I do," said Burt.

"Yeah, but I bet he knows someone who does, and just to save a bit of face, he'd probably hire one anyway," replied Mickey.

"Hmm. Well, sod it. Let's give it a go. Sounds like as good a plan as any, and if it doesn't come off, we'll just have to think of something else," announced a very impatient Dell.

Bill Winters was now a condemned man, but it was made clear that everyone should carry on as normal around him and get the fishing trip arranged. When the job was complete, Big Burt would pay Dell the money Bill had stolen, plus a few grand on top. This way, they could all stay out of jail and carry on as if nothing had happened.

But could they really? Dell had only been out of jail for two days, and already he was planning a hit. Not bad for a man who only a couple of days ago was talking about going straight! Not that anyone had taken that bit of news too seriously. When he said it, he probably hadn't taken himself too seriously either. One thing they were all taking seriously was killing Bill Winters at sea with Bart Durley as an unwilling accomplice. It was to be Terry Funnel's job to get the boat trip sorted with Bart given his twin's relationship with Bart. With everyone in agreement, the meeting ended. Bill had been convicted and sentenced to death in absentia, and he still hadn't even been paid out for his bet, and it certainly didn't look like he ever would now. So it was going to be "nice to Bill" time until the big day. The death knell had sounded and the lure was put out for Bill. The aim was to get it taken care of as quickly as possible. The main concern was whether Bart would live up to all that bragging he'd been doing in the pub of late.

CHAPTER 7

Bartholomew Nicholas Durley—the name said it all, really—was a bit of an odd character and very much one of society's misfits. Small in stature like his father, he was a former choirboy in the Catholic Church, where he had been sexually abused by more than one priest. He had then gone on to join the armed forces in his late teens, where he also had had sexual encounters with other males and had failed miserably to become the man his father wanted him to be.

He was confused and didn't know if he was coming or going half the time, and he found the best way to overcome his hang-ups was to hide behind a smokescreen of made-up stories about himself, always trying to impress his dad or anyone else who would bother to listen. Bart's dad always believed his stories as he was a compulsive liar himself and wouldn't know the truth if it hit him straight in the face. Hereditary bullshitters, the pair of them. God knows what Bart's granddad had been like. What made this pair tick? Why did they feel the need to lie about themselves, and about other people for that matter? Who knows? But the boys were about to put them to the test, well, the younger one anyway.

After the meeting in Burt's office, Burt joined Sharon in the shop and eagerly awaited Bill's appearance. The boys went to the pub for a coffee and a chat to discuss a few other business matters. As the four of them entered the pub, Bill Winters' was the first face they all saw. They had to act normal and friendly to Bill, and if the subject of his good fortune came up, they were to pretend they knew nothing about it and look surprised and happy for him. This was going to be hard, but act normal they would and did.

"Alright, Bill?" inquired Mickey.

"Yes, thank you, my ol' son. Morning, boys, and how are you all on this beautiful morning?" replied Bill, with the biggest possible smile on his face.

"Yeah, good, thank you, Bill."

"Morning, Bill, how are you?"

"Yeah, it is a nice day, mate."

"You're looking very happy today, Bill."

"You're in early today, lads. Can I get you a drink?" asked Bill.

"Well, actually, Bill, we've come in for a quiet chat amongst ourselves before the punters start turning up, if you know what I mean," replied Mickey with a wink and a nod of the head. Bill didn't need to be told twice. He got the message and stopped pottering about behind the bar, put his jacket on, left the pub, and headed straight up the High Street to Big Burt's to claim his winnings. Bill knew an independent shop like Burt's wouldn't be holding that sort of cash, and he also knew in his heart of hearts he should have placed his bet with one of the big boys. But it was too late now. He'd done it and he couldn't undo it.

Bill entered Burt's shop feeling a little nervous, to say the least, and was greeted by two stone-cold faces. "Morning, Bill," said Burt, lifting his head up from behind the counter before continuing to turn the pages of the *Racing Post*.

"Morning, Albert, Sharon," stammered Bill as he put his hand in his pocket and pulled out *the* betting slip. He handed it shakily to Sharon, trying his very best to look as calm and composed as he possibly could under the circumstances. Sharon took the slip and stared at it for what Bill felt was a lifetime and then handed it over to Burt, who did exactly the same. Burt got up and put the ticket into the till. A total of over £750,000 flashed up on the screen right in front of the pair behind the till. Sharon gasped and put her hands to her face as if in total shock. Burt looked at Bill and Bill looked at Burt. There was a moment's silence as a sort of stand-off situation emerged.

"Well done, Bill. Looks like you've just had a right touch, me old mate," said Burt.

"Oh, I did get lucky, Burt, didn't I?" replied Bill.

"Yeah, you did, Bill, and it doesn't look like you were the only one who got lucky on those horses. Very strange," said Burt sarcastically.

"Oh, really? Why? Who else backed them, then? I just picked them out myself and hoped for the best, so I did," replied Bill, his mouth now very dry as his nerves got the better of him.

Burt closed up the morning's *Racing Post* and showed Bill the headline on the front page.

"You and half the scammers in Ireland by the looks of it."

"Bloody hell, would you believe it? Us paddies think alike, you know, Albert," said a worried Bill.

"Yeah, I bet you do. You never picked these yourself, Bill. You were in on the scam, weren't you?" said Burt sternly.

"No, no, Albert. I swear to God I picked those horses myself. I promise you so I do."

"Well, you'd better come upstairs to my office, then. We'll discuss this in private," said Burt as he motioned with his head for Bill to follow him. Burt, with a rolled-up *Racing Post* under his arm, opened the door and Bill followed him upstairs to the office. He told Bill to sit down as the two men stared at each other across the desk.

"You've had me over, Bill, haven't you?" said Burt. His tone now had a more sinister ring to it.

"Albert, I would never do such a thing to you, honestly, I wouldn't. Please believe me."

"I'd love to, Bill, but that's difficult after having read this. You lot have taken the bookies for millions between ya and you want me to believe you picked them horses yourself? Don't take me for a c**t, Bill, but I know the rules. My shop took the bet, so I have to honour it. Now, a man of your intelligence must know a small independent outfit like mine doesn't hold that sort of money and you're gonna have to bear with me while I raise the funds to pay you out. As I'm sure you understand, I need time to get the dough together," Burt said, looking straight into Bill's eyes.

"Ah, so you're going to pay me then, Albert?" asked Bill.

"Big Burt always pays up. But, like I said, I need time to get it sorted, Bill," replied Burt.

"God bless you, Albert. You're a good man, thank you so much. I know you have your reputation to think of and I respect that. Take your time and I fully understand that. Thank you once again, Albert, my friend," said Bill, shaking Burt's hand vigorously.

"That's alright. Now fuck off and let me get my head around this, will ya?" said Albert, bringing their meeting to a close.

A very relieved Bill Winters left the office and almost did an Irish jig as he bounded down the stairs. Bill didn't want to go back to the Country Life just yet as he wanted to leave the boys to get on with their bit of business. So he headed back to his park bench and rang Fergus to let him know the good news. Bill was delighted. In fact, he felt every happy emotion there is. Now it was up to Dell's mob to get their wheels in motion so that they too could feel the euphoria Bill was feeling right now.

Bart Durley was the first of their targets and they weren't going to take no for an answer. Bart was in this whether he liked it or not—all that bragging was about to backfire on him. They had just finished discussing who should say what in their bid to get Bart to take them out on the fishing trip and at the same time not let on to Bill that they knew he had stolen the money from the safe when Bill walked in to discover all four men sat around the bar still drinking coffee.

"Do ya fancy something a little stronger, lads?" asked Bill.

"No thanks, Bill, we're just about to go, but thanks anyway," replied Dell.

"Ah, come on now, boys, I've had a little touch on the gee gee's and I'd like to treat you all to a few drinks," Bill said, trying to be a little more persuasive.

"We'll catch up with you later, Bill, but thanks again, mate," Dell continued, trying to be as polite as possible under the circumstances. Richards, a man of very few words at the best of times, just stared at Bill with ice-cold eyes. He couldn't wait to give Bill the burial at sea he thought Bill justly deserved. As the three of them got up to leave Mickey behind the bar, they made their way toward the door. Bill called over to Dell and asked if he could have a quick word with him.

"Yes, Bill, 'course you can," said Dell, raising his eyebrows to the other two as he turned back to face Bill.

"Err, Joey, mate, I don't know if you are aware of this, but I borrowed a few quid out of the safe just before your release from jail and I think it may have belonged to you," began Bill.

"No, Bill, I wasn't aware of that," lied Dell, trying his utmost to stay as calm as possible.

"Well, I'll be able to pay it back shortly as soon as I get weighed in for the bet I just landed, and let me tell you, it's a pretty penny so it is. Oh and I'll give you a nice drink on top for your trouble," Bill said, fiddling around with his hands.

"No worries, Bill, that's very honest of you to let me know. Who did you put the bet on with, anyway?" asked Dell as if he didn't already know.

"Oh, ah, I put it on at Big Burt's," replied Bill a little uneasily, still fiddling with his hands.

"Big Burt always pays, so you're in safe hands there, mate," said Dell, patting Bill on the back in reassurance. "Catch ya later, mate."

"See ya later, Mick," said Dell as he turned and walked out of the pub to catch up with his two pals who were waiting a little way down the High Street.

"Bloody hell," Dell exclaimed. "You should have just heard that no good thieving paddy. Reckoned he'd borrowed money from me out of the safe, but it's alright, he's gonna pay me back as soon as Burt pays him."

"Saucy cunt," Terry and Barry said in unison.

Terry immediately got on the phone to Gerry and asked if he was meeting Bart in the pub later. Gerry said he was as Bart couldn't go without his cocaine fix and was meeting him around five.

Everything was going to plan so far. By tonight they should have a date sorted for the fishing trip, as long as Bart came up with the boat, of course. Terry told the other two it was all good for later and then said, "Oh, while we were in Burt's office earlier, I had a missed call from the Swedish mob."

"Ah, yeah, are they on the want?" asked Dell.

"Probably. My phone was on silent. I'll ring him right now," said Terry.

The boys had a drug smuggling arrangement with another mob in Sweden which was a great earner. The way it worked was they would find a driver to take a couple of kilos of cocaine at a time and drive it hidden in the car door panels up to Sweden from England. After expenses, they usually doubled their money. And as it was about thirty grand a kilo, that wasn't to be sneezed at. Gerry Funnel usually did the driving, but as he had done it several times before, he had recently been replaced by a posh-speaking black fella called David Lightfoot. This replacement hadn't gone down too well with Gerry as he had been paid very well and actually enjoyed doing it, but the boys didn't want to get too complacent and thought it was time for a change. As David had legitimate business in Gothenburg, he was looked upon as a perfect replacement. David also liked the money it paid and was a more than willing participant.

Terry rang Sven from Sweden and, yes, they were on the look for a reload, so arrangements were made for a delivery the following week. Things were looking up again for Dell, only out of nick a few days and the dough was coming in once more. Apart from his little scare involving Bill and the missing money, things were getting quickly back on track.

CHAPTER 8

Later that afternoon, the boys headed back to the pub to continue making arrangements for the killing of Bill Winters. Each man had his role to play, but they hadn't bargained for how easy it was to get Bart Durley on board. They didn't realise Bart and Squeaky were desperate to be friendly with Flowery's firm. Bragging rights were the main reason. And the Durleys also thought they might be in for an earner as well. They could never have imagined in their wildest dreams that the boys were planning for Bart to be their skipper on a fishing trip.

Gerry turned up just before five and Bart and his dad arrived soon after. They stood chatting and having a drink for ten to fifteen minutes before Terry joined them. Bill Winters was sitting at another part of the bar and both parties could see one another. In the middle of this, also sitting at a table, were Dell and Richards, who could also see both parties. Keeping a crafty eye on the lot of them on the quiet and smack bang on centre stage was Mickey Staines. It was perfect positioning for all, and the scene was now set to arrange an accidental murder.

Just as Terry joined the trio at the bar, he heard Dick Durley telling Gerry that Bart was a right hard case and that he couldn't half pack a punch to which Gerry replied, "Shut up, Dick, he couldn't pack a suitcase," and then laughed at his own joke. Dick was always trying to make his son out to be something he wasn't, probably because Bart was also always making up stories about himself. What were these two hiding? It was a constant cover-up. Anyway, Terry heard the conversation and laughed along with his twin and then said, "Alright, chaps? Didn't know you were a bit of a handful, Bart. You should have said, mate." Bart looked down at his pint, embarrassed, and quickly changed the subject.

The four men chatted for some time, which was absolute torture for Terry as he couldn't stand either of the Durleys. But finally he managed to raise the subject of using Bart's boat for a fishing trip on the coast in the next few days as the weather was due to be nice and warm. He mentioned his two friends Dell and Richards fancied it too. When he heard that, Dick's face lit up and he looked at Bart and made little nodding gestures to him. The problem was that unsurprisingly Bart didn't actually own a boat, but he knew a man who did. Bart had to think fast.

"Well, it's being serviced at the moment and I'm not sure when it'll be ready to take out," Bart said nervously.

"Why don't you ring up and find out, son?" said Dick in an overexcited squeaky voice. Dick knew the fella who had the boat would let him use it if he wasn't using it himself. "Okay, leave it with me. I'll give the boatyard a ring," said Bart.

"Ring 'em now, son. I'm sure someone will still be there. It's not six o'clock yet," said Dick a little desperately. Bart went outside and called his mate, who said, "Yeah, sure, the kids are back at school now, so you can use it any day next week if you like."

Bart came back inside and announced the boat was ready. What day next week would they like to go? Terry turned toward Dell and Richards and called out, "What day ya fancy going fishing next week, boys? Bart's gonna take us out."

"Ah, nice one, Bart, that's very kind of you mate," agreed Richards.

"I don't mind. Whatever day suits you really, but I'd rather go earlier in the week. It should be quieter then," Dell said, speaking his first real words to any of the Durleys.

Mickey chipped in as arranged. "Bill likes a bit of sea fishing, don't ya, Bill?"

"Oh yeah, I love sea fishing," answered a tipsy Bill Winters.

"Well, why don't you go with these boys next week? I'm sure you'll be welcome."

"Yeah, yeah, I'd love to, if they won't mind."

"'Course not, Bill. You come along, mate, you're more than welcome," replied Dell gleefully.

Tuesday was the agreed day the following week and as today was Thursday, the boys had a few days to prepare for the demise of Bill Winters.

"That was easier than I thought," said Dell to Richards.

"Yeah, and me," Richards said in a hushed tone.

"Better go and have a drink with 'em, shouldn't we, Baz?" suggested Dell.

"I don't wanna drink with that smarmy little prick or his old man," replied Richards in his normal unsmiling manner.

"Nah, you're right. I'll send over a couple of pints and be done with it. Anyway, we gotta spend all day with the twat on Tuesday. At least Big Burt'll be pleased when we tell him," said Dell.

"Yeah, but we ain't got shot of the Irish cunt yet," replied Richards.

"Nah, but he's as good as gone now, son," said Dell, a wry smile on his face.

When Big Burt eventually turned up in the pub after what was a very traumatic day for him, the stress clearly showing on his face and in his mannerism, he ordered himself two pints. He quickly downed the first like it was a glass of water and then offered the other two a drink as he joined them, leaving Terry to keep the Durleys happy. Dell leaned in toward Burt and quietly said, "All sorted for Tuesday, Burt."

"Really?" asked Burt. "Thank God for that. It's been worrying me all day. Good boys, good boys," Burt said in utter relief. "By the way, Joey, I loved the way you explained the rule four scenario, sheer class my son."

"Easy, Burt, I've had enough practice haven't I?" said Dell with a cheeky grin.

"You certainly have, Joe, you're a good boy," Burt said as he started to gulp down his second pint in as many minutes. The weight of the world seemed to lift from Burt's shoulders as he said quietly across the little round table they were sitting at, "Accidentally. Don't forget."

"Don't worry, Burt. I've already worked it out, but I'm keeping it to myself for the time being. We'll be fine," Dell reassured Burt and Barry. Ice Cold wasn't worried in the slightest. He just wanted to get the job done and to collect his share as always.

Burt continued in a whisper, "I don't need to know the details. Just let me know when it's over and we'll have a square up." He was just happy to get out of this situation at a fraction of the cost and knew only too well he could 100 percent rely on the Flowery firm to take care of business. No more was said about it, and they all carried on trying their best to act normal.

Eventually Terry rejoined the other three and said in a whisper, "What a pair of slimy cunts. That was fucking painful talking to them all that time. Thanks for the support!"

"Yeah, I bet," laughed Dell. They all had another round of drinks before going their own ways, having agreed to meet the next day.

Albert went home to his wife a lot happier now than he had been earlier, and he was careful not to say or do anything that would suggest he'd had anything other than a usual day at the office.

Bill stayed in the pub celebrating his good fortune with a couple of the regulars, happy with his arrangement with Big Burt and looking forward to a nice day's fishing. Poor old Bill. He had taken a liberty with the wrong people and now he was going to pay the ultimate price.

Equally pleased with their afternoon's work were the Durleys, as they thought they'd gotten their foot in the door with the Flowery firm. Although Dick wasn't going, he said he did fancy a day out to the coast, as he would probably pull some young birds. *A strange comment for a man in his mid-sixties*, Terry Funnel thought. Luckily, he didn't have sea legs, otherwise he'd have really thrown a spanner in the works. So, at the close of play, everyone thought they'd had a good day, or at least it seemed that way.

CHAPTER 9

The Sopranos' Café, as it was known to one or two of the locals in this part of West London, was the venue for the next morning's meet. Joey and Barry were the first of the gang through the door, and were greeted by Mario, the owner, who was very pleased to see them. Mario was Italian, born in England, and had taken over the café from his father, Mario Senior. He looked the archetypal Italian café owner with his dark, swept-back hair, small moustache and large striped blue-and-white butcher's apron. He shouted out orders to his staff in a strong, theatrical Italian accent.

The café was strangely enough called Mario's, but for the clientele who frequented the place, it was nicknamed "The Sopranos" after the TV series of the same name about an Italian mafia family. Every type of villain you could imagine used Mario's. It was like a breakfast safe house for all the rogues on the west side of London, and the Flowery firm members were regulars, of course.

Mario hadn't seen Dell for a few years obviously, as he knew he'd been away to "college" again. With his usual warm smile and handshake, Dell was welcomed back with a big hug from his favourite café owner. As he looked around, he noticed a few familiar faces already tucking into their morning's refreshments and just about everyone greeted Dell with the respect he'd earned over the years. If anyone in there that morning didn't know him personally, they'd certainly heard of him. It was like he'd never been away and he was loving it.

"Just the two of you today, Joe?" asked Mario politely.

"Well, not sure, Mario. Terry'll be here soon, but I'm not sure if Albert is coming."

"Okay, no worries. I'll get your teas for you. Find a table and I'll bring them over."

They sat at a big table at the front of the café by the window. The pair of them always liked to be able to see who was coming in and who was outside, walking up and down the High Street, coming into the café, or just hanging about. They liked to keep an eye on things.

Terry joined them within five minutes. Mario told them to order what they liked, this one was on the house. Dell couldn't wait. He hadn't had a decent fry-up for years, and he went for the works—bubble and squeak, egg, fried bread, tinned tomatoes, mushroom, and double sausage.

"Been looking forward to this for bleedin' ages," said Dell, rubbing his hands together excitedly. "The last one I had was in here before I went away. All I had in the shovel was porridge." The others laughed as Big Burt turned up.

"Just like old times, eh boys?" said Burt as he pulled up a chair.

"Yeah, good innit? Anyway, how are you feeling today, Burt? Gotta be better than yesterday, surely?" inquired Dell.

"Yes, thank you, Joey boy, it's just that young Durley twat that worries me," he said.

"Don't you worry about him, mate, Tel done the business last night. Anyway, he'll end up in the same hole as the paddy if he lets us down," Dell assured Burt.

"Yeah, talking of them Durleys," chipped in Tel, "I reckon the old man's a fucking nonce. You should have heard some of the things he was coming out with last night. That was painful, I tell you."

"Well, it wouldn't surprise me if they both were. I won't have fuck all to do with either of 'em," replied Burt in his grisly old tone.

"Well, don't worry, 'cause after Tuesday, you won't have to. They'll be surplus to requirements," Dell reminded them.

"I hope so," said Burt, "and it's no wonder his old woman has a thing for taxi drivers."

"Who's old woman?" asked Dell.

"Dick Durley's old woman, Rita. She left him years ago when Bart was about ten and ran off with one. She came back when she got bored about six months later and Dick welcomed her with open arms, as he could not cope with Bart on his own. But ever since, she's had a thing about 'em," said Burt.

"How the hell do you know that?" asked Dell again.

"It's common knowledge, Joe. Whenever Bart gets on the dust with my brother, he keeps going on about it."

"Ooh, and the taxi fella dropped her back to Dick? That's not 'fare,'" Dell said, laughing and looking at the others, but none of them seemed to get the joke.

"Not 'fare.' 'Fare?' Get it? Taxi fare?" Dell was wasting his time. Even when it was explained, no one found it funny.

The boys scoffed down their breakfasts and ordered up four more teas to wash them down before they went about their day. Looking out of the café window, sipping his tea, Dell spotted a couple walking along the street. The man was dressed in Eastern robes and the woman appeared to be white European, dressed in clothing Muslim women would normally wear. "Look at that cunt," said Dell, pointing at the man in the robes and funny hat. "He looks like Ali bloody Baba. All he needs is a pair of them slippers with the curled-up toes," he laughed.

"Yeah, I bet he doesn't use taxis. He's probably got a flying carpet," said Terry and they all laughed together.

"Yeah, but the worst thing is, the bird with him looks like one of ours," Burt pointed out.

"What is the world coming to? This country's had it," added Ice Cold.

"You wanna see it in the shovel then. You don't know if you're in Bagdad or behind the Berlin Wall," said Dell.

"Probably suicide bombers," said Terry.

"Probably," agreed Dell as he gulped down his mug of tea. They'd just seen The Ayatollah and Cairo for the very first time.

"Well, I've gotta get down to the shop," announced Burt, getting up to pay for breakfast for everyone.

"Don't worry, Albert, it's on me today, mate,' said Mario, waving him away.

"Well, that's very kind of you, Mario. Thank you very much."

"Cheers, Mario, that was bloody lovely," said Dell, patting his rather full stomach. "Worth waiting for that was," he said with a belch. The other two thanked Mario as they all made for the pavement. Burt went one way and the other three stood for a minute discussing the Swedish move and what they needed to do to get it moving. They then walked in the opposite direction to Burt, and after that very jovial breakfast, they knew they had to get down to some serious work.

The Ayatollah and Cairo were on their way to the Islamic Centre, probably to pray or to look for prey, one or the other. Either way, they were totally unaware their movements were being monitored and the monitors had more than likely seen the boys pointing and laughing in their direction. But the truth was, these were very dangerous people indeed and a big threat to the British way of life; change was blowing in the wind.

The chill wind that blew through the spine of West London was felt by neither the Flowery firm nor The Ayatollah's terror cell as both parties carried on as normal. Joey Dell had thought the appearance of The Ayatollah amusing, but in truth, hundreds of men in England's capital dressed like him. His appearance was no longer uncommon, but to many, it was certainly unacceptable.

The Ayatollah still hadn't found a suitable target, but he had time as the fundraising scheme had only just begun and he had set no time limit. A rogue car ploughing into pedestrians didn't appeal to him—too few casualties. And anyway that was old hat and could be carried out by any nutcase, and there were plenty of those about. In his opinion, London was in need of a new kind of terror attack, and he was intent on providing it. Comrades take heed, the Messiah was active. The Western world beware.

The Flowery firm had to get the logistics of the move to Sweden sorted. They needed funds to keep their firm solvent. Did the Swedes have the money ready? Was the cocaine they needed available when they needed it? And was the driver available when they needed him? All these questions had to be answered that day. When a question was asked, these boys expected it to be answered and dealt with ASAP.

Sven, the Swede, was ready when they were but could do with his delivery sooner rather than later. The drugs were there, so that just left the driver. Terry rang him and asked him to come over to the pub that evening. They didn't like to discuss this sort of business over the phone, preferring to do it face to face.

When David Lightfoot turned up in the pub, Gerry Funnel knew a Swedish run was on the cards. He always became jealous and resented David since he had replaced him as the Swedish driver. Gerry had loved doing that job. He loved the adventure and getting away for a few days. He also loved the money. He always looked at it as a paid holiday and the easiest five grand he'd ever earn. He wouldn't have looked at it that way if he'd been caught, of course.

All those years in a foreign prison was a worrying thought that also caused David a lot of anxiety as the time drew closer to leave England for an uncertain journey to Northern Europe. But he also liked the wages of sin and once the drop-off was completed, he didn't even have to worry about bringing the cash back with him, as that was paid into a betting account set up for the Swedes at Big Burt's. Large sums of money were placed on non-runners who had been messaged over to Sweden that day and then money bet on them, so it looked like Burt was taking massive bets from them. Then the money taken for those said bets would be withdrawn and realised in cash. It was a simple way of only risking your investment and liberty on a one-way trip instead of a round trip.

Only out of prison for five minutes, Dell was already as busy as ever. Money was coming in from all directions, and he'd gotten the plan for Bill's extinction firmly worked out in his head. He had no doubt whatsoever that it would go down as an accident and none of them would be prosecuted—well, all except possibly Bart. But he didn't count anyway.

The weekend came and went and now on Monday morning, the day before the big fishing trip, another meet was arranged over breakfast down at the Sopranos' Café. This time, no Mickey and no Burt, as they didn't need to know what Dell had in mind and how the hit would be carried out. Once they had finished breakfast, the trio sat around the table with their heads down, talking very quietly about the day's fishing that lay ahead and what role each man would play. It was a simple plan that was a no-brainer after Mickey had let on that Bill couldn't swim. All three were happy with the plan and all agreed that it would look like an accident all day long.

As they sat back finishing their teas, Dell spotted *that* couple again, walking past the café. "Look, it's Ali Baba again," he said motioning toward the window.

"Cunts!" said Richards matter-of-factly.

The two were still out walking London's streets looking for their target. Although they'd seen various possibilities, they still hadn't found a target they were completely happy with. The Ayatollah wanted a 9/11 type attack, but he knew he was a million miles away from something like that. But still he was determined to cause shock and horror in a type of incident that would reverberate through the hearts and souls of the British people.

It was the big night before the last ride for Bill and the boys were in the pub in good spirits. They were calm and collected. A date with death was a date to keep as far as they were concerned. Also present was David Lightfoot. Money had to be earned, and nothing was going to deter them. Big Burt showed up a worried man. This needed to happen for him if for no one else; he had far too much to lose.

Terry had the job once again of reeling the younger Durley in and finalising the arrangements for the following day. As no one else wanted to talk to Bart, he was left alone. An early meet was arranged for the morning outside the pub and two motors were going to take the five of them to the coast. Bart was too scared to pull out, and anyway his dad was far too excited at the prospect of being involved with Dell's firm to let his boy pull out now. As they spoke, the elder Durley stood jangling the change in his trouser pockets in excitement, a habit he'd had for years and an annoying one at that. Bart was to pick up the unsuspecting Bill at six in the morning for the drive down to Poole Harbour. The others would follow in a separate vehicle.

David was also set for his journey across Europe and up to Sweden for his job that would bring a good few quid back the firm's way. If everything went to plan, it should be a good week all round.

Gerry then turned up and was a little surprised to see his twin brother talking with the Durleys, unaware of what he had planned for the youngster. He was, however, well aware of why David Lightfoot was sitting with the others. The bastard was nicking Gerry's work and he didn't like it one bit. Why had he been dropped? He couldn't see that his drug habits and his low-level drug dealing had rendered him unreliable and vulnerable as far as the job was concerned. He also couldn't see the fact that as David had legitimate business in Sweden and could provide paperwork to prove his trip was necessary (if required), he was a better choice.

All bets were now on. Even Bart declined the offer from Gerry for something for the evening's entertainment. Bart didn't want to oversleep and miss his chance to be the firm's captain, even if it was for one day only.

Bill enjoyed his last supper as only a convicted man could, throwing almost as much liquid down his throat as he was to swallow the next day. He needed to get away for a bit just to release some tension.

Mickey watched the various groups with caution. Did he feel guilty for his part? Probably not, for his partner had now become a burden and what would be would be. Whether he played a part or not, Bill's fate was sealed. Bill had been found guilty as charged and, anyway, at least he was going out doing one of his favourite pastimes. He was going one way or another, so it might as well be doing something he enjoyed. *Get it out of your mind*, Mickey told himself, *you've done yourself and him a favour*.

A very satisfied Dell left the pub around six thirty with a very relaxed Barry Richards and Terry Funnel. They had a date with death and not for the first time felt an early night was appropriate. Big Burt, a little more anxious than the rest, felt it was only fair to have a couple more with Bill as it was he who had called the hit in the end. Had he done the right thing? Did Bill really deserve this? Of course he did, the liberty-taking Irish fool. A good night's sleep was had by all except Burt. He tossed and turned all night, unable to free his mind of the day that lay ahead.

Bill slept in a semi-drunken stupor. He didn't know he was going to be the catch of the day, but he did know he was going to get up the next day and go fishing. He couldn't wait for morning to come and was in bed by ten o'clock.

CHAPTER 10

Dell was the first one up that morning, having finally fallen asleep after playing the "accident" over and over in his mind. He had to get it right or he was going to rot in prison until the day he died. Before getting up he lay there in bed for several minutes playing it back yet again, just to make sure.

Burt was also up earlier than he had to be. He didn't get much sleep at all. Burt wasn't worried the boys wouldn't do the job. He was worried for his old mate Joe. If Joey went back to prison because of this, that would be it. He would never get out again. He would spend the rest of his days there and Burt didn't want that. He kept trying to reassure himself that everything would be alright. He knew Joey knew how to kill and that he had never been convicted of such a crime. And he knew the same to be true of the other two, but he still he worried and wouldn't stop until the job had been completed, properly completed, with no convictions. In reality, Burt had nothing to worry about. Joey Dell had it all taken care of. He, after all, had the most to lose and he knew he certainly couldn't afford to mess up.

Every man turned up on time. Bill and Bart gave them a bit of a scare as they were about ten minutes late. Bill looked a little worse for wear. The boys drew a sigh of relief as the car rounded the corner. "Thank God for that. I thought we were fucked for a minute," said Dell.

"Yeah, me too," replied Funnel as they sat in Richards' Range Rover.

"Nice of you two to turn up," said Dell sarcastically.

"Ah, shut up. I feel like shit," Bill said, and he looked it too.

Bart walked over to the Range Rover "M3, then we'll get on the M27 to Poole Harbour," he said. "You got petrol?"

"Yeah," replied Richards, raising his eyebrows.

"There's a service station on the M27. Shall we stop there for a cup of tea and something to eat?" suggested Durley.

"Yeah, we'll just follow you anyway, so pull in when you want," said Dell, wanting to get away.

"Okay, see you soon," said Durley, getting back into his BMW.

They drove out of West London and picked up the M3 in no time. The traffic was pretty good at that time of the morning, and they were soon trying to keep up with Durley, who was driving like an idiot.

"This bloke drives like a cunt," moaned Richards.

"He certainly does," replied Dell, then continued, "I played out today's scene in my head loads of times last night."

"That makes two of us," said Funnel.

"Did ya? Good. But I want to talk us all through it again. And whatever happens, that little prick in front don't wanna be finding out that this ain't gonna be no accident, because if he thinks otherwise, he won't think twice about grassing us all up," Dell stated.

"Well, let's do him as well then," Richards added with enthusiasm.

"Don't be so stupid. We can't have two accidents on the same trip, can we? Anyway, this one's all been worked out, and it'll look more like Durley's fault than anyone else's. Good innit?" chuckled Dell.

Yeah, it was good, and as he went over and over the scenario time and time again, he finished with "England expects every man to do his duty," just to make sure everyone knew what they were about.

It was a bit of a crazy journey down to Dorset as Bart drove like an absolute lunatic and the boys struggled to keep up with his lane hopping. By the time they pulled in at Rownham's Services on the M27, Richards had the right hump, which was never good for anybody. Was there any need to drive like that? If there was, they certainly knew it wouldn't take too much encouragement for him to do the same thing on the boat. The idiot really thought he was the man, especially today.

Once they had pulled into the service station, Richards said, "Right, from now on, you will drive like a normal person!" poking Bart in the chest.

Durley got the message immediately. But that didn't stop him from saying cockily "Ah, what's up, can't you keep up then?"

"I want to keep my license, you moron!" replied an exasperated Richards, giving a look that left no one in any doubt about how he viewed the situation.

"Ah, oh. Okay then," stammered Bart.

They all went into the service station and got whatever they fancied, keeping the two groups pretty much separated as no one really wanted to associate with Durley and the condemned man. Dell thought it better to mix as they were more than likely to be on CCTV and he wanted it all to look as if they were all mates out for a day's entertainment. His assumptions were spot on. Richards hated the closeness as he couldn't stand either Durley or Winters. As far as he was concerned, a mark was a mark and you didn't try to get friendly. But he got the picture and did as Dell asked.

On their departure from Rownham's Service Station, Durley took it easy on the driving as he realised he wasn't impressing anybody. Once more on the last part of the journey to Poole, Dell ran the boys through the plan yet again and reminded them of the firm's old saying, "We ain't come here to fuck spiders, boys." They all nodded in agreement. They didn't really need reminding in the first place—they knew the saying and lived by its code anyway, whatever it was supposed to mean. In reality, it meant whatever you wanted it to mean. It was designed to confuse, but to unite as well.

When they reached the part of the harbour where the private boats were moored, they all parked and got a day parking ticket.

"Is there any beer on this boat of yours, Bart?" inquired Dell.

"Err, I can't remember," was Durley's reply. Of course he couldn't. It wasn't his boat.

"Well, there was a shop just down the road; I'll go and get some," said Dell. "You go and sort your things out and we'll meet you two back here. That alright?"

"Yeah, yeah, no worries," Durley said, relieved they wouldn't get to overhear his conversation with the harbour master who had been told by the boat owner that Durley was taking the boat out for the day.

"Thought I'd better get some beers for the trip, boys, even a condemned man should be granted a drink before he goes," Dell quipped. The other two agreed as they walked toward the shop.

When they returned with a couple of crates of Stella and food for the trip, Durley and Bill were ready and waiting for them by the motors.

"Everything alright?" asked Dell.

"Yeah, ready when you are," replied Durley.

"Thought we'd get you a few beers, Bill. You still feeling rough, mate?" Dell asked him.

"Thanks, Joe. No, not too bad now, but could have done with a bit longer in bed though."

"For a minute we didn't think you were coming, Bill," said Funnel.

"Ah, no. I wasn't going to miss this. I love a bit of sea fishing," said Bill with a smile.

They all admired the boat. It was a very nice boat indeed. It had a lower deck with a small kitchen and toilet and a little dining area. It could sleep six—very nice indeed.

"Well, I wasn't expecting this," Dell commented as they all had a good look around.

"Me neither. Now this is a bit of me," said Funnel.

It was a lovely September morning, the sun was out, there was a freshness in the air, and you could see it was going to be a nice day. The kids were all back at school, so it was pretty quiet and ideal for what the boys had in mind. Bart drove the boat out of the mooring area and into the main harbour channel, sticking to the required speed limits painted on the buoys that bobbed around and acted as path to the ocean. It was a fair journey out from the harbour and into the Channel passing by Sandbanks and Studland Bay; the scenery was breathtaking. As the boat entered the English Channel, you couldn't see the Isle of Wight, which meant a bit of sea mist was hanging about that would provide perfect cover. There were six fishing rods on board and Durley had purchased some bait at the hut where the boats were moored. No one even asked about life jackets, which was surprising considering Bill's inability to swim.

"When are we gonna start fishing then?" asked Bill keenly.

"Shall we pull up here?" suggested Bart. That's Old Harry Rocks over there." He pointed at some rocks jutting out into the sea like a series of old tombstones.

"Yeah, this'll do for a while. We can always move on if we don't get anything," replied Bill.

The rods were already set up, so all they had to do was attach some bait to the hooks and off they went. The boat sat there for a while and they caught the odd fish, but then they decided to sail around the corner to Swanage Bay and try their luck there.

Bill was throwing the beer down him, still celebrating his win and getting nicely drunk. He was catching a few fish to boot, perfect for what the boys wanted and probably better for Bill. It was now past lunchtime and all the food had gone as the sea air had made everyone hungry. Bart hadn't touched a drop, which was probably the most sensible thing he'd done in a long time.

The mist in the distance hadn't lifted all day, and it was therefore the perfect visibility for the deed. And the boys wanted it to be done sooner than later. Richards was getting impatient and he kept throwing "when are we going to do it?" glances at Dell. With the four of them fishing from the back end of the boat, the time was now right. Dell gave the nod to Funnel, who joined Durley at the boat's wheel. Durley really did look upon himself as the captain of the ship. All he needed was one of those caps that only a captain of a vessel was allowed to wear.

"Nuver beer?" Dell asked Winters, all the time watching Funnel making conversation with Bart.

"Yeah, yeah, why not? I'm enjoying myself," replied Winters happily.

"Go on, son! Get it down ya," encouraged Dell. Winters didn't need persuading to take another as Dell joined him for only his third can of the day. It didn't matter to him; he wasn't driving and the old wife beater (Stella) was the perfect bit of Dutch courage to take the edge off his nerves.

He had a good look around the boat and out to sea. He could see that with the cover of the distant mist no other boats were in sight. So it was time to get Bart to do a bit of showing off. "What sort of speed does this thing do,

Bart?" This was the signal to get ready, also meant to encourage Bart to give the boat some throttle. Not that he needed much persuading.

"Yeah, Bart, there's no speed limit out here and there's no other boats about, so you got a clear run. Open her up a bit," said Funnel, as he stood at the helm with the ever-capable Captain Bart.

"Yeah, alright then. Let's give it some," he said with a grin that said, "Watch me everyone, I'm the dog's bollocks." As Durley pushed the throttles forward, Dell and Richards positioned themselves on either side of Winters. Both men made a grab for Winters as the boat accelerated, each one managing to keep his footing, and with little fuss, they launched Winters over the back of the boat and into the dark blue yonder. "Aaahhh" and a splash was all the pair heard as Winters belly flopped into the wake created by the boat's sudden acceleration. He was certainly no Tom Daley nor, as they already knew, a Mark Spitz either. Winters disappeared, never to be seen alive again.

After a few seconds, the pair turned toward the front of the boat, calling out to Durley to stop. "Man overboard!" shouted Dell as soon as he was sure Winters had gone under. Durley and Funnel turned round together and the smile on Durley's face quickly disappeared as he realised Bill Winters was no longer with them.

"Stop, stop, turn the boat around. Bill's gone overboard," continued Dell.

"Bloody hell, what happened?" cried Durley, not as smug now as he was a moment ago.

"Just turn around. We need to find him quick!" yelled Dell. Richards kept quiet, holding on to the back of the boat, looking out to make sure Winters didn't emerge. He was loving this. His demeanour as his eyes scanned the waters was that of a coldhearted killer.

The boat slowed, then Durley, now panic-stricken, turned her around and went back to look for Winters. He had no idea Bill couldn't swim and was expecting to find him treading water somewhere near where he went in. If anything happened to Bill, he could be at fault, seeing as he was the captain. As the boat hurried around, there was no sign of Bill anywhere. "Where is he?" asked Durley, increasingly worried.

"God knows. He must be somewhere round here, but it all looks the same to me, Bart," Dell said, trying to show real concern. They all looked for Bill, but it was becoming more and more clear he was a gonner.

"What the fuck have you done, Bart? He's nowhere to be seen," said Funnel, the mood becoming more tense.

"Me? What do you mean, what have I done?" cried Durley, his voice now starting to sound like his dad's.

"Well, you are the captain of this boat and you did open her up a bit sharpish, didn't you?" said Dell, laying the blame firmly at Durley's door. "And when you did that, poor old Bill just flew over the back. Didn't you hear him yell as he went over?" Dell continued.

"No! How could I? I was watching what I was doing up front, not watching what was going on behind."

"Yeah, but you did it all so quickly. I don't think Bill was prepared for it. Poor sod, looks like we've lost him for sure now."

"Yeah, you did do it a bit lively, Bart," agreed Funnel.

"Bloody hell, what are we gonna do now?" Durley cried.

"Do you have a radio? We need to alert the rescue services," Dell said calmly, trying to bring a bit of order to the situation.

"Yeah, yeah, there's a shore-to-sea connection thing on this radio here. I...I mean, sea-to-shore. Ah, whatever, I'll try it," stuttered Durley. Even if the others had calmed down, he was still panicking at there being no sign of Bill. The others of course never wanted to see his ugly face ever again. Not the most glamorous underworld killing, but certainly a very effective one.

Bart alerted the rescue people and in no time at all, a search-and-rescue helicopter was out. The boat had to stay put until they were told they could do otherwise. Once they were told they could return to shore, Durley started the engine and this time the boat limped slowly back to the harbour. Durley's showing off had really done for him this time. He was as white as a ghost and looked ill.

"You alright, Bart?" inquired Funnel.

"No, not really. Poor old Bill. It wasn't my fault, was it?" pleaded Bart. "You lot told me to open her up a bit, so I did," he moaned quietly.

"Don't you start blaming us; it was an accident. But you did give some, Bart," agreed Funnel.

Dell and Richards looked at each other with a pleased and satisfied expression, and Dell gave one of those winks that says, "Nice one, mate, job done." He turned to Durley and said, "Don't you start blaming us for anything, Bart. We didn't do anything wrong, did we, Baz?"

"No, mate, nothing," replied Richards.

With the job completed, they knew they were going to have to make a statement, either to the rescue people or to the Dorset police—maybe both, but as it was such a simple incident to explain, no one apart from Durley was particularly worried. They all knew what to say as everything had gone according to plan. If Durley got charged with anything, they weren't bothered. No one liked him anyway, and Big Burt was going to be well pleased. But he wasn't going to be told the outcome until everything was cleared up with the authorities and they were free to go.

The time was getting on a bit as they pulled into the harbour, and sure enough, waiting for them were the coast guard and the police. The trio were well prepared for this, but quite obviously Durley wasn't. His chin hit the deck as he saw the officers waiting by the berth. If his mood hadn't been somber enough before, it certainly was now. He began to shake with panic. It was as if he had something to hide, and as he kept making mistakes while he tried to moor the boat, anyone looking on could easily think his actions were a sign of guilt.

As they all got off the boat, they were asked to "come this way" and led to a building a short distance away used for questioning by the coast guard. First, the boat was to be searched by a forensic team to make sure nothing untoward had taken place on it. Durley panicked when he heard this. This was serious and all fingers seemed to point at him.

They were all questioned separately, and the Flowery firm's statements tallied nicely. Durley's was a different story. His was littered with contradictions and just didn't seem to add up at all. As his tale was completely different to those of the other three, he very quickly found himself under suspicion. The authorities seemed to think he was covering something up.

Dell and his mates were released, but Durley was held for further questioning. The boys all waited around to find out where Durley was, only to be told to go home as he was being held for a while longer. This was music to their ears. They quickly left the building and headed for the motor. No one said too much until they were safely on their way out of Poole. Dell, sitting in the back, was the first to break the silence.

"Ha ha," he laughed, then sat back in the seat looking upward. "Well, it looks like poor old Bart is well and truly under suspicion."

Terry Funnel, sitting in the front passenger seat, turned to face Dell and began to laugh as well. Looking in the rearview mirror, Barry joined in as he drove steadily back to London. Once they'd all stopped laughing, Funnel asked, "When are we going to tell Albert?"

"Pull into the next service station and I'll call him from a pay phone. I bet he's worried to hell about us. Bless him!" replied Dell.

They pulled into Rownham's just before 9:00 p.m., and Dell found a payphone. All three of them stood close by as they all wanted to hear Burt's reaction. Dell dialled Burt's number and he answered almost too quickly. "Hello!" the gruff voice on the other end said.

"Alright, Burt? Weighed in, weighed in," a delighted Dell said, imitating the voice you hear on a racetrack that announces you can go and get your winnings.

"Really?" inquired Burt.

"Yeah, went like clockwork," replied Dell.

"Yeess! Good boys. I knew you'd pull through," shouted Burt down the phone as Dell held it out for the other two to hear.

"I'll come and see you tomorrow, Burt," Dell said, not wanting to say too much over the phone.

"Okay, Joe, thanks for ringing." Burt didn't want to say too much either. He was just happy it was all over. There were a couple of "get in there's" with clenched fists as the boys headed back to the Range Rover.

"Next stop, London. It's been a long day and we've done a good job," said a very satisfied Dell.

"Yet again," commented Richards. And off they went, the contract completed and the job done. Luck had been on their side. Bart Durley was the fly in the ointment, but he never saw anything, so whatever he had made up was going to carry no credibility whatsoever. It was three against one. It wasn't long before Inspector Tommy Butler of Scotland Yard got wind of the fishing incident and he wanted to know a bit more.

CHAPTER 11

Aged sixty, Butler was slightly overweight with an extremely thin face, almost weasel-looking, and a bald head with hair left around the sides and back that he kept short. He had "Policeman" written all over him and a nosy manner to match. He was five foot eleven. He had been a policeman all his working life, including at the Criminal Investigative Division (CID) in West London. He knew Joey Dell and his boys very well, and they were well aware of him too. Butler was never a fair cop and had always kept tabs on Dell's firm. He was now under the command of a much higher authority, and his secret mission was to find a well-respected criminal gang that could be persuaded to become the beacon for a new government approach to terrorist crimes.

Butler had been unaware Dell was at liberty until he'd heard about the Dorset incident. His mind immediately turned to Dell and his cronies. Now a detective chief inspector (DCI) at Scotland Yard, Butler thought of himself as almost above the law and decided to go and seek out Flowery.

Dell meanwhile had agreed to a meeting at the Country Life before opening time with Mickey and Big Burt to go over the events in brief so they were up to speed with what had happened the day before. As they were talking in the bar area, unbeknownst to them, Gerry Funnel had found the door unlocked and entered the premises to collect a jacket he'd left there the previous night. On hearing familiar voices talking in hushed tones, he stopped to listen. He kept well out of sight and stayed quiet, but just managed to get the gist of yesterday's events.

So now already someone else half knew a story they didn't need to know. This might prove very valuable for the Funnel twin if he was to get a tug from the Drug Squad. Also, it might add a bit of weight to the bullshit story Bart Durley had invented. Although, of course, Durley's story was actually nearer to the truth than he realised. Funnel left his jacket and decided to return for it once the pub was officially open. There were drugs in that jacket, and he sure as hell couldn't afford to lose them. He was unaware it was Bill Winters they had been talking about, but he now knew someone had gone missing and he hadn't just gotten lost. It wasn't until his newfound mate Bart Durley finally turned up that Gerry managed to put two and two together. Gerry was going to be a dangerous man now that he was armed with half a story about a missing partner of the pub, presumed lost at sea, but more than likely dead. He backed out of the hallway and shut the door quietly behind him, no one knowing he'd been there.

Dell and Burt left Mickey by himself and walked together to Burt's shop. They went into the office, the door firmly shut behind them. "Nice work, Joey, my son. I knew I could rely on you," Burt said, shaking Dell's hand and patting him on the back at the same time.

"Well, did you ever doubt us?" asked Dell.

"Nah, course not. But naturally I was worried. I didn't want you boys to get in any trouble now, did I?"

"*Trouble*! Bloody hell, Burt!" exclaimed Dell.

"Well, you know what I mean."

"Anyway, the Swedes have placed large amounts on the usual non-runner caper, so I assume your man has already delivered or is very close," said Albert with a knowing smile.

"Ah! Fuck me, I'd forgotten about that. Strangely I had something else on my mind," Dell said with a smile. "Well, that's good. How much did they put in?"

"Let me have a look," said Burt, getting it up on his laptop.

"Well, it was twenty but now looks like thirty has gone in."

"Okay, well, Terry better let them know today's non-runners or no-hopers. I want that squared up before Lightfoot gets back," said Dell.

Mickey had been left alone with his thoughts. He felt a bit guilty about the tale of his old partner, but comforted himself with the thought that it had been quick and Bill hadn't been hurt before his departure. Anyway, Bill had taken a few liberties, so it was back to business as usual. The boys carried on as normal and had their rendezvous at the pub at the usual time, hoping to see Bart Durley and eagerly waiting to see what he had to say about the situation. But to their surprise, it wasn't the Durleys who turned up, but their old enemy, Tommy Butler.

"Fuckin' hell, what's that cunt doing here?" exclaimed Dell.

"I don't believe it!" was Funnel's surprised answer as Richards calmly glanced around to see what the fuss was about.

"Evening all, well, afternoon," was Butler's smug greeting as he took a look around the pub, standing there full of piss and importance. "Thought you were still banged up, Joey my old mate," said Butler. He looked very pleased with himself, having caught all three having a quiet drink together.

"Hello, Mr. Butler. Haven't seen you for a while," said Dell very innocently.

"Well, you wouldn't have, would you? You've been on holiday, haven't you? My colleague here only informed me this morning that you were about again. So I thought I'd pop in and see how you were getting on," said Butler in the way only coppers nosing about can.

"Can I get you a drink, Mr. Butler?" was the only thing Dell could think of to say at this precise moment.

"That's very kind of you, Joe. I'll have a large G & T if you don't mind, and my colleague here will have half a bitter." Dell nodded to Mickey as if to say "get them two dogs a drink." This was going to be interesting.

"So, what have you boys been up to lately? Anything interesting?" Butler asked.

"No, not really, Mr. Butler," replied Dell, again innocently.

"Well, that's good to hear," said Butler sarcastically, not wanting to let on he knew already about the fishing trip.

"So, what brings you here then? Have they brought back hanging or something?" asked Dell, equally sarcastic.

"No, no, not that I'm aware of, but it wouldn't be such a bad thing if they had. No, I was just in the area and thought I'd pop in for a quick one to see who was still about," replied Butler. He wasn't bothered about the fishing incident, but he would use that to his advantage if he had to. He had bigger plans for Dell and his boys and was actually pleased to see them all still together. He sincerely hoped he could persuade them to feature in his and the government's plans. But first he had to do more homework on the boys as he didn't actually know himself what the top secret plans were to be. He was just doing as told, looking around for a suitable firm to carry out a task in the near future, and his first thought had been this mob.

Butler swiftly drank his G & T, said his goodbyes, and left, leaving no clues as to what he was doing there in the first place. As he left the premises, Dell turned to the others and said, "What was all that about?"

"Dunno, but I'm sure we'll find out soon," said Richards frowning.

"I don't like it. He's up to something," said Funnel, feeling a bit uncomfortable.

"Nah, neither do I. What you reckon, Baz?" asked Dell.

"Dunno, mate, but we ain't got fuck all to worry about, we're all staunch, ain't we?" came Richards' reply.

"True, very true. But I still don't like it," said Dell, drinking up and going to the bar to get them another and to pay for Butler's drinks.

"What you reckon, Mickey?"

"I don't know either, but it's funny, don't you think? He hasn't been round here for years and then suddenly turns up out of the blue."

"Hmm, I think we're all getting paranoid. Let's all stop worrying. Like Baz said, we ain't got anything to worry about, and we ain't done nothing to worry about, have we?" said Dell, rejoining the other two.

Burt arrived for a couple and the boys told him what had happened. Burt didn't like the sound of it either, but he was of the same opinion as Richards. "What can he prove, anyway?" asked Burt.

"Fuck all," was Richards' reply to that one. They all agreed, relaxed, and carried on enjoying a drink together.

"Has anyone seen them Durleys yet?" was Burt's next question.

"No!" was the answer from the trio in unison.

"Well, you probably won't see him for a while. I bet he's proper shitting himself," Burt said.

"Yeah, probably, but you don't know what old bollocks he's come out with, do ya?" said Dell.

"True, but the old Bill will see straight through him. So, I wouldn't concern ya'selves with him too much," assured Burt.

"No, we won't," replied Dell, his mind drifting off for a minute.

When Gerry finally returned for his jacket, he was a bit cagey, but he kept himself to himself and didn't think anything about Bill's absence from the pub. That would change once Durley reappeared. They all knew they couldn't keep that one quiet for long and that tongues were bound to wag.

It was only natural that everybody involved in the Bill Winters affair was feeling a little nervous. They had been feeling pretty good about it before Butler showed his ugly head. None of them wanted to let on that Butler's appearance had given them cause for concern. They kept reassuring each other they would all be okay.

David Lightfoot had reported back to Terry Funnel that he'd made the delivery and would be back in a few days as he was going to stop off, have a short break, and take his time coming home. As he was empty, he felt a lot safer and the pressure was off. That was good news and one less thing to worry about. Maybe things would be alright after all.

Butler reported to his superiors that the gang he had in mind was still together and under the current circumstances he was confident that whatever they had in mind for them, he could get them to take part.

"Good work," he was told. "Keep an eye on them, but don't overdo it." Butler was very happy with himself. He was certain he'd gotten the right boys. He knew they were pros and very reliable too. He was looking forward to this and thought that just maybe it could get him even further up the career ladder. Butler didn't show his face in the Country Life for a while, which came as a great relief to all involved there, and very soon his appearance had been discounted as a mere coincidence, although it had certainly ruffled one or two feathers for a moment.

Bart Durley turned up a few days later, and naturally the boys were extremely curious to hear what he had to say about Poole. For once, all three gathered around him wanting to know where he'd been and exactly what happened. Bart looked even more scared now than when he first walked in. The blood was draining from his face again, which gave him the ghostly appearance he had worn when he saw the police at the mooring. All Bart would say on the subject was, "They held me overnight and questioned me again the next day. I've been released on bail and have to go back to Poole nick in a month's time," he said, shaking like a leaf. He and his dad now realised that there was going to be no gain associating with this lot, just a lot of pain.

"So, what did you tell 'em then?" asked Dell.

"Well, I just told them what happened. I told them the truth," he replied.

"Which was what? 'Cause the truth is a bit difficult to get from you, ain't it, mate?" said Dell, with menace in his voice.

"Ah, just leave me alone, please. I've had enough of all this," said Bart politely.

"Just as long as you ain't made any bullshit stories up, mate," said Dell, turning away and returning to his seat with the others.

"He's shitting himself," said Richards in his usual eloquent manner.

"Yeah, I know, and he's not telling us the truth, is he? The truth from him is nothing like it. Noncey little prick!" said an irate Dell.

Gerry Funnel turned up and stood with the Durley's, all of them feeling a little bit more comfortable now they had someone else to talk to. But the atmosphere in the pub at that particular moment felt strained. Bart was very uncomfortable indeed and didn't want to stay any longer. He had a quiet word with Gerry on the side and asked him if he was holding any gear (cocaine). Gerry said he was and Bart suggested going back to his place as his missus had gone to stay with her mother in light of the recent events. Gerry said that was fine by him.

"What you doing, Dad? I'm going home with Gerry. Are you staying here or what?"

"Err, yeah, I'm not going home yet. I might give ya mum a call and see if she fancies coming down," squeaked Dick.

"Okay, I'll see you tomorrow then." Dick phoned Rita. She said she'd get a cab down to the pub and would be there in about half an hour.

It was no secret anymore that Bill Winters had lost his life as a result of the fishing trip accident earlier that week. You can't keep something like that quiet for long, and of course the rumours quickly started. Although no one mentioned it to the Flowery firm, people knew better than that. Some knew Bill had won a big bet at Big Burt's and hadn't been paid. And to them it all looked a little fishy.

Rita turned up as promised, having gotten her cab from Ifty's cabs and she asked for Ifty by name to be her driver. She was taking a bit of a shine to Ifty and he to her, and when he dropped her at the pub, she gave him a nice little kiss as she got out. Ifty smiled. He knew the score. "I'm in here," he thought to himself, and given Rita's history with taxi drivers, he probably was.

Bart and Gerry went back to Bart's place and straightaway they got on the gear. Bart poured the beers and off they went. As the booze and drugs flowed, so did Bart's bullshit, but he still hadn't mentioned Bill Winters, although Gerry thought he clearly had something on his mind. He was acting very strangely, and after a few lines of coke, he became extremely paranoid, looking out from behind the curtains and checking the back door.

Gerry had heard about the trip. Everyone had by now, and he could fully understand why Durley was acting like he was, and he also knew sniffing cocaine was only going to make him worse. But, as Bart had already paid him and was willing to share it with him, Gerry didn't care. Gerry certainly wasn't going to mention what had happened. He would wait until Bart brought it up, and he knew that Bart would at some point.

Gerry knew what he'd heard when he first went to pick his jacket up, but he wasn't going to say anything about Dell telling Bart and Mickey it was a "nice, clean job." Gerry also knew about the bet Bill had placed as he had kept telling everyone about it when he'd had a few too many drinks. Gerry was going to keep that up his sleeve for now as well as it might come in handy at a later date. But he was dying to hear Bart's version of events. It wouldn't be long before Bart spilled the beans. He trusted Gerry and needed to talk to someone about it.

"You haven't asked me anything about the fishing trip, Gerry. I was expecting you to," said Bart with a sad and serious look on his face.

"No, I haven't, Bart. It's none of my business, is it?" said an equally serious Gerry, the cocaine was taking effect on both of them.

"Well, is it alright if I tell you what happened?" asked Bart.

"Yeah, 'course, mate. Go ahead if you really want to." *This should be good*, thought Gerry and let Bart continue.

"We were out fishing on my mate's boat," said Bart.

Gerry thought, *Ah, your mate's boat now, is it?*

"And after a reasonably successful day's fishing, I s'pose we were all getting a bit bored. They kept egging me on to give the boat some welly." Which was partly true. It was only mentioned once by Terry and Dell, but they knew Bart wouldn't be able to resist an opportunity to show off.

"So I opened her up a bit and not very much, may I add," continued Bart.

Yeah, right, thought Gerry.

"And the next thing, I turn around to see poor old Bill flying off the back of the boat like an Olympic diver, and Dell and Richards seemed to be turning back toward the sides as if they'd just launched him over. One of 'em, I can't remember which, sort of wiped his hands together in that 'job well done' action. You know what I mean? So of course I slowed right down, turned the boat around and went in search of poor old Bill. The others didn't say much.

Well, your brother did." Bart's version of events was pure fiction, but the truth of the matter was that Bill *had* been thrown into the sea by Dell and Richards.

"So where was my brother positioned at the time?" asked Gerry, curious by now.

"Well, he was err, err, somewhere near me, I think," replied Bart.

"So he was nowhere near the others then?" said Gerry.

"No, no, he wasn't."

"So did he see the others throw Bill over?" asked Gerry.

"I don't know if he saw, but I reckon they did do it," said Bart, his mood a bit more excited. A minute ago, he'd as good as seen them do it. Now he only "reckoned" they had.

Gerry racked up a couple more lines of the devil's dandruff and they sniffed it up together. They sat in silence for a few seconds. Gerry thought for a moment and then said, "Hmm, so you actually saw them throw him, did you?"

"Yeah, threw him like a rag doll. Well, that's what I reckon," was Bart's reply. Here he went again, one minute seeing it, the next thinking it. Gerry knew this was classic Durley fiction at its best and that Bart would need to be very careful about what he said and who he said it to, but Gerry wasn't going to tell him that.

"What do you think, Gerry? Will they try and nick me for what they done to Bill?"

"What for? You didn't throw him in, did ya? What the hell can you get nicked for, you berk?"

"Yeah, you're right, Gerry. Well, I hope they don't try and charge me with it," Bart said, his eyes narrowing as if he was scheming something.

"Well, like I said, they ain't got F-all to charge you with, have they? If they did, they'd have done it there and then wouldn't they?" Gerry reassured him.

"Yeah, I suppose so," said a more confident Bart.

"So, what did the Old Bill say about it anyway?" asked Gerry, not expecting Bart's answer.

"Well, they reckoned I was lucky to get away alive myself, as my crew were the biggest bunch of brigands and bandits out there. They also used the word cutthroats as well."

Gerry, getting a bit bored with it, started rolling a joint but chuckled away as Bart said that, and replied in a matter-of-fact way, "Well, they're not wrong there, are they?"

"Nah, what a mob!" Bart said, deadly serious.

Gerry never said anything to Bart about what he'd heard when he walked into the pub that morning. What was the point? He knew what they were capable of, and Gerry didn't want to be on the receiving end. Even though his twin was part of it, he didn't think that would bother the other two too much.

The boozing and drug-taking carried on for a few more hours, and it soon became clear that Bart didn't want to spend the night alone. He was a frightened man. Scared of what would happen when he went back to answer bail. Frightened of Dell's boys and just generally worried. He was like a rabbit caught in the headlights and all this drug-taking wasn't going to do his state of mind any good.

As the night turned into the early hours, Bart's mood became more emotional and soon tears were flowing. Gerry was on hand to provide a shoulder to cry on and give him a cuddle. Bless him! As the tears flowed and the hugging continued, Bart received one or two pats on the bum, something he was no stranger to. Gerry, noticing he never complained, continued to push his luck a little bit further. Still Bart didn't complain and if he did, Gerry would just say that it was down to drink and drugs and Bart had been mistaken. Although Bart was no stranger to sexual activity with men, Gerry didn't actually know that. But he could sense Bart was no straight flyer. So, as the comforting became more sensual, the drink and drugs now taking hold, the inevitable happened and the two of them ended up enjoying a very passionate night.

When morning came, the pair woke up in the marital bed and looked at each other a little bit surprised, but not overly. "Oh, morning, Gerry," said Bart, a little sheepishly.

"Morning, love, you were amazing last night," Gerry said with a grin.

"Oh, was I? Look, I don't normally do things like that, you know, mate," said a red-faced Bart.

"No? That's what they all say, mate," commented Gerry.

"Who do?" asked Bart.

"The girls, they always say that," Gerry said smiling.

Bart got up and hurried to shower and get ready for work. He was late already and not only was he feeling rough, he was a bit sore as well. Poor old Bart, not only was his head full of old bollocks, how his arse was as well. At least this would take his mind off Bill Winters.

"Don't tell anyone about this, will you? We need to keep this to ourselves." As Gerry said this, Bart's mind flashed back to when he was a young boy. That was exactly what the priest had said to him then. It was history repeating itself—no wonder he was a messed-up piece of work, and at the end of the day, it wasn't his fault. It was always others who had put him in these positions, and quite often those others were people he trusted.

"And don't forget to change the sheets before your old woman gets home either," mentioned Gerry, matter-of-factly.

"Just get dressed, please, mate, will you?" pleaded Bart. "I gotta go to work. Where do you want dropping off?"

"Anywhere on ya way'll do mate," was Gerry's answer.

Bart wanted Gerry out of his house as soon as possible and he needed to meet up with his dad. Work was about the most important thing as he didn't want to upset his old man. Gerry was dropped off and walked off with not only his head spinning with contradictions but also with a hand he thought he could play.

CHAPTER 12

On the other side of town, ISIS fanatics were getting themselves some reasonable ideas. The big targets—landmarks such as Big Ben, London Bridge, the Tower of London, and Tower Bridge—were well out of their reach and they began to look elsewhere. A school looked like the easiest target, one that would bring the most carnage and have the biggest effect on the British people. After all, how many schools had been hit in Syria and Iraq and all the other countries in the Arabic world?

Cairo was in favour of hitting innocent children and their parents. She was embittered and could see no wrong with inflicting on others the emotional damage she'd suffered. The Ayatollah loved this trait of hers, and he knew he'd found the perfect female partner. She was cold, callous, and evil. Although she hadn't been born that way, life had made her that way. Funny old world, isn't it?

They didn't have the money to fund any operation right then, but they had the knowledge and commitment between them. Of that there was no doubt. But with the fundraising activities and their new connections with drug addicts and Gerry Funnel, it wouldn't be too long before they had the ingredients required to do whatever they wanted. Gerry and Ifty actually had no idea of the cell's political leanings or that they were part of a cell in the making. It was, in fact, at that time an innocent way for everyone involved to earn a few quid. How times were changing. The whole situation on the surface looked like people trying to survive. The death and destruction motive wasn't obvious to Gerry and Ifty at all. But it was well and truly obvious to observers.

*   *   *

There had been no sign of Tommy Butler for a while and that kept the Flowery firm happy. But that didn't mean they were out of his thoughts. A message had reached him, but he was still none the wiser as to what it really concerned. All he knew was that he'd identified the team and his superiors were happy to let him or his team of trusties deal with it.

The country as a whole was fed up with the terrorist situation, and this meant increasing pressure on the government. They too were far from happy about it and as they had been voted in to deal with Brexit, that also meant protecting the borders against murdering religious fanatics. They were on the nation's side. It was time to act and act in a very different way than they had in the past. The command was therefore passed down from the Home Office. Find us an independent team that can help sort this problem out. One that can appear independent of government. Tommy Butler was the messenger who in the long run hoped to be regarded as the man who found the Holy Grail. And in his case that was Joey Dell.

Since Dell's release, everyone from here to Timbuktu seemed to require his services one way or another. For a one-time public enemy, it looked like his star was in the ascendency. Heroes come in all shapes and sizes, but in this particular case, the nation's unknown heroes were going to stay just that—unknown. Generally heroes don't become household names until they've been dead for at least half a century. Joey Dell a national hero? It didn't seem likely. Although he might be a local legend, a national legend was far beyond anyone's imaginings.

Tommy Butler was the chosen one, chosen to be the go-between for his higher-ranked civil servants and what they regarded as lower-ranked workers and doers. But they would all become to realise that at the end of the day, they were all going to need each other. But it would require all parties to cooperate and it was Butler's job to see they did just that. But this wasn't going to be an easy task by any stretch of the imagination. Butler was going to have to dig deep to pull this one off. These boys weren't going to trust him or any other representative of the law, so a lot of planning and thought were needed to get these boys on board. But if anyone knew a way, it was Butler. The game was on, but it would take time and cunning. Time was something Dell wasn't short of serving and cunning he had plenty of. So this was going to be a battle of wits. Let the game begin.

Tommy Butler knew he needed to arm himself and put together a decent squad of his own. He'd have to keep himself out of Dell's way for a while and send someone Dell wouldn't know to observe things and see who his associates were these days. Butler still didn't know what it was all about. It was all top-secret stuff, but his superintendent had told him he'd be informed "all in good time." He didn't know MI5 was also involved, and he certainly knew nothing about a terror cell plotting something in Dell's manor.

David Lightfoot had returned from his trip to Sweden, and he thought he'd drop by and see the Flowery firm in the Country Life, both to let them know everything had gone smoothly and to pick up his wages. Dell was already aware everything had gone alright as the Swedes had paid up in full. David rang the pub and asked if Dell was there. Mickey, recognising his voice, told him he was. "Tell him I'll be over shortly please, Mickey."

"Okay, will do, mate," said Mickey, hanging up. Mickey leaned over the bar as Dell and Richards were both standing there and said quietly in Dell's ear that Lightfoot was coming in. That was alright by Dell, and they carried on chatting. When Lightfoot arrived, both of the Funnel brothers were there. One was with Dell at the bar and the other was sitting alone at a table. The trio greeted Lightfoot with handshakes and smiling faces. He got a pat on the back from Dell, and "whatever he wanted to drink" was quickly shoved into his hand.

The Funnel brother sitting by himself and pretending to read the paper was not quite so happy to see Lightfoot. That should have been him over there getting a warm welcome and a good few quid in wages. Gerry watched carefully and was envious, but was careful not to let it show. As if coming to rescue Gerry on his white steed, the gallant Bart Durley turned up just at the right moment with his dad right behind him. "You alright, Bart?" asked Dick as he followed him in, looking at his son's backside.

"Yeah, why?" replied Bart curiously.

"Well, you're walking a bit funny. Thought you might have piles or something."

"Am I? Well, I do need the loo a bit desperate, Dad. Can you get these? I need to go," said Bart, trying to show no pain as he minced off to the toilet. Gerry heard all this and had a quiet laugh to himself, shaking his head in disbelief as he watched the embarrassed Bart Durley rushing off red-faced toward the gents. This certainly took his mind off what was going on at the other end of the bar. *Oh well, I suppose things could be worse*, he thought as he sat there grinning from ear to ear.

"Alright, Gerry, what you smirking at?" Dick asked him.

"Ah, nothing, Dick, I was just thinking about something, that's all. What's up with Bart? Has he got a stomach bug or something?" Gerry asked cheekily.

"I don't know. He's been acting strange all day. I don't know what's up with him, to be honest," squeaked Dick. Gerry got up and joined Dick at the bar, where he was still waiting patiently to be served. "I'll get these, Dick," said Gerry, thinking it was the least he could do.

"Ah, thanks, mate," said Dick, needing no encouragement whatsoever to stand down and let Gerry take over the round. Bart came back and his dad said, "That was quick, son."

"Yeah, well it was desperate. Shut up about it, will ya!" he grimaced, again red-faced.

"Alright, don't bite my head off. See, I told you, didn't I, Gerry?" said Dick, as he looked at Gerry and pulled a face.

Gerry just smirked and said to Bart, "Alright, mate, what you want?" reaching into his pocket for some money.

"I'll just have my usual, thanks, Gerry, and don't take any notice of him. I'm alright, thanks. You?"

"Yeah, I'm good, mate. Come on, let's have a drink," was Gerry's reply. He was feeling completely relaxed.

"I'm only gonna have a couple tonight, mate. I'm bloody knackered," said Bart in a "you know what I mean" way.

"Yeah, me too," replied Gerry, raising his eyebrows.

Bart whispered into Gerry's ear, "And I've gotta change the bedding."

"Yeah, I know, but won't the missus get suspicious?" Gerry asked him.

"Probably. I'll just say I had an accident. She can ask the ol' man if she doesn't believe me. He knows I got a bad stomach." The pair of them burst out laughing.

"What are you two laughing at?" asked Dick in all innocence.

"Nothing!" they both replied.

"Nothing, my arse," said Dick, and the pair giggled again.

"What now?" said Dick, holding out his hands in a gesture that said, "What are you two children up to?" This cheered Gerry up even more. He quickly forgot about the Swedish thing, and the banter had also made for a much easier first meeting with Bart after their previous night's encounter.

As Lightfoot was getting up to leave, Gerry heard Dell telling him to see them in the café tomorrow morning at ten and they would square him up. As he stood there thinking, Gerry watched Lightfoot leave and then an idea struck like a bolt of lightning. *What a great idea*, he thought. He turned and looked at the Durleys, thinking they would never know it was him, and then turned back to look at his brother standing at the other end of the bar with Joey and Barry. He murmured to himself, "And neither would they." He drank up quickly, said his goodbyes, and went home to think more carefully about his cunning plan. *Brilliant*, he thought to himself as he walked out onto the street. On his way home, he stopped off at the corner and bought a few different red-top tabloid newspapers to take home and read. He was looking for the part that says, "If you have a story, ring this number."

Once indoors, Gerry started scanning the papers for the numbers, which were usually just inside the front page. He got on the phone and to his surprise, a couple of them were interested in what he had to say. No loyalties here. Gerry had not only fucked Bart, he was metaphorically about to do him again. Only this time, he was going to get paid for it. *Nice work*, Gerry thought. Now Gerry was whoring himself and he didn't care one little bit. All Gerry cared about was making some money, and he wasn't too bothered how he earned it.

The next day came quickly as Gerry fell asleep early, thinking about the story he was to tell the press. Bart would be named and shamed, but he would think very carefully about who else he would name. He wasn't that brave, and he certainly didn't want to follow in Bill's footsteps, found floating down the Thames or dead in a ditch somewhere.

Bill's body had been found washed up on a beach somewhere in Dorset and it had been reported in a couple of national newspapers that morning. This would add considerable weight to Gerry's story, and he could therefore now demand a nice few quid for his version of events, which he could claim had come straight from the horse's mouth. This really would rub salt into the wounds of Bart, who was fast becoming the second victim in this sorry episode. All the others seemed to be profiting from Bill's death except Bart, and who knew what effect this would have on him? Mentally he was very fragile and this could push him over the edge.

Gerry had his meetings that day and both reporters seemed more than a little interested in what he had to say. Gossip sells and Gerry had now made up for losing out on his old Swedish job. Managing to keep his name out of the story and being able to remain anonymous made the whole thing even better as it was going to keep everyone guessing as to who had actually leaked the story to the press in the first place.

When the story finally broke a couple of days later, it caused widespread pandemonium in the pub. No one had expected it and Gerry took great satisfaction dropping the relevant papers on the bar. It was no secret there what had happened, but no one dreamt of it becoming national news. As soon as the local papers got wind of it, they decided to run a story of their own. The Durley boy became inundated with reporters, exactly the opposite of what he wanted. No chance. Everyone now wanted to know, was Bill pushed or was it an accident? Or plain murder?

Gerry had put the cat among the pigeons. Bart wouldn't go home as reporters were camped at his front door, and the pub was buzzing with new faces all the time. Gerry was quietly loving it, although he hadn't expected all this fuss and certainly no one suspected it was he who had gone to the papers.

CHAPTER 13

With all these new people turning up in the pub, nobody noticed a couple chatting in the corner. They looked just like any other courting couple who had popped in to get the gossip, but this pair remained regulars, even after all the fuss had died down. Not surprisingly both the Durleys were keeping very low profiles. Bart was close to his breaking point.

He refused to give interviews and all he had to say on the matter was that it was just an accident and that no one was to blame, certainly not him. And the Flowery firm had told a group of journalists and reporters who haunted the place in no uncertain terms to *Go Away!* Social media was alive with stories about Bart and his dad. Gerry hadn't done them any favours whatsoever. Gerry's life went on as usual and he even had the two local jihadists, Badini and Dasti, come into the Country to talk about further drug deals. This hadn't gone unnoticed by the undercover police couple who had strict instructions to keep their distance from Dell's mob as they would suss them straightaway. But Gerry also was fast becoming a man of interest.

As things quieted down a bit and yesterday's newspapers became today's chip papers, the Durleys skulked back into the pub with their tails between their legs. The bullshit flowed once more. But the melee surrounding Bart in the papers and on social media had stirred up a few ghosts the Durleys had thought would remain in the closet forever. With photos being bandied about, one or two memories were dragged up from many years before when the pair had been cleaning windows at an all girls' convent school.

In the wake of the Jimmy Saville scandal, lots of children involved at the time had come forward as adults and reported indecent assaults, rapes, and other vile acts of depravity. Also, the government had vowed that anyone implicated in this type of behaviour would be thoroughly investigated and, if found guilty, imprisoned. This was an extremely bad situation for the Durleys, as one by one, women filed complaints about them from the days when they worked at the school. All in all, about a dozen people came forward, and before they knew it, the Durleys were the subject of yet another police investigation. Bart was very fond of using the phrase "what goes around comes around"; he was a great believer in karma.

Rita started to meet the Durleys on a more regular basis down at the pub, saying to others that she had to keep an eye on her boys. Of course in reality, she wanted to keep her eye on a certain taxi cab owner she requested each time she went on one of her pub visits. Not only were the men in this family a devious pair, but the mother was also. No stranger to straying from her husband's side, she was determined to bag herself yet another cabbie.

What's good for the goose is also good for the gander, at least that was Rita's opinion, and she knew of her husband's past. Revenge is sweet, so they say, and Rita was certainly going to make sure she got her share of the candy. Although her husband's and son's past had yet to be widely exposed, woman's intuition told her Dick had probably been up to something, somewhere most of the time, during their marriage. But she was no saint herself and was determined to get her own back. Her sights were on Shifty Ifty. This was a dysfunctional family by anyone's standards. What a sorry state of affairs, but none of them knew any different. They were all in it for themselves. Rita was totally unaware of the social media campaign implicating her husband and son in pedophile allegations dating back a couple of decades, but she was fully aware they were both capable of anything of a sexual nature, no matter how depraved it might be.

CHAPTER 14

Big Burt was satisfied that, for now, the fuss surrounding the death of Bill Winters had died down, but he couldn't help thinking there was more to come from that event. Although he didn't say anything to Dell and Co., it kept eating away at the back of his mind. After all, he'd been around a lot longer than the others. He knew about other hits the boys had gotten away with in the past, but this one seemed a different kettle of fish altogether, and he couldn't help but think this one was going to come back to haunt them. *Anyway, onward and upward for now, and we'll cross that bridge when or if we come to it*, he thought. He was well aware Bart had said it was an accident when approached by the press, but Bart had also been telling different stories about that day to other people. Then again, who would take Bart seriously? Everyone knew he didn't know his arse from his elbow. It was the timing of Butler's appearance that gave Burt cause for concern, but none of the others seemed bothered about it. Big Burt had a gut feeling storm clouds were building and it might be time to batten down the hatches.

Whenever Burt expressed such concerns to his old pal Dell, he was always told he was worrying unnecessarily. The Winters case was over and done with, lost at sea as it were. However, the two Jihadists who had become very friendly with Gerry Funnel were a mystery to the firm, and they were wondering where Gerry had been introduced to them. Why all of a sudden had they started using the Country? When they saw them shaking hands and talking to Shifty, as if they'd all known each other for a long time, the boys assumed they must be related or something, and Gerry must be conducting business with them.

The extremist pair made sure to keep their political views and intentions to themselves. They dressed like any other people of their age, wearing the latest fashions like ordinary Londoners and blending in. They drank, smoked, and did drugs and were even seen coming out of the toilets wiping their noses and checking each other to make sure they had no residue visible on their noses before reentering the bar. They acknowledged people around them but generally kept to themselves as much as possible. They didn't want to arouse suspicion any more than the boys did, and they kept down to the end of the pub Gerry used. They never thought about venturing up to the other end. That lot up there looked like trouble.

They had popped in only now and then to start with, to see Gerry, but they had begun to get other ideas about this nice, big pub on the High Street. They had decided to check it out to see how busy the place actually got. The Country was a typical suburban pub. Probably once it had had a snug and a saloon bar, but now it had just one large, U-shaped bar with a couple of beer engines and oddly sized and shaped tables and chairs scattered about. Moderate food was served, but customers generally came for the drink and the company. There were the regulars, lunchtime, early evening, and late, and a weekend crowd who came to watch football and horse racing. Mickey put on a DJ or live music on Friday and Saturday nights, and Badini and Dasti discovered the place was full to the rafters with revellers partying and generally having a good time.

This place, or maybe a similar venue, seemed to them a possible target, and they would mention it to their leader. There was one slight problem with targeting the Country. They would have to get past the hostile mob assembled at the other end of the bar. That lot ran security and had searched them already when they'd ventured in, and they were sure to search them every time, as they viewed anyone of Asian descent as a potential threat. In this case, they were right. This would take a lot of serious thought and careful planning, but it should at least be considered, they felt. And to hit all those innocent infidels out enjoying themselves on a Saturday night was a mouth-watering prospect. They did think about trying to use these nights to sell their drugs for the fundraising campaign but then thought better of it. They would more likely become the victims if they did that, and being killed by the Flowery firm wasn't in their plans. Allah wouldn't want that and neither would they, so they would have to deploy different tactics.

The Ayatollah and Cairo were not only looking for prospective targets, they were hard at work with their hate preaching. Possible recruits at London colleges and universities were prime targets of theirs. Young, vulnerable, disenchanted Muslim students were of particular interest. The pair were also very busy attending Islamic extremist rallies in places like Bradford and Rochdale and even one recently close by in High Wycombe. Until they had sufficient funds for their commitment, they would carry on exhorting the "Big" picture. In their perfect world, England would become a Muslim state under Sharia law.

The writing was now on the wall and one of these days swords would be crossed, but who would be the victors and who would be the victims? Only time would tell. Big Burt's inner feelings may have been right, but he had no idea in what shape or form his fears would manifest. Hindsight is a wonderful thing, but prophesying an event before it actually happens is a completely different story. Burt wasn't anxious for no reason, but even his anxiety couldn't predict what the future held for his beloved Joey Dell and his band of brigands.

To a stranger, Dell and his inner clique looked like men who worked in the city. They were always well dressed, and they were always very respectful to people, and because of that they had gained the respect of others. But if they didn't like you, you would get the picture pretty quickly, which the Durleys failed to understand.

Gerry knew the score and after he was pushed out of the inner circle, he knew it was best to keep out of the way. He knew only too well how they operated. Once they got the hump with you, you needed to keep your distance. He knew his saving grace was his twin brother, but if he overstepped the mark, even that wouldn't be enough. He managed to keep half a foot in by getting his gear from Dell, but even this was indirectly as they kept far away from everyday involvement in drug dealing, but it came from them all the same.

London's answer to "murder incorporated" had put the memory of Bill Winters' fatal accident out of their minds, but the Durleys couldn't shut up about it. They would talk to anyone who could be bothered to listen, and almost every time they did speak about it, the story was different. Most people didn't take any notice, but the couple who had recently started using the Country were all ears. They kept their distance for now, but were keen to listen to what the pair was saying. The seeds of weeds had definitely blown into the pub and one man was very quick to pick up on it—Albert Kinsley. He'd noticed the couple as soon as they had started to become regulars in the pub, and his sixth sense began working overtime. He knew the Old Bill when he saw them and the more he saw of them, the more he was convinced. He never liked the Durleys either and liked them even less when he kept hearing what they were saying about Bart's nautical adventure.

Burt needed to get Dell by himself for a serious chat. He rang and asked him if he could come over to his office as he needed to get something off his chest and, most importantly, would he come alone? Dell was only too happy to meet Burt. If Burt wanted to talk, Dell was all ears. He entered the shop and Sharon indicated Dell should go upstairs. He didn't need to be told twice. He winked back at her and made his way to Burt's office. He found Burt waiting at his desk. Dell gave a little knock on the door and let himself in.

"Alright, Burt, what's up?" he inquired.

"Ah, Joe, my dear boy, come in and sit down. Fancy a drink?" Burt got up and walked toward a small cabinet he kept a few bottles of spirits in.

"Go on then. I'll have a brandy, if you've got one," Dell replied.

"'Course I have, you want ice with it?"

"Don't mind, mate, as it comes," said Dell.

Burt poured them both a drink and they sat down opposite each other at a very regal desk, the type you would expect men like these to grace, with paintings of the Queen on one wall and Winston Churchill on another. The mood was serious as Big Burt started the conversation. "I don't like it Joe, there's too much activity."

"How do you mean, Burt?" asked Dell, taking a sip of his brandy.

"Up until Bill's accident, all was quiet and rosy. Now it's different. We've had all sorts of stories flying about, we've had the media hanging around the pub, stuff in the papers, a visit from the dreaded Butler, and let me tell you, that was no coincidence. And that won't be the last we see of him, trust me, and during all the melee, we've now picked up ourselves a pair of undercover 'coppers' who seem to becoming residents in the pub," said Burt in a slightly raised voice.

"Ah, you mean that couple who came in when all the fuss about Bill was going on. Yeah, we've clocked them. What do you reckon on it?"

"What do I reckon? I reckon Butler's planted them there and I reckon the water is looking very murky indeed and either that fishing trip is coming back to bite us in the bollocks or they're trying to set us up for something. I don't know; I just have this strong gut feeling that a darker force is at work and that we're going to feel it one way or another."

"Well, don't worry about the fishing thing. You're not involved in that. Only two of us saw what happened there, and we ain't saying a word. You should know that," said Dell.

"Yeah, I know that, but I don't like it one bit, and I can't shake off this feeling I have. It's not natural," said Burt, doing a sort of shivery shake of his shoulders. Dell looked at him and could see he was a worried man.

"Burt, you've got nothing to worry about, mate, just relax. If anyone it'll be me they're after, and they haven't got F-all on me. We'll take things easy for a bit and keep our eyes on the situation. They'll get bored after a while and piss off, you watch," Dell replied, referring to the two undercover cops in the pub.

"Well, you just make sure they ain't got anything on you and that you haven't got anything around you that'll cause you any problems, if you know what I mean. I don't want anything to happen to you, Joe. I look at you as the son I never had, you know that, don't you?" said Burt with a little tear in his eye. He thought the absolute world of Joey Dell.

"I know that, Burt, and I look at you as a father figure too. Ever since my ol' man passed away you been there and I've got your back too," replied Dell.

"Good boy. Just be careful out there 'cause there's too much activity for my liking," repeated Burt.

"Don't worry, Burt, I will," said Dell with a little smile. The pair stayed in the office like men do, reminiscing and generally enjoying each other's company. Both needed this and both needed the reassurance of their special bond.

CHAPTER 15

Dell left Big Burt's with the words "too much activity" ringing around in his head. He was trying to keep an open mind on everything going on, but he couldn't help but think Burt might well be right. He needed to go home and think the whole thing over alone. Besides, Burt had summoned some ghosts by talking about Dell's mum, who had lost her battle against cancer when he was just a boy of ten. Not long after that his dad had hit the bottle. He died of drink when Dell was just nineteen years of age. Big Burt had been a father figure to Dell ever since those dark days, and all he had wanted to do was look after him. Even though together they had gone down the road of heavy villainy, Burt still only wanted the best for his "boy." Burt and Joe's dad had been great friends, and Burt had only been able to stand by and watch as Joe's dad had slowly but surely destroyed himself, leaving his only child alone.

On his arrival home, Dell poured himself another brandy, lit up a cigar, and turned on some music. He sat back in his favourite armchair, put his feet up, and began to reflect on his life gone by. This was something he'd always tried to avoid as he always looked forward, not back, but as he sat there in deep thought, he came to realise that the past had shaped the present and what had happened to him was not his fault, but maybe the person he'd become was. Or was it just he'd become that way as a result of the past? He asked himself many questions but found few answers. Where did he go from here? Dell didn't know the answer to that either.

One thing he did know was that he wanted to be there for his son. But he was too scared to ask of his whereabouts because he was frightened of what the outcome would be. He knew he was lucky to have his boys around him, but that was all he seemed to be living for. He loved that and so did they. But he really longed to be reunited with his son. How was he going to achieve that when he didn't know where either Harry or his mum were? For the first time in his life, he'd come to realise he was actually a lonely man despite all the people he had around him. This had to change, he told himself. After what seemed like hours and hours of contemplation, Dell fell asleep in his chair and dreamt of a different way of life where there wasn't going to be "too much activity."

Dell woke up in the early hours of the morning after a night of mixed dreams. On the one hand his son, Harry, and a happy family environment, on the other, murder and prison and yet more prison. He sat up in his chair and thought about yesterday's conversation with Burt. It weighed heavily on his mind. This is no way for a man to feel, but at least he could see a better future, which hopefully involved his son. He knew only too well the feeling of abandonment and that was not what he wanted for his boy. Dell had started to feel guilt for the very first time and he didn't like it. Burt had planted the seed, but there were many rivers to cross before he could even think about reuniting with young Harry. A guardian angel would come in very handy if there were such a thing. Big Burt was probably the closest thing to that. Dell needed something altogether different. Dell needed a change of direction and his chat with Big Burt had made that more apparent. Too much activity was taking its toll.

CHAPTER 16

Operation Desert Storm was what they called it, and soon Dell and his boys were going to find out all about it. But first a certain policeman by the name of Butler had to be told of the plan before wheels could be set in motion. He was called to a secret location on the South Bank for a briefing. Dark forces were now at work, and none other than Tommy "Bloody" Butler was the chosen on. He was about to get a real lesson in policing and policy.

Butler had been the scourge of Dell's younger years and he was about to return with the long arm of the law, this time with a different agenda. He was about to receive orders from above that would shock not only Butler himself, but also Dell, the Flowery firm and the whole nation if they were ever to find out the truth. This was going to be the first operation of its kind in the UK, but not necessarily the last, and Butler needed not only to prove his position in Scotland Yard was justified, but so was his choice of accomplices. Only time would prove him right or wrong.

Butler sat down at a big oval table in a room that overlooked the Thames. Seats had place names in front of them on the table, but he noted a couple of positions had none, which he found strange. His superiors were here. Maybe he was being demoted or, worse, maybe he was being sacked. He grew nervous as everyone around the table looked extremely serious and important. He had been asked to pick a capable team for a secret operation. Had he messed up somewhere along the line? He hadn't even disclosed who his choices were. All he'd done was check that they were still a team and still associating with one another. He knew in his own mind that whatever their mission, he had the right team for the job. As they sat around the table eyeing each other up, Butler grew increasingly anxious, his mouth becoming dry as he tried to hide his nervousness. What was this all about and why was he here amongst what appeared to be such important officials? If Dell had done something he didn't know about and had ruined his career, he was going to make his life hell.

A man Butler had never seen in his life coughed and stood up and said in a very authoritative way, "I suppose one or two of you are wondering why we are all gathered here today. Let me explain."

Butler fidgeted in his chair, fiddling with his nameplate. He reached for a jug of water, shaking as he did so, and poured himself a much-needed glass.

"What I have to say is strictly confidential and for all involved in this covert operation, it is a matter of life and death," the faceless man continued. "This is for Queen and country and every man sitting here today has been carefully chosen to carry out his duty as England and the whole of the UK expects.

"I am here to tell you about a trial operation that has been sanctioned by the Home Office and it is for the men in this room to carry out in a right and proper manner. Are we all clear so far?"

Tommy Butler was trying to keep his cool and his nerve as he swallowed what seemed like a tennis ball-sized lump in his throat. *Oh my good gawd, what have I been roped into here?* he thought to himself. *Why me? And what the hell is he going to come out with next? Bloody hell, why did I think of Dell's mob? This sounds like it should be something for the SAS, not for the likes of me and the toe rags I had in mind.* As the grey suit continued, Butler thought it must be a fantasy, something out of a James Bond film, and therefore certainly not something he should be involved in, let alone Flowery Fucking Dell. Then without warning Grey Suit turned to Butler and asked who he had in mind for his part of the operation. Butler only got as far as J... - when Grey Suit produced a series of photos of Dell and the others, to Butler's amazement. Who were these people? How did they know who he'd selected? Then, while pondering these questions, a close-up of Gerry Funnel was shown with two Asian men Butler, much to his embarrassment, didn't know.

"Get to this man first before you try Dell and his mob. He'll give you what you need to know to get them on your side," said Grey Suit, pointing at the picture of Funnel.

What don't these people know? Butler worried. He felt well out of his league and very uncomfortable. He'd paid one visit to the Country and only had one drink in Dell's presence. How did these people know so much? And again, who were they? Times were certainly changing, and this was a power way above Butler. All he could do was honour his election into this secret society and carry out his orders to the best of his ability, and carry them out he would. The establishment was not happy with the state of the nation, and now it appeared they were about to take a very different stance indeed. Butler was now on the front line and he was going to take Joey Dell and Co. with him. But it was going to take all the cunning he could muster. He was going to have to draw on all his experience as a policeman as he knew he was going to have one hell of a fight on his hands. Dell was an experienced criminal who would not be prepared to help the "Filth" at any cost. Butler was going to have to prepare himself for a Battle Royal of wits and he knew it wasn't going to be an easy task by any means. Dell was certainly no fan of the establishment, but on the other hand he was certainly no fan of Muslim terrorists.

The men in the grey suits had given him the heads up on Gerry Funnel, so maybe, just maybe, Butler held the trump card. But he was going to have to find that out for himself. He'd already gotten a pair of undercover cops in place in the Country and so far they'd come up with nothing on Dell. They would have to turn their attention to Funnel and see what could be dragged up on him. So far, all they had reported was the constant moaning from the Durleys and how they were getting their solicitors involved in the case of Bart's arrest. *Some people just don't know when to let matters drop and be thankful that no charges were ever made*, Butler thought.

Operation Desert Storm had just gotten off the ground but was very much in its infancy. It seemed Butler was pretty much the last man to know just what it involved. While the plan had gotten out of the traps and already hit the first bend running, it seemed to Butler as if he was only just leaving the gate. He had a lot of ground to make up if he was going to finish a winner. Right now, though, he was feeling very much like an also-ran.

There was a good reason for this lack of information. He didn't need to know the full details until just before the off. He knew something was going on. He'd been asked by his governor to find a capable team of villains, but he didn't know what for. Now that he'd been briefed on the matter, he could get going and catch up with the rest of the "in the know" crowd, although there weren't too many of them. The target, the recently formed terror cell led by The Ayatollah, was also very much in its infancy and Butler knew two of its party should have stood trial for war crimes in Syria. It had been decided to watch them to see how their radical views developed. The British government saw them as involuntary guinea pigs. They were part of the prize Butler was aiming for—not that he knew that at that moment. What he did know was that he didn't have long to assemble his team.

He'd left the meeting under no illusion of the expectations of the grey suits. He was well aware he'd been the last person in the room to know about Operation Desert Storm and also that England's expectations rested on his shoulders. The "England expects" was a bit strong, Butler thought, but at least the message had been got over as to how serious the establishment was taking this. At one point, Butler had visions of being told to take a short holiday and spend his time at Plymouth Hoe, keeping his eyes on the horizon for an invasion of foreign ships while he played a relaxing game of bowls. But never mind, he'd got plenty to get on with now. As he walked away from the meeting, his head was all over the place. With much to think about, he needed a stiff drink. At this particular moment, he would have loved to walk into the Country and ruin the Flowery firm's day, but he knew that was off limits. So, once back over the Thames, he got himself comfortable in a nice old pub not far from Scotland Yard and had a couple of drinks and a good long think about the best way to tackle this. This was completely out of the ordinary.

Big Burt's proclamation of "too much activity" was going to ring true for Butler as well now. Like most men in his position, he liked everything nice and quiet and peaceful, and as there were now a bunch of terrorists looking to change all this, he was not a happy man. One thing that did please him, though, was the fact that all the criminals he needed all drank in the same establishment. The police loved it when all the usual suspects drank under the same roof. It made their lives so much easier.

One such suspect of course, was Gerry Funnel, and he had now hit the front of the pack. He would be the first to feel the long arm of the law, but not before observation was set up on him. Butler wanted to be armed to the teeth with evidence so that Funnel would talk and give him enough on Dell's firm to get them on his side. And he knew he'd never needed the help of a criminal gang as much as he did now. He also knew getting Funnel to talk about a gang of professionals that included his twin brother was not going to be easy. One thing Butler did know was that Gerry Funnel was not just a drug dealer, but also a frequent drug user, a possible addict, and those sorts of people by and large were only too keen to help as they were normally desperate for their next fix. He hoped Gerry would prove to be no exception.

For Gerry, too much activity was a good thing and the more activity, the more he liked it, as it meant he was earning and he liked earning. Since he had lost out on the Swedish move, he'd struggled, but now business had picked up for him and he was getting back on top a lot quicker than even he'd imagined. One reason for his change of fortune was his introduction to the Afghan pair by Ifty. They had started to order big and their preferred drug of choice, crack cocaine, was a very good earner indeed as the end user had to keep feeding his addiction. This meant orders were becoming more frequent and bigger. Not only was Gerry earning it in cash, he was also getting his hands on a lot of stolen goods as the users had to turn to theft to satisfy their cravings. This suited Gerry down to the ground as he could offer rock bottom prices for goods like expensive watches, designer handbags, jewellery etc. The Durleys loved to buy such items as they thought they were getting a good deal and for some reason or another, they trusted Gerry. They still hadn't put two and two together and realised Gerry had spoken to the newspapers and it was the newspapers fees that had set him up properly in the drugs trade. One day, Dick Durley in his squeaky little voice had asked him if he gambled as he was a little bit curious as to where this money had suddenly come from. Gerry's reply was, "Don't be a cunt, Dick, you know what happens to people round here if they win money on the horses, they end up floating in the Channel and I don't fancy that mate. Would you?"

"No, I wouldn't, thank you," squeaked Dick in reply.

Gerry could have gone on dealing for years had he not been introduced to the fundraising department of the local terror cell. He was now well and truly on the radar. He was very careful not to let on to Dick about his drug dealing, as he didn't trust him one little bit, and if he found out Bart was a regular customer, there was no telling what sort of stories he'd tell about him.

One person who didn't mind a bit of shady dealings going on in the pub was the landlord himself, Mickey. He'd buy the odd bit of Tom (jewellery) himself and because more money was being spent in his place, especially by Gerry, he turned a blind eye and let them get on with it. After all, worse things happen at sea.

Big Burt's words still played on Dell's mind and he too was getting a strong gut feeling that something was on the horizon. He seemed to think that whatever it was, was going to include himself and it was going to get messy. He therefore thought it was about time he spoke to the boys about it, and a Stewards Inquiry was called.

CHAPTER 17

A ten o'clock breakfast and a chat down at the Sopranos' Café was the venue. His two trustees, Richards and Funnel, made up the stewards along with Dell himself of course. Dell was feeling a little anxious to say the least, and he wanted to get things out in the open. This wasn't going to be easy, but in his view it was best spoken about. Much to Dell's surprise and relief, the boys had been thinking along exactly the same lines. And one of their concerns was the two new punters who seemed to have become a little too regular in the Country.

"Yeah, that's what me and Burt thought. Do you think they're wrapped up with Butler?" asked Dell.

"Wouldn't surprise me," replied Funnel.

"Me neither," said Richards.

"Well, boys, we need to keep our wits about us and I think we should shut up shop for a while," said Dell. They all agreed.

After a long pause Dell completely unexpectedly changed the subject to his ex-missus and his son, Harry. This was very hard for Dell as he didn't like talking about his private life and certainly didn't like to show any emotions.

But he needed to know where they were and he wanted to know now. Neither Richards nor Funnel knew anything about their whereabouts, but Funnel did tell Dell he knew her dad was still chairman of the local Royal British Legion and he knew this because his old man used the Legion on a regular basis. He also said Dell's father-in-law, so to speak, spent most of his time at his villa on the Costa del Sol, Spain.

"Spain, God, I'd forgotten about his place over there," said Dell.

"Well, no one's seen your old woman for a couple of years now, Joe, so maybe she's over there with them," said Richards.

"Yeah, you could be right, Baz. You couldn't get your old man to find out for me, could ya, Tel?" asked Dell.

"Yeah, 'course I can, leave it with me," replied Funnel.

As this Stewards Inquiry concluded, another one down the road was just starting. This one was chaired by The Ayatollah at the Islamic Centre. A number of things were on the agenda as the four-man Desert Storm Terror Cell or the DSTC sat around a table in a back room of the Centre. The Ayatollah spoke in his heavy, Middle Eastern, broken English accent on subjects including hate preaching and raising funds to buy weapons and bomb-making equipment. He asked the group if they thought they should recruit more members for their cell or encourage others to follow their lead. It was agreed that a four-man cell was perfect for them as they wanted to remain as secret and undercover as possible. They didn't need any newcomers infiltrating the group who might increase their chances of being exposed. So it was agreed they'd remain as four but would continue to encourage and promote extremism to the best of their ability. Next on the agenda was the target for destruction, and so far the best idea they could come up with was a school. They were not all agreed on this, but The Ayatollah had something to say on the matter.

"What I have to say on the subject of a school as our target is this: having carried out many reconnaissances with Cairo here, I see that many pupils who attend the schools in these parts are in fact Muslim children and that targeting a school here would only be an attack on our own people. And this we do not want. So we will have to keep looking. Do you agree with me, my brothers?" asked The Ayatollah with his arms spread wide. The other three sat looking at him, nodding in agreement. All they wanted to do was wreak havoc, and if The Ayatollah said it was okay by him, it was okay by them. Other things were discussed but as the meeting drew to a close, The Ayatollah remembered a potential target Cairo had brought to his attention earlier. "Brothers of Islam," he said, "I almost forgot that Cairo has come up with a potential target. Would you care to explain, sister, your brilliant idea to the others?"

"No, no brother, you explain," she replied obsequiously.

He nodded and continued, "Sister Cairo has suggested we target a British Legion Club on Remembrance Sunday, and this year they celebrate one hundred years of the end of World War One. We have such a club on our doorstep, and it is a big club and plenty of people will be there to celebrate. These are all infidels and enemies of Islam. What you say, is this a good idea or what?" beamed The Ayatollah as he looked at Cairo, who couldn't contain her joy. She grinned from ear to ear. The others were smiling too and they agreed this would be an ideal target and as it was still a couple of months away, they'd have plenty of time to raise the funds needed to organise themselves properly.

So it was agreed: they would hit the soldiers of the past and present as they gathered on a Sunday morning to pay their respects to their war dead over the past one hundred years. Brilliant! The Centre of course had been bugged by MI5, so all this latest intelligence was passed down the necessary channels until it reached Butler. Now was the time to act.

*   *   *

Gerry Funnel's business had quickly grown to a very substantial enterprise, but now he was about to get what every drug dealer dreaded—a raid. One was planned for Funnel, but not until surveillance was sure he had enough drugs in his possession to put him away for a good few years. This way he was sure to provide enough information on Dell's firm that could get them arrested and into Butler's capable hands. But first, he needed Gerry in his pocket to ensure this happened.

Gerry carried on his dirty work without a care in the world and as his business grew, so did the size of the drug delivery he would pick up at any one time. He was now buying two kilograms of the finest cocaine—top grade— almost one hundred percent pure from a supplier with a very good reputation. It came through the Flowery firm but was purchased from an outlet that kept the firm very much out of the picture. With Gerry under observation, it was only a matter of time before the Drug Squad pounced on him, and that would be when he was carrying enough of the drug to earn himself at least ten years in prison.

*　*　*

The Durleys' problems were also just beginning. Several women had come forward with reports of a sexual nature and with Rita growing ever fonder of Shifty Ifty their little world was about to fall apart. If Big Burt thought there had been too much activity before, he hadn't seen anything yet. But one thing was certain: that gut feeling he had was correct and half of the punters in the pub were about to fall victim to that feeling. He must have a sixth sense.

Bart was the first of the Durleys to get his collar felt by the local constabulary and when he was asked to accompany them to the local nick, the only thing he could think of was the Range Rover he had stolen while at a George Michael concert a few years earlier so he could pull an insurance scam. But that would be very hard to prove. He left his house with two officers and wasn't too worried. The Bill Winters investigation had been dropped, so what was there to worry about, anyway? At the station while the desk sergeant was checking him in, he was very calm until a loud commotion startled him. In walked his old man kicking up a right stink, hands cuffed behind his back, squeaking away like a piglet. *What's the old man done now?* thought Bart to himself. *This must be why I'm here.*

Bart racked his brains for all he was worth, trying to work out exactly what it was all about as the Old Bill wouldn't tell him. Then he thought about all the other insurance frauds he'd pulled off on other motors in the past, but that was nothing to do with his dad. The old man didn't even know about them. But his father had a rough idea why he was there. The police had said to him this business was of a sexual nature, hence all the shrieking and girly high-pitched shouting. Before the pair could speak to one another, Bart was carried off to the cells and locked up until his interview. He told himself again he didn't have anything to worry about. It would all be sorted quickly and he would soon be on his way.

Bart sat in his lonely cell and began to let his mind wander. As he did so the old recurring panic attacks started up again. It's funny how your conscience comes back to haunt you, but at this particular time, Bart didn't realise why. It wouldn't be long before he found out what his old man had already concluded.

CHAPTER 18

Dick got put in a separate cell well away from Bart's. In fact, he was in the women's cells and he knew only too well he was in mire up to his neck. It didn't matter how many Hail Marys he said or how many times he crossed himself—not even the big fella could save him now. He may as well have prayed to Allah for all the good it was going to do him. He sat with his head in his hands as the cell door slammed shut, leaving him alone with his thoughts. What would Rita say?

He thought back to those days when he had cleaned the windows of that convent with Bart, who was in his early teens at the time. Dick had genuinely thought those girls fancied him and he'd not actually done anything wrong. Those young innocents had flirted, encouraged, and egged him on. He had simply obliged. But like his son he'd been abused as a choirboy. Had he encouraged that? He didn't think he had and he felt it was alright to take advantage of school kids since it had happened to him.

Had Bart been through the same experience? Maybe he had. Bart had indulged in those perverted acts the same as Dick had. The more Dick thought about it, the more he began to shake, sweat, and panic until he came up with a very simple answer to the problem: blame Bart. It was his son, not him, who had sexually abused those girls. Yeah, that's it, blame Bart. Dick actually managed to convince himself it was his son who did the dirty deeds and as loyalty was not something the Durley family practiced, it wouldn't matter if Bart took the blame so Dick would not have to spend the autumn years of his life in jail. So that was what Dick decided he would do when the police questioned him. He'd blame his son.

As Bart's panic attack eased, the police cautioned him and then told him the reason for his being there. They started questioning him. They didn't get very far because as the accusations sank in and the questions started coming, true to form, Bart had another panic attack and this time a doctor had to be called. His dad meanwhile was left rotting in his cell until he too came down with a "Durley attack." It must be a hereditary problem and it didn't seem to be the only thing passed down through the Durley genes. The panic attack saga dragged on, but that only delayed the inevitable and kept the pair at the police station for much longer than was necessary at this stage of the investigation.

Rita was obviously aware of her husband's arrest and after having spoken to her daughter-in-law, she was also aware of her son's. Although at this point neither of them knew why their men had been arrested, they both knew it had nothing to do with the boating accident. Dick wouldn't have been taken in for that as he wasn't there. But Rita did learn, after phoning the local nick, that neither of the men would be released any time soon due to unforeseen circumstances. They would probably be kept overnight. Although a little bit concerned, the coldhearted Rita decided to seek a little comfort from Shifty Ifty.

She reached for the phone and dialled Ifty's office. Much to her joy, the man himself answered. Rita looked up and mouthed the words "Thank you, God" and explained Dick's situation and how lonely and frightened she'd become. Could they possibly meet up for a drink? Ifty said he would send a cab and to meet in the Country at seven o'clock but to make it look like a chance meeting. Rita agreed readily. With Dick incarcerated for the night and no Bart to poke his nose in, she was free to have the night with the man she had developed a need for. Dressed up to the nines in saucy stockings and suspenders, Rita was going out to enjoy herself. *Sod the old man*, she thought. With Dick and Bart's continuing issues with panic attacks and the unfortunately unobtainable solicitor they'd been recently bragging about, it looked like they would be spending a bit longer at the local nick than they first thought.

Rita got to the pub early, looking very much a woman ready for action. Her extremely tarty appearance didn't go unnoticed. She was in her mid-sixties with dyed auburn hair covering her natural greying ginger. Five foot six, with a pallid complexion, she had never been a great looker at any stage of her life, but she was noticed by many as while not overweight, she did carry a substantial backside.

One or two eyebrows were raised when Rita strolled into the Country and leaned against the bar, looking around as if to say, "I'm here boys, what d'ya think?"

"Bloody 'ell, look at Durley's old woman. She looks like an old brass," commented Burt.

"Cor, you're not wrong, Burt. That'll do you, mate," laughed Dell.

Big Burt gave his mate Dell a funny look and said gruffly, "You can fuck off. Anyway, I fancy a drink tonight. I've got the taste for it and when that happens—you know the old saying?"

"Yeah, I know it alright. One pint's too many, a hundred's not enough," Dell laughed. "Yeah, actually, I fancy a few myself too. Cam on let's have another."

As Dell got up, he saw Gerry sitting at the other end of the bar near the spruced-up Rita. As their eyes met, Dell said "alright" to Gerry and nodded toward Rita. The pair smirked as Gerry pulled a face that said, "Jesus Christ, I know what you mean."

As Dell ordered the drinks, Gerry got up and started to talk with Rita. "Where are the boys tonight then, Rita?"

"An' don't talk to me about them," she said matter-of-factly.

"Why? What have they been up to then?" Gerry asked.

"I don't know, but they've both been nicked and they won't be home tonight," she said in a tone of voice that said it all.

"Sorry to hear that, Rita," said Gerry.

"Well, don't be, my love. I'm gonna have a few tonight and forget all about it."

"What have they been nicked for?"

"I don't know and I don't really care," came her sharp reply.

Dell overheard the conversation and hurried back to the table where he and Burt were sitting. Handing Burt his pint, he was laughing as he said to Burt, "I just heard Durley's old woman telling Gerry the pair of them have been nicked."

"What, Dick and his soppy son?"

"Yeah, and she reckons they ain't getting out tonight either."

"Oh yeah? What they been nicked for then?"

"She don't know, but I bet that's why she's all tarted up, Burt. Go on, my son, get in there."

Burt pulled a face and shook his head in disgust.

"Probably been nicked for noncing, it wouldn't surprise me," said Burt.

"Nah, nor me, to be honest. Anyway, looks like Rita's doing a bit of noncing herself. Look, Gerry's drooling all over 'er," laughed Dell.

"Don't be silly. He wouldn't be interested in an old granny like that, would he?"

"Fucked if I know. Ah, look out, he's got competition now. Look, Shifty's just turned up and I bet he's wearing breadcrumbs," said Dell, still laughing.

"Breadcrumbs? What are you on about?" asked Burt.

"Aftershave, Burt, breadcrumbs, the birds love it," said Dell, slapping his face with both hands as if to apply the smelly stuff. The pair laughed out loud.

Burt said, "Breadcrumbs, you cunt, I like that one. I'm gonna have to use that myself."

"What and cop a bird like Rita? I knew it," teased Dell.

"That ain't a bird, more a vulture, I s'pose. Look at it. The whole family's fucked. No wonder the boy's an idiot," Burt said seriously. "Mutton dressed up as fucking lamb. Mind you, you can't blame her—the old man's a bloody prick."

"Looks like Shifty don't mind a GILF though, Burt," said Dell.

"Go on then, what's a GILF?" asked Burt.

"Granny I'd like to fuck. It's an acronym. GILF," chuckled Dell.

"You ain't well, Joey boy, breadcrumbs, now GILF. Anyway, I said there's too much activity going on around this place, didn't I? Now those two have been nicked. Who's next? I bet they're coming out with some stories between 'em," Burt said, a very serious look on his face.

"Yeah, well, let 'em. They don't know F-all about us lot," said Dell, his face also serious.

"That won't matter. They make it up as they go along."

Shifty greeted Rita with the old "Surprised to see you in here by yourself, Rita," routine and she replied accordingly. The pair put on an act for a few minutes in an attempt to make their meeting look like a chance one. She only briefly mentioned her old man's arrest before getting stuck into the large gins Shifty and Funnel were buying for her, both men now seemingly competing for Rita's attention, which seemed a bit out of character for Gerry, considering his sexual preferences. Perhaps he, as one of Bart's most regular customers, was trying to find out the real reason for Bart's arrest. Anyway, it was Shifty Rita wanted—her intentions were crystal clear—and she didn't know the reason for Dick and Bart's arrests, so Gerry wasn't going to get anywhere. All the same, the three of them drank the evening away as did Burt and Dell.

While Rita was setting out her stall for the evening, things weren't quite so romantic for the other two Durleys over at the local police station. Neither man had yet been questioned, but both had been sedated by a doctor. As the pair relaxed and slept with only their dreams for a bit of comfort, their wife/mother was planning on heading back to the family home for a night of excitement and passion with the renowned boss of the local Shift's Lifts taxi company.

It was getting a bit late now. Rita's head was spinning a little and Big Burt was starting to feel a bit hungry. Dell looked at his watch, a nice top-of-the-range Rolex, and saw it was ten fifteen. He then said, "Yeah, I could do with something, Burt, what ya fancy?"

"Well, after watching them two all night I don't fancy Indian, Joe. What about you?"

"Nah, neither do I. Makes ya feel sick dun it, a woman of her age behaving like that? Mind you, none of our business, Burt. Let 'em get on with it. What about the Turkish place up the High Street? Fancy that?"

"What's that like? I haven't tried it," said Burt.

"Yeah, it's alright. Plenty of meat and rice nicely done out and the beer's good. You'd like it," Dell replied.

"Cam on then, drink up. We'll have a stroll up there then," said Burt as he threw the remains of his pint down him as if he were in a race. Off they went, saying goodbye to the bar staff as they left. Mickey was not behind the bar tonight. He was relaxing upstairs in front of the TV. They glanced at Rita and Shifty schmoozing at the bar and both men shook their heads as they walked out the door.

Rita looked at her watch and then asked Shifty if he was hungry, to which he replied he fancied a little nibble on something, but he wasn't hungry. "Okay, let's have one for the road and you come back to mine with me," said Rita, seductively rubbing at Ifty's chest through his shirt. The pair giggled like teenagers. They both sipped slowly on their last drink and waited for one of Ifty's drivers to take them back to the marital home of the Durleys.

Gerry, having left the pub, was not the only one going to wake up in the morning with more than a headache. He'd gone home to turn a sizeable amount of cocaine into its purist form, crack, the popular choice of the fund-raising section of the DSTC and its growing clientele. Gerry's job tonight was to process half a kilo, but after he had broken a bit off and chopped it into lines and sniffed it up himself, he couldn't be bothered. Instead, after a couple of goes on it he decided to give one of his "boys" a bell and see if he would like to join him for a bit of fun. The other man accepted Gerry's offer and the pair of them spent the night together high on drugs and indulging in sex.

CHAPTER 19

When the sun rose over London the next morning Gerry found himself still in bed with his friend and in a bit of a panic as he remembered he had a ten o'clock appointment and he hadn't gotten even half of the order prepared.

Rita woke up with her head banging and then turned and saw Ifty beside her. Looking under the duvet, she saw the pair of them were naked except for Rita's stockings and suspenders. She knew she needed to get rid of him quickly, just in case they let the old man out. She didn't want the neighbours to see him either, so Ifty got rushed out of the Durley residence a bit lively.

Joey Dell woke up at his usual prison time, although he was beginning to sleep in a little longer. But he couldn't rid himself of the guilt he was feeling over his son and the longing to see him seemed to be getting ever stronger.

The Durley men woke up to find last night's bad dreams were actually today's nightmares. It seemed the only way they could rid themselves of these nightmares was to blame the other. No loyalties here—it was every man for himself. That's how these people thought. Look after number one was their policy because they had no choice but to face questioning. Panic attacks would not be accepted today. The police wanted answers from this pair and were not in the least bit impressed by the previous day's performances. Waking up in a police cell frightened the life out of Dick and he started to have visions of spending the rest of his days in prison. If he was found guilty of whatever, they would throw the book at him and he was getting on in years. Bart was therefore going to have to carry the can.

In another cell Bart was not quite as perturbed at waking up in a cell as his father, as he'd done exactly that only a while back when being questioned over Bill's disappearance. But he was thinking along the same lines as his old man. As Dick was getting on a bit, Dick could carry the can. He'd had a good life and it wouldn't matter too much if his last few years were spent in prison. Bart didn't fancy prison at all. Surely Dick would bail him out again.

Rita knew of her son and husband's ability to talk bullshit on any subject volunteered to them, but try as she might she had been unable to stop it. It appeared hereditary and in her heart she knew she was always fighting a losing battle. Both men believed their own lies and that was dangerous. Had she known the charges her husband was about to face, she wouldn't and couldn't have changed anything. Ifty was always going to be her jockey. She was sure he would go the distance. And anyway she had been thinking about leaving her husband for years now.

Dell meanwhile had gotten on the phone pretty soon after his breakfast to ask if Terry had found time to ask his old man about his ex's old man. He was told his former father-in-law was spending most of his time in Spain at the villa on the Costa del Sol, but as of yet Terry didn't know whether Harry and his mum were living there too.

Gerry had managed to process his cocaine parcel in time for the pre-arranged meet and had then inadvertently done the deal right in front of the MI5 observation team. Things were heating up for certain people in this part of London and the epicentre of the forthcoming eruption would likely be the

Country. The big question was, which client would be next? Gerry was looking a strong favourite and if he went along with the Durleys, there was no telling who'd go after that. Poor old Mickey might lose all his regulars in a very short space of time.

* * *

First up for questioning was Dick and as his cell door opened he turned to face PC Jones. Jones noticed he'd hardly touched his breakfast and what he had eaten was mostly still stuck to his chin.

"Sleep well, Sir?"

"No!" squeaked back Dick.

"Not fancy your breakfast then, Sir?"

"No, it's disgusting," replied Dick, self-pity on his dopey-looking face.

"Well, you might have to start getting used to it, mate. You're wanted for questioning upstairs now, so you'd better get washed and come with me."

"I'm not answering anything until I've seen my solicitor, Cuthbert Knipe," said Dick smugly.

"Gutters is upstairs waiting for you, Sir, so we can proceed."

Knipe was known to police as Gutters—as in guttersnipe—due mainly to the type of defendant he represented. The Durleys were excellent examples of the quality of his clients.

Durley cleaned himself up at the basin in his cell and attempted to make himself look presentable, but he failed miserably. Jones looked on, grinning at the disheveled Durley. He was the proverbial rabbit caught in the headlights.

In the interview room Durley met up with his slimy-looking brief, who looked more of a pedophile than Durley did. He had long, greasy, uncombed black hair that hung down to his shoulders and that he kept slicked back. It made people's skin crawl. All who met him wondered when he had last had a bath. But the Durleys still thought the sun shone out of his backside. On first appearance most people wouldn't ask him to clean their lavatory, let alone represent them in a court of law.

Durley went through the usual process of having his rights read before the two officers present started firing questions at him. Dick looked terribly confused as different names came up of young girls from about twenty-five years ago who had recently come forward to lodge their complaints. None of the names meant anything to him now as that part of his life had been erased most conveniently from his miserable little memory.

He continually looked to his brief for support, but it wasn't forthcoming as Knipe couldn't advise him on such matters while on camera and audiotape. It was down to Dick to answer the questions as he saw best and the only way he saw fit was to blame his son and repeat time after time that the police must have the pair mixed up, a likely mistake as at the time Dick would have been in his early forties and Bart would have been in his early teens. The worst questions were about two boys from the church football team who both claimed Dick had molested them when they were aged between ten and eleven and played on the same team as Bart. He couldn't blame Bart for those, could he? Dick realised he was in it up to his neck. He began to wonder how long you had to go before your past would leave you alone. Obviously longer than this. And had he not gotten his picture in the *West London Gazette* because of Bart's inability to sail a boat, all of this would probably not have occurred. He decided to carry on his interview with "no comment."

Bart had to wait for his father's interview to conclude before it was his turn. Dick had stopped answering police questions about his sexual behaviour with the under-aged, but he couldn't help but make up stories about his son. One minute Bart was the sexual deviant they should be looking at. The next minute he was harder than Mike Tyson.

When PC Jones, the jailer on duty that day, opened Bart's cell door, it was no iron man that stood before him, but a quivering plate of jelly. Bart looked at Jones with the usual Durley frightened face and all signs pointed to an upset stomach. "Phwoar!" Jones greeted Bart as the smell from the cell's toilet hit him like a brick wall.

"I ... I've had Delhi belly," stuttered Bart.

"Jeessuss, you're not kidding. Let me fetch the air freshener." Once Jones had fumigated Bart's cell, he grabbed Bart by the arm and, without wasting any more words, led him to the interview room.

"Where's my solicitor?" Bart asked.

"Don't worry. He's here," snapped Jones. Jones felt extremely uncomfortable around Bart and knew there was something about Bart he didn't like at all. Jones knocked on the door of the room where Bart's solicitor was waiting with the two officers.

"Got Bart Durley here, Sir," said Jones, showing Bart into the room. "Oh, and be careful. He's got an upset stomach," he quipped with a little snigger.

"Thank you very much for the warning, Jones," said Jim Drayton, the officer in charge.

Bart entered the room, looking like he was about to burst into tears as the two officers eyed him up and down. This wasn't the hard man his dad had described in his contradictory statement, but Bart did look like the sex pest Dick would try to put the blame on. Durley sat next to his brief and with his sweaty palms shook his hand and greeted him with the usual "Hello, Mr. Knipe." Knipe asked if they could have a few moments alone and Drayton agreed as he fancied a cup of tea anyway.

As Drayton and his sidekick, Bob Harris, left the room, they both had their eyes firmly fixed on this smarmy-looking Durley. These two officers were trained Pedophile Online Investigation Team officers or POLIT for short. They both certainly knew a wrong'un when they saw one and they saw two in this pair. As they entered the officers' mess, Harris put the kettle on then turned to Drayton. "Well, Jim, first impressions?"

"Well, Bob, my experience says that just on looks alone that slimy little creep next door is as guilty as sin—as is his old man. Anyway, three million lemmings can't be wrong, can they?" said Drayton.

"My sentiments exactly, Sir. Let's see what codswallop he comes out with. If he's anything like his father, it should be very interesting. I can't wait, but we'll have to try and not laugh. This is a very serious matter."

"Right. We'll have this tea then and take our seats for a couple of hours' entertainment," said Drayton with a grin.

Cuthbert Knipe looked at Bart and said in a very serious tone, "It doesn't look good, Bart, and you should think very carefully before answering any questions. A lot of women have made statements against you and your father."

"What? What women and from where? Who are these women and when were these things supposed to have happened?" asked Bart frantically.

"Well, they were young girls at the time of the alleged incidents, all of whom attended a convent you and your father were supposed to have cleaned windows for some years ago. And to make matters worse for your father, a couple of men have also put in a complaint from when they played on the church football team your dad helped run," said Knipe.

"Shut up! That was twenty-odd years ago and they were all willing participants!"

"Yes, that may be, but they were all under age, some of them very much so. All this would probably never have come to light had it not been for the publicity you received over that boating accident. It seems a few skeletons have been rattled," said Knipe glumly.

Bart put his head in his hands and said in a tearful voice, "I don't sodding believe it. This is a nightmare. What am I going to tell my wife? She'll go bloody ballistic," sobbed Bart.

"I think your wife is the least of your problems at the moment, Bart," said Knipe, putting his hand on Bart's shoulder in an attempt to comfort him.

Once they had finished laughing, Drayton and Harris went back to the interview room to start questioning Bart. They weren't about to take the panic attacks as an excuse. They knew from experience Bart would melt like an ice cream. They couldn't wait to hear the crap he was about to come out with. He didn't let them down. Once the questioning started, so did Bart's bullshit. He quivered like a guilty man. They knew he was banged to rights, but they still had to go through due process regardless.

As the questions started, Bart began to panic, but that didn't stop the lies queuing up to get out of his mouth. Bart was gripping his seat and sweat poured from his brow. He became more and more uncomfortable with the interrogation tactics of the two officers in front of him. Several girls' names were mentioned that Bart honestly couldn't recall. One or two silly answers Bart gave prompted the odd cough and a few nudges from his brief, who wasn't at all impressed with Bart or his father in the face of adversity. Neither one held himself up at all. Bart even resorted to blaming his dad for the events of all those years ago. "Like father, like son" was the expression and these two were its living proof. This was exactly what Drayton and Harris expected from the pair of them. It certainly made it easier to bring charges, especially when they mentioned a certain girl Bart had had a serious crush on back in the day, Madaline Bedfont. The officers held her as an ace up their sleeves, so to speak. When this name was mentioned, Bart's expressions and mannerisms gave the game away completely. Bart couldn't contain himself on this one; his body language said it all.

Madaline had two older sisters and they lived in a big house with their parents. All three girls were a catch for anyone. Bart fancied himself the man to bag himself a Bedfont, but as the older two were too well educated and streetwise for Bart, he focused on the youngest sibling. A girl of thirteen and a half surely would be very flattered by the attentions of an older man, he reasoned, (even though Bart was only sixteen himself). Madaline was seemed to agree and at the time appeared happy to accept Bart's advances. Her name was still firmly embedded in Bart's memory and it was a great shock to him that Madaline, out of all of them, should file a complaint about him. He thought they had had something special between them and that their little illegal romance would remain a lasting secret memory. Bart couldn't hide the shock and disappointment on his face.

"So then, Mr. Durley, you remember this girl very well, don't you, Sir?" said Drayton knowingly.

"Err, err, well, the name does ring a bell, sort of," stuttered Bart.

"Too right it does. You had a full on romance with this poor innocent underage girl, didn't you? And you took away her innocence in a vile forced way, didn't you, Mr. Durley?" said Drayton, sternly this time.

"No, Sir, I didn't. I wouldn't do such a thing, Sir, honestly I wouldn't. That sort of thing just isn't in my blood, Sir. I swear. I'll take the oath, Sir," said Bart tamely and very unconvincingly.

"Well, you just might have to, my son, and what about young boys? Are they in your blood, sonny boy?" inquired Drayton, knowing full well there hadn't been a complaint against Bart from any boys, unlike his father.

"Young boys? What are you talking about? Are you trying to fit me up or what?"

"Ah no, Sir. You've hung yourself anyway. And just for the record, sonny, fitting people up isn't in our blood either," said Harris, joining in the fun.

Bart had an idea but looked at his trusted brief for support as he leaned across the table to put his plan to the two officers who stared coldly back at him. "What if we could do a deal here between the four of us? No one would need to know. You know, I scratch your back, so to speak," asked Bart in a slimy manner.

The two officers looked at each other with blank expressions. Both men raised an eyebrow and shook their heads in disgust.

"So, basically you want to grass people up to us for a bit of leniency, do you, Mr. Durley?" inquired Drayton.

"Yeah, that's right. I give you a few names and you let me go, that sort of thing," said Bart smugly.

"Oh really? Well, in this sort of case, we'll have to review it because this is a very serious situation, Mr. Durley. I hope you understand these things aren't taken lightly," said Drayton, regarding him as a slime bag. "Who exactly do you have in mind then, Mr. Durley?"

"Well, for starters, there's Gerry Funnel, a top drug dealer," replied Bart.

"Whoa, whoa!" interrupted Knipe. He knew Bart would need a lot of evidence to even try to make a deal and this was anyway clearly a case where a deal couldn't be struck at any cost.

"Oh really? And what evidence do you have to back up your accusation then, Mr. Durley?" chipped in Harris.

Bart was clutching at straws, but deep down he had begun to suspect Gerry might have been the source of all the media attention. This would possibly be a way to get even.

CHAPTER 20

Rita by now was fully aware of her men's situation and she knew only too well neither man was coming home any time soon. This gave her another opportunity to entice Ifty, seeing as he had "ridden" her so well the night before. Her mind cast back to Marcus, the cabbie she'd left Dick and Bart for many years before when Bart was still a young boy. How she'd love that sort of relationship again, but Marcus had settled down again with his wife. But Ifty could be a good replacement. Rita was looking for a second go, knowing what a dog her husband was, but not knowing fully just yet what a complete dog he really was.

She was getting herself very worked up at the thought of another night of passion with Ifty. She reached for her phone, hoping Ifty hadn't looked at the previous night as a one-off. To Rita's delight, Ifty actually felt the same as her. They arranged once more for a meeting at the pub for a few beverages before going back to Rita's for a repeat performance.

While Rita was tarting herself up, Bart sat in front of the two POLIT officers, reeling off names he thought would get him a quick release. Although

Drayton and Harris took great delight in listening to the names he'd thrown into the pot, it wouldn't do the no-good nonce any good.

In fact, Bart had come very close to confessing to all the cars he had stolen for insurance purposes, until he realised it was other people he needed to give up, not himself. Cuthbert Knipe was quite disgusted at his client's behaviour and no matter how he tried to advise Bart, he couldn't stop the flow of tales coming out of Bart's desperate big mouth. He was fast becoming an embarrassment as a client and that really was saying something for a man like Knipe.

Rita's meeting with Ifty just happened to coincide with a meeting Gerry had arranged with the two fundraisers for the DSTC. This pleasant gathering was once again observed by the Drug Squad and as Ifty and Rita happened to be in their company, they were now on the list of people of interest.

"Evening, Rita. You here alone again?" remarked Gerry.

"Hello, Gerry. Yeah, thought I'd pop in for a couple, seeing as Dick and Bart haven't been released yet, and I bumped into Ifty here who very kindly got me a drink," replied Rita matter-of-factly.

"Careful, Rita, people'll start talking soon," said Gerry.

"What? About Dick and Bart?" asked Rita sarcastically.

"No, about you and Ifty. Anyway, why are they keeping 'em in? What the bleedin' hell have they done?"

"Well, love, I don't know what they're supposed to have done, but they did tell me both of 'em had panic attacks yesterday and they were unable to interview them. They are going to keep 'em in until they can interview 'em, darling," explained Rita.

"Panic attacks!" exclaimed Gerry. "That doesn't sound very good, does it?"

"Ah, don't worry, darling. They're both drama queens, but I think you'll find my son is worse than his father."

Gerry started to worry a bit. Bart knew a little bit about his drug activities and if he was getting all panicked out down at the station, then he might start talking. As he took a bathroom break, in walked his two ISIS pals for a meeting and a possible reorder. Gerry's mind would soon get back to business.

"Hello, boys. You here to see Gerry?" said Rita slightly provocatively.

"Yeah, love," said Badini, his face hidden beneath a baseball cap.

"Alright, boys?" said Ifty, smiling.

"Yeah, you alright, Ifty? Where's Gerry?"

"Gone to the toilet, mate," replied Ifty.

The four of them made small talk until Gerry returned, all the time observed by persons unknown.

Over at the other side of the pub sat Dell with Terry Funnel and Richards, very quietly chatting about another trip regarding the Swedish. This time there were going to be a few changes. These changes were not going to suit everyone, but they were certainly going to be more profitable, a lot more logical, and a lot less likely to allow the product to be lost at Border Control. The Swedes had requested a change of dispatch and Dell thought they were starting to get a bit complacent with the whole thing. A change was as good as a rest. Anyway, a meeting was going to have to be called with the newly recruited David Lightfoot and a new deal discussed as he might not be in agreement.

Down at the local police station, the Durleys were settling in for another night of discomfort before appearing before the local magistrate. At this point the police were going to object to bail and Knipe was pretty certain his clients couldn't make bail anyway. A chain is only as strong as its weakest link and these two were very weak links indeed. Rita wasn't overly bothered about their situation at this particular point in time. Tonight all she was concerned about was getting home for round two with Ifty.

Dell asked Terry to set up a meeting with David as soon as he could and told Terry he didn't want to meet in the pub. Somewhere a little more private would be required to discuss what he had in mind and what the Swedish had asked for this time around.

Gerry had gone home, satisfied with his order of yet more crack from his new Asian pals, but on his mind and very much a worry was the situation regarding his associate Bart Durley. Gerry just couldn't get it off his mind and he thought two nights in the police cells for a pair like this seemed like a long time. There must be something more to it than Rita was letting on.

CHAPTER 21

Gerry spent a very restless night and paced the room several times before finally getting up at five. He wanted to speak to Rita and fast, but it was too early to ring her. Gerry made himself a cup of tea and rolled his first cannabis joint of the day. As he was engulfed in a sickly smelling cloud of smoke, he inhaled as he sat pondering. He was becoming almost obsessed with Bart's situation, but it was more out of self-preservation than concern for Bart and his dad.

Ifty had an early shift that morning and he rose early as he did most mornings. But he had the semi-naked Rita next to him, so he decided to wake her up with his version of Turkish Delight. Rita loved it. It had been years since Dick had woken her up like that. Now that she was wide awake, she got up and made coffee. As the pair sat in the kitchen, Ifty's phone made a noise and as he glanced at it, he saw it was Gerry texting him. Gerry was asking if he had Rita's number as he wanted to speak to her urgently. Ifty waited to reply until he'd left Rita's, just to be on the safe side. He drank his coffee quickly and made his way to work after giving Rita a peck on the cheek and a squeeze on her ample backside. Once well away from the house, he rang Gerry to find out what it was all about.

"Morning, Gerry, my good friend. This is early for you isn't it? What can I do for you?"

"Have you got Rita's number, mate? I need to find out what's going on with Bart and his old man."

"Err, I don't have it myself, Gerry, as I'm sure you know, but it might be in the office. When I get there, I'll have a look for ya."

"Cheers, Ifty. How long do you think that'll be, mate?"

"Oooh, ten or fifteen minutes. Leave it with me, Gerry, mate."

"Thanks, mate. Speak to you soon."

Ifty rang Rita straightaway and asked her if it was okay to pass her number on to Gerry and explained why Gerry had phoned. Rita was alright with that and thought she probably should have done a bit more to find out what was going on, but under her circumstances with Ifty, perhaps it was a good idea that someone else took the reins for a change.

Ifty left it a while before ringing Gerry back and went through the pretence of the old "took me ages to get it" trick before passing Rita's number on. Once Gerry got the number, he wasted no time ringing her. Rita quickly sensed Gerry was concerned about her husband and son's welfare, so she promised she would ring the police and get an update as soon as she could.

She rang the station immediately after she'd hung up with Gerry and asked what was happening with the Durleys. She was shocked to find out they were appearing in court at ten that very morning. Why hadn't her daughter-in-law called her to let her know? Maybe Sebrina didn't know herself, or perhaps she had been doing what Rita had, enjoying a couple days off with another lover.

Rita got back to Gerry and explained what was going on. She told him the telephonist didn't know what the charge was, so if he didn't mind, could he get to West London Magistrates' Court and find out what it was all about for her? Gerry said he didn't mind at all and he'd let her know as soon as he had any information. As Rita got off the phone, she paused for a moment before calling Sebrina. Sebrina's phone rang for a while before the answering machine kicked in. Rita left a message and without too much worry carried on with her day. It was still early, so she didn't think it was unusual that Sebrina hadn't picked up. But Rita's idea about her daughter-in-law living up to her name of Sexy Sebs was along the right lines.

Gerry got himself over to the courthouse, only to be greeted on arrival by Mr. Drayton himself, who on seeing Gerry promptly walked up to him and, looking him up and down in a distasteful manner, came out with, "And what is a horrible little man like yourself doing here, Funnel? I haven't noticed your name on the program of artists appearing at these premises today. So what are you doing here?"

"Morning, Mr. Drayton, nice to see you too. No ... no, you're right. I'm not on stage today, just a social visit, I'm afraid."

"Ah, yeah. That's what Hitler said when he invaded Poland."

"Well, I'll try not to disappoint you, then." Gerry looked around for a friendly, familiar face.

"You've come to find your grubby little oppo, Durley, haven't you?" said Drayton, raising a knowing eyebrow.

"Well, as it happens, Mr. Drayton, Sir, yes I have, as it goes. Where is he then?" asked Gerry, still trying to find an excuse to get away from Drayton.

"In the cells beneath here. Best place for scum like that. I knew you were low life, Funnel, but admitting to knowing filth like that takes you very low, even for a man like you," said Drayton, still displaying that pained expression.

"I was a kid when you nicked me, Mr. Drayton. I've changed since then."

"Really, Mr. Funnel? I very much doubt it. If you're coming here looking for Bart Nicholas Durley, that says it all."

"I'm not sure what you're talking about, but what is the charge?" asked Gerry.

"You'll have to ask his equally horrible slimy brief that, won't you, my son?"

"Well, I would if I knew who's representing him, wouldn't I?"

"Who else but the one and only Guttersnipe? Your old mate Cuthbert," said Drayton.

Now Gerry knew this was a case of a sexual nature. Knipe had represented him when he was caught in a position of indecency by Drayton himself. Knipe was renowned for that type of case, not being too straight himself, but Gerry didn't know he was the Durley's brief, period. This alone was very odd as your everyday man who leaned to the criminal side, no matter how slightly, would not use a solicitor with Knipe's reputation. This got Gerry's attention and he wanted to know more. But whatever they were charged with, Gerry felt vulnerable. Being seen talking with Knipe wasn't going to do his street credibility any good, and what the hell would Bart possibly be prepared to say about him, or anyone else for that matter, that might help get him off?

Gerry thought it best to ask the clerk of the court what number courtroom Bart was appearing in and go and find out the charges himself. But it was also important for Bart to see him there as Bart would more than likely think he'd come to offer moral support and hopefully keep his big mouth shut.

The Durleys were bought up from the cells into Courtroom No. 2, handcuffed together and to security guards. As they looked around the room, hoping to see a familiar face, both spotted Gerry sitting in the front row of the gallery. Gerry nodded to each of them in such a way Bart wished he wasn't there as he was about to hear the multiple charges against them. The ignominy of it all would be too much for the whole family to take. But at least he'd turned up. That was more than the Durley wives had done.

Gerry at this point was still unaware of the charges the pair were about to face and as they were read out, Gerry sat there wide-eyed and open-mouthed and said to himself in a whispered tone, "*Fuckin' hell.*" He couldn't believe what he was hearing. He looked over toward Drayton, who smiled a smug "told you so" back at Gerry. Gerry wanted to leave and he began to sweat a little. He knew his behaviour at times was unacceptable, but this was really something else.

The Durleys only spoke to confirm their names and addresses and were remanded in custody for a week. After that they could apply for bail.

Gerry got out of there as quickly as he could and got on the phone to inform Rita of what had happened. But he wasn't prepared to tell her of the charges, in fact, he couldn't remember all of them. She was going to have to call Knipe herself. Once the news of the pair's crimes got out, the Durley family would be even more reviled than they already were and Gerry couldn't wait to call his twin brother and tell him all about it.

CHAPTER 22

Dell, Richards, Terry, and Lightfoot were in a meeting at Dell's place to go over the rearranged plan for their Swedish connection. Sven, the Swede, had requested that the cocaine he required now be dropped to him not in kilo lumps as before, but in street form—tiny one-gram plastic balls tied up in a bag and cut down to size so that the cocaine was ready for retail. This would mean more work for the couriers and more expense, but it also meant they could charge by the gram and therefore earn more profit. Dell had given this proposition a lot of thought and as he had been involved in similar situations abroad, he had plenty of ideas on how this should work. He looked at Lightfoot. "Remember a mate of ours, Ronnie Slaughter?"

"Err, no not really," was Lightfoot's reply.

"Well, you might know him as Viagra Ron."

"Ah yeah, I know him, a right villain," smiled Lightfoot as he looked around at the others in the room who were nodding and smiling at his answer.

"He couldn't help being a villain with a name like that, could he? Anyway, me and him started out together years ago doing the same move, but in Spain, on a slightly smaller scale to start with. Well, we didn't have that much money at the time. So what we did was, we'd buy a bar of change (nine ounces of cocaine) and smash it up into 0.8 of a gram with a bit of bosh in it, of course, and sell in the pubs and clubs of Marbella. But we made sure the apartments we'd used as factories were away from the area we would be selling it in. I've given it a lot of thought, David, and I've got a mate who lives in Holland—and it's not Amsterdam—who you can meet, get the gear from him, conceal it in your motor and head up north toward Sweden, where we'll have an apartment rented for you and a mate to do the business in. What you reckon?"

"Yeah, sounds alright, as I won't have to take anything out through customs here, but what about the money? It's a lot of dough to have to take out of the country, innit?" said Lightfoot, looking a little concerned.

"No, you won't be carrying any dough out with you. I'll sort that out the usual way as I do with Sven," replied Dell.

"Ah okay. Well, yeah, sounds alright, Joe. When do I go?"

"Not just yet. Sven was just marking our card and finding out if we'd do it like that, which is why we're all here. I just wanted to know if you were up for it."

"Yeah, and I reckon my brother'll come with me too, but do you reckon we'll look a bit dodgy? Two black men driving up through Europe with a load of gear on us."

"Nah, don't be daft. One man in a motor is a bigger tug than two in this sort of work. Anyway, they're too politically correct to go pulling you boys over there," replied Dell.

"Yeah, you're not wrong there, Joe," grinned Lightfoot.

"Okay, well, we've got a good couple of weeks at least to have a think and find a suitable place for you to work. Oh yeah, and you'll need one of them vac-pack machines to make your parcel smaller and easier to hide. Ah, and another thing, you'll only be grabbing one kilo, but with a bit of bosh and doing up at 0.8s you'll get best part of two out of it," explained Dell.

"How long do you think it'll take us then, Joe?"

"Well, if two of you work all day and into the evening with one measuring the gear out and the other one tying up the bags and cutting the long bit off, I reckon two days, but allow three to be on the safe side and we'll hire the place for a week. So when you're finished and cleaned up, you can leave when you want. How's that sound?"

"Yeah, sounds good to me. I'm up for it," said Lightfoot, smiling once again.

"Okay, good boy, and you'll earn a bit more for your troubles." Dell smiled back and put out his hand to shake Lightfoot's. The pair shook on the deal and both men seemed happy with the arrangements.

The timing couldn't have been better, as just then Terry's phone rang. It was his twin calling about the plight of the Durleys. His reaction to what he was hearing caused everyone in the room to hush up and stare at him as he laughed and said, "F-U-C-K-I-N 'ELL, we all said they were wrong'uns."

"I take it it's to do with them idiot Durleys?" asked Dell.

"Yeeaahh," laughed Terry. "That was my brother. He's been to court and seen and heard it all."

"Well, I was warned about that pair of pricks on my release. Big Burt had them two sussed from the off. Just hope they don't think they know about us, 'cause I still have a few good pals in the shovel and if them batty boy wankers feel like talking, it'll be their last chat, *ever!*"

"Apparently noncin' over a long period of time. Gerry said there were too many charges to remember," was Terry's reply.

"Well, no surprise there. That means they'll be on a special wing. I ain't got no pals down there, obviously, but we can get to 'em if we have to," said Dell.

As Dell paused for thought, he suddenly remembered what Burt had said about the Country and his gut instinct. *Hmm*, he thought to himself before turning to the others. "I don't like it, boys. If they've been remanded for a week, that means they still have to try and make bail the following week. While they're banged up, they are potentially more dangerous than when they're on the outside. God knows what stories those two are concocting as we speak."

"Yeah, he's right. They love a story," said the ever-quiet Richards. Barry was forty-four with cropped hair and he looked like he had spent time in the army. He was over six feet tall, in good shape, and strong. He wore a permanent frown, liked a drink, and liked hurting people when the opportunity arose. Not that he went out of his way to find trouble, of course. So when he spoke the others listened and considered and realised this had the potential to be very dodgy indeed, but what none of them knew was that it was too late for them anyway. In the end it would have nothing to do with the Durleys—it would all come down to fate.

* * *

As the surveillance on the DSTC intensified, Gerry would become of greater interest, as unbeknownst to himself, he was their biggest source of income. But the local Drug Squad would lay the groundwork.

Cairo was instructed to start frequenting the Royal British Legion (RBL) in nearby Greenford and to get feedback on how many people were expected to attend the one-hundred-year commemoration service on Remembrance Sunday. She was to do the reconnaissance work there because (a) it was her idea in the first place and (b) she wouldn't stand out as on the surface she was one of them. She accepted this task with great pride. She would revert to plain Karen White and carry out her mission. When spoken to, the innocent-looking young woman would tell her sad story to whoever she conversed with. This would gain trust as well as sympathy from the unsuspecting members who attended the club, whose sole purpose was to support the military and who no doubt had similar stories of their own. She was the most perfect undercover sister of Islam imaginable. She believed in what she was planning. These people and everything they stood for owed her a living, she thought. They had taken her life away, but now she was reborn and she would take away theirs.

Now the DSTC was infiltrating the enemy and the tracks were rolling nicely on their tank. For now the hate preaching would stop as they needed to keep a low profile. Only the money-making machine would continue. They needed more funds for weaponry and bomb-making equipment and as the cash machine was doing very nicely, thank you, everything was heading in the right direction. All was looking rosy in the garden of extremism.

CHAPTER 23

Tommy Butler was ordered to make his acquaintance with his team and as Dell and the boys were on his first team starting lineup, it wouldn't be long before he paid them a social call once more. Big Burt's gut feeling was quickly becoming reality.

Gerry kept himself busy plying his trade in total ignorance of any potential problems, but it was only when he was fully loaded with narcotics that he would feel the full force of the law. The Durleys roasted in prison until Knipe could get them bail and Rita carried on her affair with Ifty. She really was enjoying the break; it was bliss for her.

It was now time to choose sides. Cairo had made her choice and Butler knew what side his team would choose without even asking, but it was going to take a bit of cunning to get Dell's boys on board. They wouldn't be in any mood to cooperate with the authoritative enemy, but he was more than sure they would team up with him and the rest of their country to destroy the now common enemy who would do everything and anything they could to destroy traditional English freedoms and the lives of people close to their own hearts.

Butler knew Dell's former father-in-law was the president of the Greenford RBL and the Funnel boys' father was a regular patron of the club. In his mind, it wouldn't take too much to convince them to join his crusade. The deal certainly had to be right for Dell's mob to get involved, but Butler was more than confident that his first elected four were more than capable of pulling off the job he intended for them. Or was this too good to be true? That he was going to have to find out for himself, but at whose cost? This was the imponderable.

Butler knew a little more homework was necessary, but he thought he had one or two winning cards. Or at least on the surface he did, but who would have THE trump card, him or Dell? Previous experience told him this was going to be one hell of a hill to climb and Joey Dell was no mug by any means. If Butler could get Dell on his side, he knew he would be almost there.

Dell was beginning to heed Big Burt's feelings and was more cautious than ever, but he still needed to earn a living. Nothing on the doorstep was his opinion. The Sven connection would do for now and then he would wait and see what happened after the dust had settled. With prejudice polluting the land, no one was comfortable as the terror threat was more present than ever. It seemed the vast majority of the country was more determined than ever to come together to combat these people.

CHAPTER 24

Seeing as Dell had recently mentioned his old mate Ronny Slaughter, he thought maybe it was a good time to make contact again, knowing his ex-in-laws had a place on the Costa del Sol and that Ronnie had resided there for a few years. Maybe it was a good idea to take a long shot and ask if he might just possibly have seen Harry and his mother over there in Spain. No one had seen them locally for a good long time.

Dell put a call into his old ally and good friend. They'd learned their trade together in the eighties in Spain, gaining a rapport with the South London bank robbers who ruled the roost at the time. Unfortunately, the robbers had faced extradition, but Dell knew full well Ron was still a face in those parts and if his boy was living there, he'd find out. Terry had also asked his dad to find out for him via Dell's former father-in-law, but he hadn't come back with anything as of yet.

As Ron's phone rang, Dell felt excitement and also a little nervousness about what he might hear.

"Hello," said Ron cautiously. "Who's this?"

"It's Al Pacino," Dell chuckled.

"Bloody hell—it's Flowery Dell. You out of the shovel, son?" bellowed Ron, very happy to hear from his old mate.

"Yeah, 'course I am. How are ya, Ron?"

"All the better for hearing from you, mate. What's happening, my old mate?"

"Well, this and that, Ron. You know me, not one to let the world pass me by when I have the chance."

"Ah, so good to hear your voice. When you coming to see me then, Joe boy? You'll love it over here, mate."

"Well, Ronnie boy, I've not been out too long and I was wondering, seeing as our missuses were great friends back in the day … has she heard from her or seen her and my Harry by any chance? I'm really concerned as to their whereabouts and no one around here has seen hide nor hair of either of 'em."

"Well, as it happens, my son, the old woman bumped into them a few weeks ago down the harbour in Puerto Banus, and the saucy little fucker was wearing a Chelsea shirt!" joked Ron.

"Good boy. Still got a bit of taste then. I was a bit worried he might have turned Manc or something in my absence. Anyway, Ron, was there another fella about, do you know?"

"No, not that I'm aware of, mate. Anyway, don't worry about that. Where's the boy's Millwall shirt is what I wanna know."

"I'd rather that than some northern shit on his back. Do you know if they're living there, Ron? All I thought about in the shovel was him. She never brought him to see me once and I … well, you know, I miss him," said Dell, turning the conversation serious.

"Hang on a minute. I'll ask the old woman." Ron shouted for his wife, Lizzie.

"No, Ron! Don't let her know you've spoken to me. I don't want Chrissie knowing I'm trying to find his whereabouts," pleaded Dell.

"Ah right, okay then. Tell ya what. Leave it with me. I'll ask Liz on the snide and I won't let on that I've spoken to ya. When I find out a bit more, I'll get hold of ya. Is this your number and is it alright to save it?"

"'Course it is, yeah, cheers Ron. Just keep it between me and you for now. Anyway, how's things over there, mate?"

"Yeah, alright, Joe, thanks. We would never go back to London. We love it here. You should come over, or are you too busy running Murder Incorporated's London branch?"

"Nah, mate, not up to much at the moment. There's a strange smell in the air, so we're keeping it a bit quiet. Anyway, I ain't going back to the shovel again. I'm too old for that now and I wanna see my little Harry again."

"Good boy! You must be the sharpest dresser in West London, though, Joe, surely to God?"

"Yeah, yeah, 'course I am. You know me, son. You still living up to your name, Ron?"

"Nah, I don't need to do that anymore. Just enjoying it over here and I would like to see you again soon, mate," said Ron, back to a serious tone.

"Well, Ron, I'll get over as soon as I can, mate, but in the meantime, could you do a bit of research on the boy for me, please, mate?" asked Dell.

"Yeah, 'course I will, anything for my old mate Flowery Dell," Ron said smiling.

"Cheers, Viagra. Been nice talking to you and I'll get over there as soon as I can, mate. Speak to you soon," said Dell as he bid farewell.

"And you, Joe, bye, mate."

Dell sat down feeling a lot happier and relieved now that Harry and his mum had been spotted and were safe. Maybe he'd be able to settle down to the quiet life after all, as long as she wasn't attached. But even if she was, at least he could reunite with his son, hopefully. Dell wasn't about to get his hopes up, but he was pleased he'd made contact with his old mate Ron. He thought back and chuckled at how he got the nickname Viagra Ron.

Ron had gotten himself a pharmaceutical license years ago, with the intention of entering the drugs game legally, but Ron, being Ron, couldn't help himself. When the chance presented itself, it was at the time Viagra first appeared on the market. It became popular with recreational drug users after a night on cocaine and other substances, so Ron ordered a very large shipment of both Viagra and Valium to help the users not only with the obvious, but also to help them sleep. Ron sold the lot in bulk to another villain he knew on the side. He shut the company down, didn't pay for any of the order, sold up, and went to live in Spain. "Valium" Ron didn't have the same ring to it, so "Viagra" Ron stuck after that venture!

Ronnie was a boy without any doubt, but he was concerned about his old mate. He remembered the days of the paramilitaries and how once upon a time they'd been approached by persons unknown to help with the Northern Ireland conflict. He now thought about his mate and wondered if perhaps the same old tactics were being considered, but it was only a thought. He knew full well what Dell was capable of and how he worked.

Ron decided he should call Dell back.

"Alright, Joe?" asked Ron. "Do you remember when we were in Gibraltar?"

"Yeah, yeah, 'course I do. Why? What's up, mate?"

"You remember the men in suits? Same war, but different mob. Well, you just be careful because I've got a notion they're gonna come back at ya!" was Ron's reply.

"Really? Not you as well. Big Burt has a strange feeling too."

"Yeah, but you know how you work and so do I. Please, Joe, keep your wits about you. You know the tea caddies ain't the problem no more, but that ISIS mob are," said Ron sincerely.

"Hell, Ron, I thought you had news about my boy. What the fuck have that lot got to do with me?" asked Dell.

"Don't matter, mate. Obviously you're still the boy over there. They will come at ya, mate. They did it when we were wrapped up with the paddies," replied Ron.

"Yeah, but we were grafting with the paddies. I ain't grafting with that mob, mate."

"Well, just be careful, mate, 'cause you will still be on the radar," said Ron.

Ron couldn't get out of his mind the time they were approached by persons unknown while in Gibraltar back in the day. It kept playing on his mind and he felt the need to remind his friend of past events, whether or not it turned out to be relevant.

Dell started to wonder about the people around him. Who out of his mob was working with a terror firm? No one he could think of. Well, there was Gerry, but he didn't have much to do with Gerry anymore, in fact, nothing at all, and those two who came in to see Gerry in the pub hardly looked like ISIS terrorists, but then again, how would one look anyway? They wouldn't have a T-shirt advertising the fact now, would they? Dell put it out of his mind and decided to go over to Big Burt's and have a look at the racing in order to take his mind off things.

Don't be bitten twice, Dell suddenly thought to himself. But why was he thinking this? No, this wasn't happening, was it? Just other people's thoughts. *Speak to Big Burt and go and have a drink, then everything will be alright.*

Dell strolled into Burt's shop. It was about pub time, he thought as he walked up to the counter and spoke to Sharon. "Alright, Sharon. Is he about?" Dell asked.

"Upstairs," said Sharon.

"Alright to go up?" he asked. *Forget the racing. I need a drink.*

"Yeah, I would think so," she said.

Up he went and tapped on the office door. "Albert, you there?"

"Yeah, come in Joe. What's up, mate?" Burt knew when Dell referred to him as Albert he was in a serious mood.

"Fancy a beer, mate?"

Burt looked at his watch. It was four thirty. "Yeah, why not? I'm done here for today." He got up and moved toward the door. Dell was out in the hallway anyway and let Burt out as he locked up. The pair headed for the Country. They sat at the bar and both Burt and Mickey could see Dell had something on his mind. "What's up, Joe?" asked Mickey.

"Eh? Oh nothing, just thinking about something. 'ere, Mick, you remember Ronnie Slaughter, don't ya?"

"Yeah, 'course I do. You couldn't forget a bloke like him in a hurry. You and him were good pals back in the day."

"Yeah, that's right. Well, I've been speaking to him today."

"Oh yeah? Everything alright?" asked Mickey, now also wearing a concerned look.

"Yeah, yeah, it's just that he rang me back after I had spoken to him an hour or so ago and he reminded me about something that happened years ago when we were up to no good in Spain. I'd completely forgotten all about it. So I'm just trying to put it all back together in my mind, that's all," said Dell with a real distant look about himself.

As the three men continued chatting at the bar, Lightfoot walked in and was quickly spotted by Gerry, who was also having a quiet drink.

"Alright, Joe? Can we have a quick chat? asked Lightfoot, looking around at the other two in Dell's company.

"Yeah, 'course, don't worry about these two. What's up, mate?" asked Dell, having seemingly snapped out of his daze.

"Nah, nothing. Just, I spoke with my bro and told him the job and he's in. If that's alright with you?" said Lightfoot.

"Nah, that's alright, mate. Thanks for letting me know so quick. Oh, and it might be sooner than we thought," said Dell in a hushed voice.

"Yeah, no worries. That's alright with us, mate. Get Tel to bell me and we'll meet up," said Lightfoot with a wink.

Gerry watched Lightfoot as he walked back out of the pub and he instantly knew a Swedish move was imminent.

Lightfoot's visit on the other hand seemed to snap Dell out of his trance as after their brief chat he got involved with a couple of pints of bitter and had a laugh and joke with the other two. People always thought it uncharacteristic that Dell drank bitter as most of his associates were lager men, which is what you might expect. But Dell was always a little bit different.

Just as the three were relaxing, who should walk in but the dreaded Tommy Butler and his sidekick, Frank Wilson, heading straight for them.

"Jesus Christ!" said Dell, putting his head down as he turned away from the unwanted visitors.

"Afternoon, gents. It's alright, don't get up on my account," said Butler, trying to make a joke.

"Don't worry, we weren't going to," replied Dell.

Now everyone felt uneasy and it also affected Gerry over at the other end of the bar. He drank up pretty quickly and left immediately.

"No need to look so worried, boys, this is a social call," said Butler snidely.

"Fuckin' 'ell, the last time you said something like that to me, I didn't come home for about three years," said Dell.

"Well, Joey, my son, it was you I've come to see, actually," replied Butler.

"Yeah, I thought it might be, strangely enough. What can I do for you, Mr. Butler?"

"I have a very tempting proposition for you, but we have to discuss it elsewhere, *alone*."

Dell's face dropped as Ronnie's words went through his head once more.

"Not interested," Dell replied quickly.

"Well, you don't know what I'm proposing yet, do you?" said Butler, as he turned and looked at Wilson, who had a puzzled look on his face as he often did.

"I didn't mean the proposition. I meant coming to meet you in the first place, Mr. Butler."

"Well, let me put this another way. Either we arrange a meeting now or you won't have a choice. We'll come and get you anyway and then it'll be on our terms, if you get my drift!"

Dell gritted his teeth and cursed Butler under his breath.

Ron's warning and Burt's gut feelings were becoming reality. Dell didn't like this one little bit. Butler leaned over and whispered in Dell's ear. "It'll be well worth your while." He then stood back and said, "Well, as it's a social call, who'd like a drink? On the Old Bill of course."

Dell and Burt looked at each other. Dell said, "Well, what do you think?"

Butler continued, "I think it would be rude not to, don't you, Mr. Wilson?" Wilson nodded his approval.

"Yeah, go on then. I'll have a pint, please Mr. Butler," conceded Dell. Burt followed suit. Dell looked over and noticed Gerry had made a quick exit. He knew Gerry would alert his brother who, in turn, would tell Richards and hopefully neither of them would turn up in the pub that afternoon. All hoped Butler wouldn't hang about, but unfortunately he fancied doing a bit of male bonding, much to Dell and Burt's displeasure, and Mickey's for that matter. Butler wasn't good for business.

After a begrudging hour or more of Butler's company, Dell looked at his watch and then called out to Mickey to get him a cab. "Don't worry, Joey me ol' son, we're about to go anyway," said Butler before Mickey had a chance to answer.

"Well, to be honest, I thought it was later than that, Mr. Butler," said Dell, doing a quick shake of his head to Mickey to stop Mickey ordering the cab.

As Butler and Wilson turned to leave, Butler said to Dell, "I'll be in touch again very soon, Joe. Seriously I've got some business to put your way."

"Ah, that's nice of you, Mr. Butler," said Dell with a quiet aside of "Can't fuckin' wait," glancing secretly at the other two as he said it.

They all shook hands like old mates and after Butler and Wilson had gone, Dell looked at Burt. "Thank God he's gone. What's he want with me anyway?"

"Fucked if I know, but I told you I've been getting bad feelings, didn't I?" replied Burt.

"Ron could be right. Perhaps I am still on their radar after all," said Dell, thinking out loud.

"You'll never be off it, Joe, I'm afraid," said Burt.

"Nah, Ron, meant a different radar." Dell went on to explain how years ago two men claiming to represent the British government had tried to get them to wipe out some IRA men planning something or other, and how they gotten out of Gibraltar a bit lively. In fact, out of Spain altogether. Was history about to repeat itself? Is that what Butler wanted to talk about? Was Ron's hunch right? Dell's head was spinning once again. All sorts of things were going through it as he, Burt, and Mickey dissected Butler's unwanted appearance. After a lot of deliberating they were none the wiser, but they all knew it wasn't going to end with good news for poor old Dell. That the Durleys had just been remanded in custody added to their worry.

CHAPTER 25

Rita had entered the Country while Dell and Burt were chatting to Butler. She was all tarted up, waiting for Ifty's arrival, seemingly unfazed by her husband and son's unforeseen incarceration. She had found out what they were being charged with. There was no way Gerry was telling her. He pretended he'd gotten there too late to hear the charges and suggested she call the solicitor. Rita was not only unsympathetic but also appalled and disgusted by what Knipe had told her. She was even more determined to build upon her relationship with Ifty. She wasn't even that surprised. She knew what her husband and son were like. Anyway, her idea to leave Dick was a more concrete plan than ever now. If he was to make bail before the case was heard, he'd have to cope by himself as she would no longer be there for him. This was the final nail in his coffin.

As for Bart's missus, that was up to her. She took him for better or worse and it couldn't get much worse. But the pair hadn't spoken about it yet, so for now Rita was going to carry on with her taxi ride and hope Seb would be doing something similar.

After much discussion amongst the trio, Dell decided he wasn't going to let things bother him too much. In fact, the idea of a new challenge and maybe a new adventure quite excited him and he was beginning to feel a bit more relaxed about the whole thing. If Ron's thoughts were anything to go by, he'd welcome the idea, but he really didn't know why Butler would want to do business with him. Butler's "It'll be well worth your while" kept resonating and the more he played it back, the louder and more meaningful those words became. "This might not turn out as bad as we first thought," he told himself and he began to tell the other two of his thoughts.

"No, true, it might not. But then again, it could be worse," said Burt.

"Yeah, true, but why come and see me in the pub? Why not wait 'til I'm indoors?"

"Because you weren't at home. You were here," said Mickey, half serious and half joking.

"No, think about it. He's not gonna come in here talking about me and him as if we've been lifelong partners in front of people, is he? Don't get me wrong—he's definitely up to something, but I've got a trick or two of my own," said Dell, winking at his two pals.

Gerry had snaked back in now that the coast was clear, having rescheduled his meeting with Badini and Dasti. He spoke to them away from the bar at a table not too far away from the prying eyes and ears of the now almost residential undercover lover cops. After ear-wigging on Gerry's conversation, the pair were now fully aware Gerry was about to receive his biggest parcel yet of cocaine, ready to be transformed into crack. This was the moment they'd been waiting for. The night departments were informed and all eyes were now on Gerry, who was expecting his special deliver. His soon-to-be arrest would throw further confusion into the mix.

* * *

The following morning Dell received another call from Ron, who had a bit of news about his boy and his ex.

"Alright, Joe boy?" asked Ron.

"Yeah, not bad, Ron, thanks. I got something to tell ya!" said Dell.

"Well, I got news for you too," Ron said.

"Ah yeah, what's that then?"

"Well, Chrissie and Harry are livin' over here now at her parents.'" Ron was pleased with himself for getting the information off his missus without suspicion.

"Well, I did half suspect that, mate, to be honest," said Dell, rather taking the wind out of Ron's sails.

"Yeah, and what's more they're coming over to the UK with her old man for the one-hundred-year commemoration at the Legion her dad's president of."

"Ah, nice one, Ron, that's f**kin' brilliant, mate, well done. I can go in and have the surprise meeting. Does Liz know you spoke to me?" asked Dell, excited by what he'd just heard.

"No, don't be silly, mate. I wouldn't let on, but I thought you'd be pleased to know. Anyway, what did you want to tell me?"

"Ah, nothing, really. Well done, Ron, that's the news I wanted to hear. I'm so pleased, mate, you've made my day, Ronnie, my son!"

"No, go on, what did you wanna tell me? We're on the phone now, so you might as well," Ron encouraged.

"Okay. Do you remember an Old Bill called Butler?" Dell asked.

"Err, not really. Why's that?"

"He was local filth but now he's with the Yard. Well, he turned up in the pub yesterday with another muppet called Wilson, trying to be all friendly, but he wants to do a bit of business with me."

"Oh yeah? What sort of business?"

"Dunno, but he said it would be worth my while."

"Well, just you be careful, son! Remember what I said. They still come at ya. Different face, different name, but still the same ol' game."

"Yeah, well, I've taken all that on board and have a plan myself, Ron. I ain't about to fall for their old tricks, mate," Dell said, more serious than ever.

"Yeah, I know you're nobody's fool, Joe, but, like I said, make sure you tread careful," was Ron's equally serious reply.

"Don't you worry. I intend to. Anyway, thanks for that bit of information. You don't know how happy you've made me, mate!" exclaimed Dell.

"Oh yeah, and don't forget when they come over, her mum and dad are gonna be there too," Ron reminded him.

"Yeah, well, they never liked me anyway. In fact, they are, or were, the best part of my problem in the first place."

"You must remember that boy's your son, not theirs. You do what you gotta do and go careful, 'cause I wanna see you over here and soon," said Ron.

"I will, Ron, even more so now you've told me that. Thanks, Ron, I'm most grateful."

"Yeah, I know you are. Take care, my son," Ron said sincerely.

"Will do, Ron, and you, mate. Thanks again," said Dell, hanging up the phone.

As Dell put the phone down on the kitchen worktop, he stood there for a moment and sighed a deep sigh. He felt so many emotions at once. Elation, excitement, and for once he actually felt he needed to be loved. This was it. He was going to plan the chance meeting with his estranged son he so longed for. He felt bulletproof. This was the news he'd been waiting for. Forget Butler and what he had in mind. Joey Dell had something else in mind and Tommy Butler wasn't going to ruin this one chance.

"Fuck him!" said Dell out loud in the kitchen of his apartment. "I'm gonna see the boy, my Harry, and no c**t's gonna stop me! Fuck 'em. Fuck 'em, lah diddly dee, no more rascal's life for me," he sang as he danced round his kitchen. Dell all of a sudden was one happy man.

Whatever Butler had in mind for Dell, Dell didn't care. Nothing was going to stop his reunion with his son and if Dell thought Butler would get in the way, he would have to go, Dell told himself. Perhaps he was a little too excited, but there was no getting away from it, if that's how he felt. Good luck, Mr. Butler, because this boy wasn't here to f**k spiders. Dell wallowed in his excitement for the rest of the day. He cracked open a few cans and decided he wasn't going to leave the premises. He wanted to savour this moment and get as much out of it as he possibly could. This was his moment and he was going to cherish it. There was just over a month to go and he had plenty of time to think it out. He didn't want to ruin his chance. As Terry's old man went down to that Legion, happy days, he would get Tel to go with him and it would look like a normal Memorial Sunday.

Of course another little firm had rather different ideas for that place.

If Joey Dell thought this was going to be a happy reunion, he'd better think again.

CHAPTER 26

Gerry had sold out of his most profitable merchandise and was awaiting another delivery of his precious goods: two kilos of Columbia's finest and purest cocaine just waiting to be turned into crack. But of course he didn't know there just happened to be another mob, dressed in blue, waiting just as eagerly to get their grubby little hands on the delivery. Only this lot weren't going to pay for it. But first, they wanted Gerry to sample the merchandise. After that, he would be very vulnerable. Gerry hadn't become complacent by any means. The cocaine was only intended to be in his house long enough for him to complete the manufacture. He'd just gotten unlucky in getting caught up in the crossfire between terrorism and government.

Gerry sat back after sniffing a great big line of the substance and as the drug took hold, there came a dreaded knock on his front door that had the familiar rat-a-tat of the police. Before he had a chance to move, let alone to get up and answer it, the door was smashed off its hinges and the nasty sound of lots of size twelve boots and loud voices filled Gerry's home and scared the life out of the poor man. Before Gerry knew it, his house was filled with police officers running amok, swarming all over the place like a plague of rats. What could he do? He was caught red-handed. He was shaking like a leaf, frightened to death, and completely overcome.

Shit. That's it. I've had it, thought Gerry as he sat frozen with fear at the dining table. He stared at the mayhem around him as his place, not to mention his world, was completely turned upside down. *This is down to them Durleys.*

The illegal parcel of two kilos of the purest cocaine was sitting on the table for all to see, so why was his home being wrecked? The officers kept on turning the place upside down, looking for God knows what while placing various items into large plastic bags and carting them outside into an waiting van. Eventually handcuffs were put on him and he was also carted off, having not said a word. He was too off his nut to say anything at this point and frightened out of his wits.

A confused and devastated Gerry stood handcuffed in front of the desk sergeant and the first words he said were his name and date of birth. For Gerry that was hard to work out as the effects of the cocaine were still as strong now as they were when he had first sniffed it. He stared vacantly into the face of the desk sergeant in a complete daze, but he finally managed, "Please don't put me in a cell. I can't handle that right now."

"Sorry, Sir, but I'm afraid we're going to have to," replied the sergeant.

"Really? Can't you spare me that? I'll be cooperative," stammered Gerry.

"Well, we can't interview you in your condition now, can we?" said the man as he looked up at Gerry while at the same time trying to fill out the paperwork in front of him.

"Please, I'll tell you everything. Just don't lock me up in this condition."

The sergeant threw him a disgusted look. "Oh, I'm sure you will, Mr. Funnel. But first you'll have to sleep it off, won't you?"

Gerry was almost in tears. "Sleep? Your jokin', aren't ya? I can't sleep. I won't be able to do that for ages."

"Well, you'll just have to deal with it, won't you, Sir? You should have thought about that before, shouldn't you?"

How right he was and how Gerry wished he hadn't sampled the goods. Not only was he in big trouble with the law, he was also in big trouble with his state of mind. This had turned into his biggest nightmare ever. Once an officer had read him his rights, Gerry was thrown into a cell to see through his nightmare.

In the meantime, Butler was told of Gerry's incarceration and received the news with great glee. Now he could get on the move and Gerry was going to have the delight of a little visit from Scotland Yard once he had come back down to earth.

CHAPTER 27

Over at Wandsworth on remand was an equally panicked Bart Durley. He hadn't been there a week yet, and already he had been placed on suicide watch as he kept suffering panic attack after panic attack. The prison officers weren't convinced one little bit, otherwise he'd have been put in the prison hospital. His father was behaving in a similar fashion. The pair made a specially odious duo and even on the sex offenders' wing the inmates despised them. It didn't seem to matter where these two went, they were always disliked. Now they were marked men into the bargain. Neither man would mix with other prisoners and both were reluctant to leave their cells. They thought themselves too good. But fortunately for the Durleys, Knipe was working tirelessly behind the scenes to get them bailed. He actually succeeded and at their first bail hearing the pair was released. All in all, they had only to spend a week in custody, but that was more than enough for both of them. To hear them talk once they were out, you would have thought they were a pair of proper old lags.

Rita, for one, was not very happy about her husband's release, having enjoyed the most blissful week of her life. Now he was out of prison and the pair of them had been put on a tag, which meant Dick had to be in the house by six every night as part of his bail conditions. This was too much for Rita and as she'd been unhappy being married to Dick for years, now she decided she would leave him for her taxi driver. This suited both Rita and Ifty, but it certainly didn't suit Dick. Bart was far from happy about the situation. He decided to distance himself from his mother and the pair's relationship would never be the same again.

Bart's missus had once again fallen for his lies and she decided to stand by her man. She was so blind she believed everything he told her.

Rita's departure from the marital home had a devastating effect on Dick. He began to feel even lower than he had when in prison and the fact that his wife had left him for another man added insult to injury. Never mind all the misery he had caused his wife and all those poor kids over the years. As usual Dick just thought of himself. How was he going to cope on his own and, if he was forbidden from going out after six, what was he going to do? Even Bart couldn't keep him company as he was bailed to his own home address under the same conditions. He put his head in his hands and wept.

CHAPTER 28

After spending all day climbing the walls of his cell, Gerry was slowly coming back down and fully expected to be joining the Durleys in the next day or two.

After Gerry had spent a few hours stewing and pulling his hair out, his cell door opened and an officer asked, "Gerry Funnel?"

"Yeah, that's me," said a wary Gerry.

"Good. Someone wants to see you," said the officer, leading him out of the cell and into the corridor. He took Gerry's arm and led him into a room with a table and a chair on either side of it. Gerry thought this a bit odd as it looked like an interview room for just two people. He was told to sit down and wait. Gerry did as instructed and sat at the table facing the door and watched the officer leave the room. Gerry was left alone and now was as nervous as hell. Then the door opened and he got the shock of his life. Tommy Butler entered and sat on the chair at the opposite side of the table.

"Evening, Gerry. Got ourselves in a little bit of trouble now, haven't we?"

"Hello, Mr. Butler. Just a little bit. Who grassed me?"

"Nobody, Gerry. You should learn to keep better company or you wouldn't be in this mess," replied Butler.

"What do you mean? Is it the Durleys you're on about?" asked Gerry.

"Who are they? They're no one, my son, but you have been keeping company with a couple of very unsavoury characters, haven't you?"

"Don't know, have I? Like who?"

"Never you mind, but let me tell you something of great importance for your future. If you listen to what I have to say and comply, we could keep this situation of yours very quiet and if you're a very good boy, we might even lose that two kilos of Columbian for ya. If you're a good boy, that is, Gerry. What do you say?" asked Butler.

This was music to Gerry's ears, but first he had to hear what Butler had to say.

"I'm listening, Mr. Butler. Go on. I'm all ears."

"Well, Gerry, this pleasant and reasonably safe community of ours is under threat of being disturbed somewhat and it's my job to keep it nice and safe and peaceful. Do you follow me?"

"Yeah, I understand, but who or what is threatening our community?"

"Well, I am not at liberty to disclose that information as of yet, but in order for me to keep our community safe from harm, I am going to need some cooperation from a few little toe rags like yourself, Funnel," Butler explained.

"Well, if I don't know who is threatening our peace and safety, how the hell can I help, Mr. Butler?"

"Let's start with your old mate Joey Dell. I want as much information on him as possible so I can control him like a puppet," said Butler as he leaned toward Gerry with a menacing look.

"Shut up! Dell? I don't know anything about him, Mr. Butler," cried Gerry. "He dropped me out of his firm ages ago. Anyway, since he came out of the shovel, he's been keeping his nose clean. Alright, there was that boating accident, and I think that put the wind up him."

"Put the wind up him, don't be so fucking daft. Nothing puts the wind up Joey Dell, I can tell ya. Everyone knows he's the main man this side of London. In fact, he's probably the top dog in the whole of bloody London," said Butler through gritted teeth, banging his fist firmly on the table.

"Alright, Mr. Butler, calm down. I think you might have got that wrong. He don't do anything. Anyway, I've heard he wants to get back with his ex-old woman and play the family man," said Gerry, now sweating up a bit.

Butler continued, "Well, you can be compliant or defiant, but let me tell you, the latter will hurt you more than it will hurt me. So the choice is yours, Mr. Funnel. I'll give you a bit of time to think about it. But it's down to you, my son. We ain't having our backs put against the wall."

Gerry sat there and thought for a while after he was left alone. If Tommy Butler of the Yard was taking the case over, this was a serious situation. He concluded cooperation was his only option. He wasn't the only one left with his thoughts. Butler went to make himself a cup of tea. *Dell, family man, what is this prick talking about?* As the kettle was on the boil, Butler suddenly had a humanitarian thought and went back to the room where he'd left Gerry.

"You fancy a cuppa, Funnel?"

"Ooh, yes, please, Mr. Butler," replied Gerry, who was on the rough end of a comedown. He needed something to pull himself back from his irritable state. He realised there could be a deal on the table and he certainly didn't want to blow probably the last chance he would ever get.

Butler, in a one-off compassionate moment, asked, "What you fancy? Tea or coffee and how do you want it?"

Gerry was completely astonished at even being offered a bit of refreshment from the notoriously unaccommodating Butler, let alone being given a choice.

"Tea, three sugars, please, Mr. Butler."

"Yeah, no worries, Gerry. You continue having a little think to yourself and I'll be back in a sec."

Gerry thought about Dell the family man and about the position he was now in. What the fuck did he know about Dell since his release? There really was only one thing to say. Butler returned with two cups of tea, one for himself and a nice sweet one for Gerry, who was craving something and it wasn't tea, but for now that would have to do.

"There you go, Gerry, now let's get down to business," said Butler with a smile. Gerry thought, *Bloody hell, it was Funnel a minute ago, now it's Gerry. Best I listen and listen good. This sounds a bit too good to be true.* This just didn't add up and all of a sudden Butler seemed almost human.

"Right then, my son. What can you tell me about Dell?" asked Butler as he sipped his tea. "Let me remind you, you are in a very tricky situation. A very tricky situation indeed and you could end up with a very long stretch. Now, do you want to play ball or get banged up for the foreseeable future with a load of Islamic fanatics and Eastern Europeans who would make the next few years an absolute bloody misery for you? Or would you rather work with me for a brighter future for yourself and all the rest of us?"

"Well, of course I would, but I don't follow you, Mr. Butler." He was confused. *What did Butler mean, all of us? What is he trying to get at?* "Okay then, Mr. Butler. If you want me to tell you what I know, I want some sort of guarantee that whatever I say is going to remain here with us and no way can it ever get out that I've been cooperating with you. Please, Mr. Butler, if it ever got out that I've talked, I'm a dead man and you know it!"

At this point, a presumptuous Butler produced two legal documents, one for himself and one for Gerry, that gave the prisoner total immunity from prosecution if they both agreed to the terms and signed it.

"Shouldn't I have my brief here to look this over?" asked Gerry just before he put pen to paper.

"Yeah, you could do, but for one, this is an agreement between me and you and it might take a good few hours before your legal man gets here. Now, in your state, do you really want that?" asked Butler.

Gerry paused as he browsed over the papers and tried to take it all in.

"No, but I'm not sure how I can help you, Mr. Butler."

"I'm sure you can, Gerry, and I'm pretty sure you know you can as well, don't you?"

"Well, you might be a bit disappointed as all I can tell you about Dell is his Swedish move," said Gerry limply.

"Swedish move! What do you mean, Swedish move? What, as a family man? I didn't even know he had kids, let alone a bleedin' family, and now you're tellin' me he's moving to Sweden. Don't take me for a cunt Funnel, or you are a fuckin' goner!" screamed Butler.

Now it was back to Funnel. Bloody hell, the Ol' Bill were so fickle. *He was makin' me tea a minute ago!* thought Gerry.

"No, no, I didn't mean he was moving to Sweden. It's a move he's got going on in Sweden. He exports cocaine over there!"

"You better not be tellin' me porkies, Funnel. But before we get into that, what's all this about Joey Dell wantin' to be a family man? I think you're lying to me already, young Mr. Funnel," said Butler, curious about what had been said earlier.

"Mr. Butler, you must know Dell has a young boy with a girl called Christine Hathaway, surely? Everyone knows that. And now he wants to keep his nose clean in order to see his chavy," said Gerry in utmost seriousness.

"No, I didn't know that. Just in case it's escaped your memory, I'm no longer local plod. I work at the big office now. Did you know that, you little prick?" Butler puffed out his chest like he was some sort of heavy-weight champion.

"Yes, of course I did. You won't let us forget it, will ya!" exclaimed Gerry.

"Hathaway, you say? Sounds a little bit posh for a Joey Dell bird, don't you think?"

"Well, yeah, maybe, but how the hell should I know? All I know is my ol' man knows her old man from over the Legion," said Gerry.

"What Legion?" asked Butler.

"You know, the big one over at Greenford," said Gerry in complete innocence.

"Greenford British Legion! Are you fuckin' kiddin' me, Gerry?" asked Butler.

"No, why would I? I didn't realise them boys that fought two world wars were a threat to our community."

"No, I don't think they are. And your old man drinks over there, does he?"

"Yeah, has for years. Why?" asked Gerry.

"Well, Gerald, my old son, if what you're tellin' me is the truth, we can be in business. Let me think about this for a while. You could be of a lot more help to me than you actually realise," said Butler excitedly.

"Really? Why's that then?"

Butler got up and asked Gerry if he'd like another cup of tea, which Gerry was greatly appreciative of, but he couldn't work out why Butler was so excited about the fact that his dad and Dell's former father-in-law used the Legion. This was all too much for Gerry. What was the significance?

Butler returned shortly with two cups of tea. "Well, forget about the Legion, Gerry. Now you tell me all about this Swedish thing, because in case you've forgotten, you're still in a bit of bother."

"I thought we had a deal and we'd both agreed on it."

"Yeah, well, we have. Now, you just keep talkin' my son, 'cause I want you as a pawn in my game," replied Butler.

Gerry continued to tell Butler everything he knew about the move to Sweden. How they took a big chunk of cocaine out there from here concealed in the panels of a car and then delivered it to a man called Sven in Stockholm, and that no cash was exchanged on delivery as it was paid to the firm via other means, which Gerry had no knowledge of. Gerry even told Butler a black man named David Lightfoot was now in charge of the delivery operation and the reason he knew this was because he once did the drive himself. In fact it was that regular that Gerry considered it a full-time job.

Butler was half interested in Gerry's story and took notes on the subject, but by his reckoning, Gerry might have already given him the most important information of all. The only problem was that it wouldn't be enough to convince Gerry he'd given up enough information, so Butler had to follow due process, listening to Gerry trying to spill even more beans about Dell and his boys.

Finally Butler decided he'd heard enough. "I think we might have enough for now. Thank you, Gerry. What I'm going to do now is put you back in a cell while I get your bail sheet typed up."

"Mr. Butler, please, not the cell," pleaded Gerry again.

"Look, you're gonna get bail, you lucky little git, and this will all be kept hush-hush for now. But from now on you're mine, so just consider yourself lucky and report back to me in one week. Now go back to your cell until all the formalities are done."

"Okay, Mr. Butler, but ..."

"No buts. Just shut up and do what you're told and I don't want to hear no more about it," said Butler, passing Gerry over to the officer who had let him out in the first place.

Gerry knew he was having a result for the time being, but it couldn't be that simple, surely. What more information might Butler want from him? Gerry knew full well this wasn't the end of it. No way.

As Butler typed up the bail sheet, he too thought about the result he was having. At that moment Wilson knocked on his door and asked Butler what they were to do with the two parcels of cocaine. As this was a covert arrest and everything was to be hushed up, it hadn't been logged. So now in the station were two kilos of cocaine no one had actually claimed responsibility for. Butler sat for a few moments and then said, "Get hold of it and bring it to me and let me have a think. I don't want uniform or the Drug Squad getting' hold of it."

"Okay, Tom, leave it to me," said Wilson.

CHAPTER 29

Cairo spent a couple of hours that evening being seen and forcing herself to acknowledge various people in their targeted Legion in Greenford, West London. She played her role perfectly and was back to plain old Karen once more. She mainly kept to herself and sat alone, but she spoke and was polite whenever she was spoken to. Only sipping on soft drinks with the odd bag of crisps here and there, she took her job very seriously indeed. She scanned the place and imagined the attack that would engulf it. These thoughts always put a sick evil little grin on her face.

The Ayatollah couldn't have been happier with his team. The boys had raised enough money to buy bomb-making equipment and a couple of fire-arms, including terrorists' mandatory AK-47. He was in an Islamic heaven right now, dreaming of historical notoriety amongst his equals. But one of his team's dreams was more evil and vindictive than all the rest of them put together.

Cairo had been tormenting herself at the servicemen's club looking at all the military honours and paintings from various wars on display. These put an end to any compassion she might have once felt. As she plotted her mission, her mind's eye was playing out the events of Sunday, November 11, 2018. It was like watching a film as many, many people she was looking at right then were slaughtered by her and her beloved cell of killers. This was going to be bigger and better than 7/7, and she would forever be remembered by her extremist brothers and sisters. She herself would become a legend, going down in history as the most evil and best mastermind killer ever to work on British soil. She would be the hero honoured on walls around the country, maybe even around the world. These unknown faces on canvas that she saw on the walls around her weren't heroes or soldiers; they were just morons taking orders. To hell with their armies, to hell with their families and children. She would become the hero she deserved to be, a soldier fighting against the bullies of this world. These people had ruined her life, but now she'd gotten her purpose back, thanks to Allah the Great. People must pay and they were going to suffer for what she had been put through. They must all die and she was the one elected by Allah to carry out this much-needed cleansing.

This woman may have been a victim of circumstance, a perfect candidate for brainwashing, an easy target. No one in the Legion would ever have guessed this innocent and lonely little thing was possibly one of the most evil and hateful women who ever walked the planet's surface. Even the brothers in the DSTC had no idea how vile and calculated she could be. She was a walking time bomb likely to explode at any moment.

She watched the standard-bearers practicing for the service. Her blood boiled, but she showed no signs of anger whatsoever. In fact, if she had had a gun with her at that moment, she would have put a stop to their little game there and then. But she had to wait. The big day was only a few weeks away. She had to be patient.

CHAPTER 30

Dell had been thinking about his conversation with Tommy Butler and decided he should go and pay his solicitor, Petey Doyle, a visit. Dell had a plan, a trick up his sleeve, and he wanted the opinion of his man in the legal profession who had given much sensible advice over many years. The two of them had become good friends. Petey was one of the best in the game and Dell felt he could tell him anything. He was a very trustworthy man, sharp as a razor, and highly respected by Dell and all his associates. You could say he was in the firm. He was a large man with a full head of white hair, immaculately dressed like Dell with a red polka dot silk handkerchief in the breast pocket of his recently pressed pinstriped suit.

They sipped a nice French brandy, which always warmed the heart and sharpened the brain. They exchanged the usual pleasantries.

"How can I be of help today, then, Joe?" Pete finally got around to asking in his assertive voice.

"Well, Petey, it's like this," said Dell and he went on to explain the situation with Butler and how he didn't have the slightest inkling as to what he wanted to discuss. Dell told Petey about his tactics for when he met Butler

191

and asked if he should go ahead. As Petey knew Butler probably even better than Dell, he agreed and said he thought it a great idea and that he should use this approach at every future meeting he and Butler had from now on. Dell thanked Petey for his advice and left feeling more confident of his forthcoming date with Butler.

Butler meanwhile had released Gerry back into the community as quickly as he could, but not without conditions, hoping people had not noticed his absence. One minute Gerry looked like he would do a long stretch and the next he looked like a man who had just won the lottery. This only came to be as Butler had received an order from MI5 telling him what should be done with Gerry. They didn't want to rock the boat. Gerry was now in their pockets, even though he had absolutely no idea of what was actually going on. Everything seemed to be going to plan, so now it was essential to have that meeting with the big fella.

Dell was enjoying a nice jolly drink with a good few of the boys and this included David Lightfoot, as Terry had told him the Swedish job had been brought forward a bit and they just wanted to make sure this was alright with him. It was, so now everyone was happy and it was nice to relax. Everyone was happy. Well, almost everyone. Gerry, over on the other side of the pub, looked at Lightfoot. *It's right on you, you cunt. I've put you right in it.* But the jolly atmosphere soon changed as the dreaded duo walked in.

"Ah, for fuck's sake," said Mickey as he looked at Dell and the boys and the nice crowd he'd got in, who he expected would leave now that Butler and Co. were in the house.

Dell looked up and saw Butler and Wilson. "Fuck him. We're all enjoying ourselves. Don't no one go anywhere. Don't worry about them pricks. It's me they wanna pester. They can fuck off."

As the pair approached Dell's crowd, they sensed the hostility and decided to tread carefully.

"Evening, gentlemen," said Butler, looking around at the faces in front of him. One or two nodded and one or two just glared at them as if to tell them to fuck off.

"Is this a bad moment, or are you lot holding a wake?"

"Mr. Butler, a wake or not, it's never a good time for a visit from you or any of your mob. What do you want?"

Time was running out for Butler and his cause, but he now felt uneasy around Dell's firm as they made him and his partner feel very unwelcome. Butler, for his part, didn't quite know how to approach Dell. He was desperate to talk to him and start arrangements, but Dell was enjoying himself and looked at him in a way that made Butler feel very uncomfortable. For once in his life, he didn't quite know how to handle the situation. He needed Dell now more than ever, but Dell strangely didn't feel the same. He just wanted Butler out of the way.

Dell was holding court and enjoying the company of his boys and Butler was a commodity he could well do without. Eventually Dell turned to Butler as he stood there trying to fit in. "Yes, Mr. Butler, what can I do for you? You obviously want something, so spit it out."

"Err, err, it's probably not the right time, Joe," replied Butler, realising he had arrived at just the wrong moment.

"Correct. How very observant of you."

"I really do need to speak to you, but only when it's convenient with you, of course."

"But as you're here, would you like a soft drink and a packet of crisps, mate? Oh, and what about your fuckin' monkey? The same for him, or would he prefer some peanuts?" goaded Dell.

"Thank you, Joe, but I think we'll pass for now," said a humiliated Butler.

What were they going to do? The clock was ticking and Butler needed Dell and his boys on his side and quickly. He'd cut it a bit fine, but he was still confident he'd get Dell on his side once he got to chat to him. But it wasn't going to be today.

Butler turned around and left the band of brigands, as he referred to them. On the way out, he passed Gerry. "Is the black one Lightfoot?"

"Yeah, that's him."

Butler walked out of the Country with Wilson, more than a little disappointed with his visit. Once out of sight Butler threw a temper tantrum just like a little kid. He knew time was against him now and he hadn't got his timing right with Dell. He was going to be putty in his hands if he wasn't careful.

"What's all that about, Joe?" asked one of the boys.

"Fuck knows!" said Dell and he didn't really care. He could see Butler was under pressure and as far as he was concerned, it wasn't his problem— for now.

Tail between his legs for the time being, Butler had to ponder his next move.

* * *

Time was also running out for Dick Durley. His past had caught up with him and his wife had left him in his darkest hour and he couldn't cope with it. Bart was okay. He had once again managed to pull the wool over Seb's eyes. She liked the lifestyle Bart provided and was more than happy to appear oblivious. Pretending was just as easy for her as it was for her husband.

Rita on the other hand was making herself comfortable with her lover and had gotten her feet nicely under his table.

* * *

Butler, having received orders to let Gerry resume business and keep up the flow of crack going to the DSTC, had explained to Gerry he could continue to earn, but on the understanding that the majority of the money he received from the two kilos, which had been returned to him, was to be paid to Butler so he could use it as blood money. This arrangement suited Gerry, but he knew he had to keep his mouth shut and hold up his end of the bargain. He would have his freedom and no one would be any the wiser about his arrest.

All Butler needed to do now was arrange a meeting and get Dell's boys on his side. Then Operation Desert Storm could become a successful prototype mission. He therefore set out with Wilson, hoping to bump into Dell and get this meeting set up by trawling a few of his usual haunts. They started off down at the Sopranos' Café at around nine thirty in the morning. Both had a full English washed down with several cups of tea while they read the newspaper from cover to cover. But there was no sign of Dell or his cronies Funnel and Richards. But there were plenty of uneasy faces that weren't too happy having to start their day breakfasting in the same establishment as Butler and his sidekick. No one eating there that morning would ever come close to Dell and his firm's capabilities. Butler required the assistance of numero uno and he'd set out his stall to make sure he got him and get him he would.

CHAPTER 31

While Butler and Wilson hung around like a bad smell down at the café, making most of the patrons extremely uncomfortable, Dell, Richards, and Funnel were at Dell's apartment preparing the final arrangements for Lightfoot and his brother to go to work in Sweden. Dell was on the phone to their Dutch connection, making sure what they required would be ready and waiting for the brothers to pick up on their arrival in Holland. As this was confirmed, they could now give Lightfoot the nod to leave the following morning and head to a place an hour south of Amsterdam, where Dell's old mate "the witch doctor" or just "Doc" for short now conducted his business.

Doc was a one-time drug dealer from West London who had worked with Dell in the past, but had now set up in Holland, helping out a lot of his old London pals in the narcotics trade from his base in Utrecht. He got his nickname for (1) dishing out drugs and (2) because his family were from the Dominican Republic in the Caribbean. The Lightfoots might well know him once they met up, but Dell didn't mention who they were to meet.

Funnel spoke to both Lightfoot and Sven to let them know everything was in place and that Sven should expect a delivery in about a week. Everything was set to go and if all went well, there would be another nice payday for all involved.

As the trio had a coffee and a chat, Richards was looking out of Dell's first floor window. He watched a car pull up to the gated entrance of the apartment complex and a man got out. His passenger remained in the car. The man walked up to the gates and looked at the keypad on the wall that had the numbers of each resident. It was Butler.

"Joe, I think we've got a visitor," said Richards.

"Who?" asked Dell.

"Butler and his mate by the looks of it," replied Richards.

"Fuckin' hell. He's persistent, I'll say that for him," said Dell, annoyed.

Butler had gotten fed up with waiting in the café and listening to all the snide remarks about him and Wilson, so he had decided to try Dell at home. He knew for certain Dell wouldn't be very happy about it. But what was he supposed to do? He was under a little bit of pressure himself and he desperately needed the support of Dell and his two mates.

The intercom buzzed in Dell's flat and he picked it up. "Mr. Butler, what can I do for you?"

Butler, not expecting that reception, asked, "How did you know it was me?"

"I could smell you, mate," said Dell as he winked at the others with a grin.

"Ha ha, very funny. Look, Joe, I need to speak to you about that thing I mentioned to you the other day in the pub," said Butler with a bit of nervousness in his voice.

"Ah, yeah, that thing," said Dell, having spotted the nervous tone in Butler's voice. "Well, I'm a little busy right now, so we'll have to arrange another day, mate."

"What if I came back this time tomorrow?" asked Butler. Dell thought if he had two Old Bills around his place at the same time, they might try and bug him.

"I tell you what we can do. You come around on your own and we can have a chat, but if you bring any of your colleagues with ya, forget it," said Dell.

"Okay, Joe, no problem. It'll just be me, I promise. Cheers, Joe, I appreciate this. See you tomorrow then, mate," said Butler, relieved.

"Ah, yeah, and not so much of the mate. Alright?" said Dell as he put the intercom phone down and the three of them laughed.

Butler got back into the unmarked car a happy man as he felt sure that once he'd explained the facts to Dell, he'd join forces with him.

"What the hell does he want with me? The snide prick!" said Dell.

The other two men shrugged their shoulders. Funnel said, "Well, you'll find out tomorrow, mate, won't you?"

"Yeah, well, he seems pretty keen to talk and he doesn't seem to want me at the station. I wonder what he's up to," said Dell, curious. "Anyway, anyone want another tea or coffee?" His guests both refused. "Right then. Let's pop over to Big Burt's. I wanna let him know we're gonna have to release some dough from the betting account and put it into Doc's account, but only when we know everything's alright."

As they entered Burt's shop, he was behind the counter. Dell promptly told him about his unwanted visitor.

"Well, he poked his head in here earlier," said Burt, looking up slowly from his *Racing Post*, giving one of those knowing looks over the top of his glasses that said everything.

"Oh, yeah, what did he say?" asked Dell.

"No, nothing. Just opened the door, looked about, then went," said Burt.

"Well, he's meeting me at my place tomorrow. On his own," said Dell, nodding at Burt as he said it.

"Oh dear, Joe. Well, just you tread carefully, my son," replied Burt.

As the shop was empty, Dell explained the reason for his visit. "You don't think that's what he's sniffin' around here for, do ya?" asked Burt suddenly.

"No, no! He wouldn't know anything about that. No one does. Only us and we ain't treadin' on no one's toes. I don't know what he wants, to be honest, and I can't wait to find out."

The trio hung around the betting shop for a while, looking at the day's racing and watching the morning dog racing as the Lightfoot brothers prepared for their trip. They'd agreed on the rented accommodation they were to use for getting their bits ready for Sven's request and they'd got the addresses they needed and the vacuum packing machine. All the rest of the equipment would be purchased once they had reached their destination. Nothing now was going to stop them. They turned in around nine thirty, ready for an early start in the morning, and hoped to catch the first ferry out of Dover. Then it was on up to Holland and an overnight stay somewhere before the final push into Sweden.

They rose as planned, packed the motor, and headed off for the Channel crossing to Calais. They chatted about the trip as they drove out of the darkness into the dawn down the M2 through Kent. David, putting his younger brother at ease, told him that before this one, he used to drive to the port with two kilos concealed in the truck and related how he had to go through two customs stations before he'd even gotten on a French road. He explained how this way was so much better as they were leaving Old Blighty as clean as a whistle, and even if they did get pulled in, they'd soon be let go as they had nothing on them.

As they went through passport control, sure enough, the Kent police were at the checkpoint and flagged them down straightaway.

David stopped his pick-up truck and let the window down. "Morning officer," said David with a smile.

"Morning, Sir. Would you mind pulling in over there?" The officer pointed to the big customs shed.

"No, not at all," said David as he drove the short distance to the entrance and turned to his brother. "Fuckin' 'ell, I've never had this before. But don't worry."

They parked and got out of the vehicle as instructed. They weren't the only ones to get pulled in. They watched another car having a good going over by the customs men. But they did get alarmed when the police followed them in and got out. The usual questions followed. "Is this vehicle yours?" "Do you know why we've pulled you in?" But what they thought was a bit odd was that the police who were with them were not bothering with any of the other vehicles. They were subjected to a very intense search and the officers looked extremely puzzled as they'd found nothing incriminating whatsoever. They even put two sniffer dogs over the truck, one at a time, and still came up with nothing. At one point David quipped, "Perhaps they can smell intent."

The officer in charge looked the pair up and down and disappointment showed as clear as day on his face. The information they had received from one of Butler's team had proved inconclusive.

"Why did you pull us, officer? Is it because we're black?" David asked cheekily.

"Never you mind, son. On your way and enjoy your trip," said the officer.

As the pair drove out, the officer from the Kent Constabulary got in touch with Scotland Yard and shared with Butler what now looked like misinformation. This came as a shock. As he prepared for his meet with Dell, Butler needed something concrete on him and his boys to force them on board if they wouldn't volunteer. Now he was going to have to rely solely on Dell's patriotic side and hope to God he would play ball.

The Lightfoot boys missed their ferry and had to hang around for the next one. Once they got in the queue, David rang Dell and told him what had just happened.

"Really? What the fuck was that all about then?" asked Dell.

"I don't know, Joe. But we were the only ones the Old Bill were lookin' at," replied Lightfoot anxiously.

"Stroke of luck, though. Bloody good job everything got changed round, really, wan' it?"

"Yeah! It was. Shall we carry on, or do you want us to abort?"

"Nah, don't worry about it, David. You'll be alright to carry on, won't ya?"

"Well, that's what I'm askin' you, Boss," said Lightfoot.

"Yeah, bollocks to it. It was probably just one of those things."

"But if you hear anything, let me know, please, Joe?"

"Yeah, 'course I will," replied Dell as he suddenly thought about Butler's appointment. Were the two a coincidence, or were they linked? He'd do his best to find out.

Dell made all the appropriate preparations for Butler's visit and sat waiting for him. As expected, he turned up bang on time. This was going to be very interesting indeed. The intercom buzzed and Dell let Butler in. As Butler entered the apartment, he took a look around and said, "Nice place you got here, Joe."

"Well, what did you expect, Mr. Butler?"

"Only the best for the top man, eh?" was all he could think of to say.

"Well, what can I do for you, Mr. Butler? You seem pretty desperate to get hold of me, so what do you want?"

"Well, it's like this, Joe, and this ain't easy for me. I'd like you to listen very carefully to what I have to say, and you being a reasonable man, I'm sure you're gonna understand," said Butler.

"Hold on a sec, Mr. Butler. Would you like a drink or somethin' to calm ya'self? I can see you're a bit on edge," said Dell, now putting himself firmly in control.

"Err, err, yes, please, if you don't mind. Could I have a Scotch on the rocks, if you have it?" asked Butler.

"No problem. Sit down and make ya'self comfortable." Dell went to his drink cabinet and pulled out two frosted glasses. He poured out two large measures of whisky and then dropped in a few ice cubes. Dell sat down and handed Butler his drink. He then pushed his in the direction of his guest and the two glasses knocked together in the usual ritual. "Cheers," they said together. The two men sat opposite each other, sizing each other up, and Butler began.

"Well, you're probably not aware, but there's big surveillance going on in this area."

"Wow, wow! Let me stop you there, Mr. Butler. This better not involve me, because since my release, I'm not involved in anything. All I'm interested in is finding my son and being the father to him I should have been from the start."

Dell was wearing a poppy, much to Butler's joy, but it didn't seem to fit in with his immaculate appearance.

"I see you're wearing a poppy," said Butler, getting off the subject slightly.

"Yeah, so what! I have respect for the fallen and so should you," said Dell bluntly.

"Oh, I have. I have and I'm glad to see that you do too, Joe," said Butler, starting to feel a little more at ease as he gulped back his Scotch. It wasn't meant to be him that felt nervous. It was meant to be the other way around. But he was in Dell's domain now and felt humbled.

"Get to the point, will ya? I'm doin' you a favour here, givin' you my time. Not you doin' me one," said Dell firmly.

"Right. Like I said, the surveillance thing has nothin' to do with you or any of your boys. There happens to be an active terror cell working on your manor, Joe, and we'd like your help," said Butler bluntly, getting back to business.

"Now, there's a surprise. What the fuck do you expect? There's enough of 'em around here. Who is it? Muslims, Polish, Russians? Who? And what the fuck would I know about any of 'em anyway? I keep to myself, as you of all people should know."

Butler picked up his glass and looked at it as if to say, "I'm empty."

"Would you like another?" asked Dell, getting up and grabbing Butler's glass before he could answer. Dell poured him a big one and slammed it down on the table in front of him as he sat back down. "Go on then, tell me. What's all this got to do with me?"

"Well, it's a bit delicate and highly confidential," Butler replied, sipping at his drink.

"Yeah, well, it always is with you. Isn't it, Mr. Butler?" interrupted Dell.

"Please let me speak, Joe. This isn't easy for me, but there's been a change in government policy and they've decided they need people like you to combat the terror threat to this country," said Butler, taking another sip of his drink.

"Ah, yeah. Well, go on then, I'm all ears. Tell me why and what they want from me. Is this some sort of prison PPI where I get all my sentences back?" said Dell sarcastically. Then he continued, "I know what you're tryin' to say. You want to hire people like me to do the dirty work for people like you. That's right, innit?"

Butler looked at Dell in complete shock. "Whatever makes you say that?"

"I've heard it before, years ago when I was in Spain. But back then, the problem was with the tea caddies. Now it's with whatever piece of shit wants to come here and take over our country because we stand back and let 'em," ranted Dell.

This was just the sort of attitude Butler expected and wanted, and added to the fact that Dell was sporting a poppy a few weeks before Armistice Day, he was getting the feeling it wouldn't be too hard to win him over.

"What do you mean, you've heard this story before?" asked Butler.

Dell got up and walked around a bit and then told Butler about when he and Slaughter had been approached in Spain by who they thought were government men who wanted the pair to rub out a key IRA man. As Butler listened, it all made sense. The men at the meeting a couple of weeks before had told him who he was intending to use for this mission before he had had a chance to tell them. Joey Dell was on their radar anyway. It was all coming together.

Butler was convinced now that he'd selected the right man, but he had to convince *Dell* he was the right man. The men in Gibraltar must have known something about him even then, but he was nothing more than a kid at the time. What had he done for them to approach him? And how could Butler find out? He wasn't going to try to find out today, but he was determined to at some point. Today he was just going to do what he'd come to do. The way Dell had preplanned this meeting out with Butler, there was no way he would incriminate himself with anything from the past anyway, so if Butler thought he would, he'd have to think again. Dell was far too clever for that, as Butler would eventually find out.

Back in the mid-eighties, when Dell and Slaughter had been in their late teens, they had spent half a year ducking about on the Costa del Sol. Although they'd had a bit of experience in drug dealing at home, they'd decided it would be a good idea to ply their trade in sunnier climes. During their time there, they not only earned some good money, but they also made some good contacts. As they built up their little business, their operation grew a lot more quickly than they'd imagined, and a very well-known Spaniard took a liberty with them. The Spaniard had made a big mistake and paid with his life, and it was Dell who had ended it for him. That was when he and Ronnie Slaughter had bolted off down to Gibraltar, and the rest, as they say, is history.

When Dell had finished his story, Butler again commented on his wearing a poppy. "Oh yeah, well, as I say, I like to pay my respects to all the men who fought for this country. Mind you, if they saw it now, they'd wish they hadn't bothered."

"Yeah, I know what you mean, and a lot of men and women in the force feel the same way," replied Butler.

"Well, you can't blame 'em, can ya?" said Dell.

"You never cease to amaze me, Joe," said Butler, sipping at his Scotch once more.

"Oh yeah, and why's that?" Dell asked.

"Well, I didn't have you down as a patriotic man," Butler replied.

"Oh now, so what did you have me down as then?"

"Well, you know. A man with a reputation like yours," said Butler a little uneasily.

"No, I don't know. Anyway, spit it out. What's this all about then? I'm still none the wiser," said Dell, starting to get a little impatient.

"Well, as I was sayin' earlier, right on our doorstep we have an active terror cell. They're planning something in our community that will affect a lot of people nationally, but most of them will obviously be local people. People we all know. Some of them will be people close, people we love and have known for years. It'll affect all of us, especially here in West London. In fact, what they're plotting will touch the world and probably make them heroes and martyrs to their kind."

"Yeah, alright, Mr. Butler, but again, what has this got to do with me? Anyway, why don't you nick em?"

"Well, that's just my point. We're looking for people like you. A sort of underworld resistance to combat this scum. People with fight in 'em, people with guts. Not many men carry the sort of clout you do, Joe," said Butler, hoping to press the right buttons. "You're a highly respected man, Joe, and highly influential."

"Don't talk stupid, Mr. Butler. So I was right in the first place. You've come at me with the same offer as that lot years ago, haven't you? Why the fuckin' hell do you lot come to me? Why me, eh? Do you lot think I am a mercenary or something?" said Dell angrily, gulping his drink down. He reached for the bottle and poured them both another.

"Not at all, but you know as well as I do that you're the man who makes things happen. You and your boys are pretty much untouchable. Even the fuckin' Eastern Europeans won't go near ya, and don't you try and tell me otherwise," said Butler.

"What are you talkin' about, you cunt? That drink's gone to your fuckin' 'ead."

"Look, Joe, me and you go back years, don't we?" said Butler in a sort of plea.

"Yeah, that's right, we do, but who always cops the bird? I fuckin' do, that's who!" replied Dell.

"Okay, okay! I agree, you have done a bit of time, but only on silly things. We never got you on the proper things. You were always too clever. Do you know how many men have put their time and careers into trying to get you weighed off for life?" shouted Butler, now trying to get into Dell's face.

"No, I don't and I don't care." Dell then stopped and thought for a moment. He thought back on the things he'd actually been responsible for that could well still be on file as the cases had never been solved. "Okay, okay, you start talkin' and tell me what the fuckin' deal is, then. And don't fuckin' lie. I want it straight."

Butler gulped another one down as he slammed his glass on the table as if to say, "Fill it up then." Dell obliged and Butler braced himself to tell him the way they wanted it to be. This meeting was rapidly turning into a bit of a drinking session as both men were eager to hear what the other had to say. Dell thought he had Butler up against the ropes. He could tell Butler was out of his comfort zone and he needed Dell right now a lot more than Dell needed him. Another bottle of Scotland's finest was opened as Butler started. "The powers that be want results and they don't want to lose any more men than have been lost already, if you get my drift."

"So you want me to take the fall, do ya?"

"No, not really. They want you on their side, but let me tell you, when your pal Lightfoot got pulled this morning, it was no coincidence," said Butler, feeling he was now holding all the aces.

"Ah yeah? So what did you think you got from him that might link him to me?"

"You know, we got fuck all but we're all over that move, mate."

"Really? You done well there, Mr. Butler. Poor bloke was going away for a few days' holiday with his brother and you lot thought you were gonna put something on me? You're fuckin' good, you lot. No wonder this country's fucked if we have to rely on people like you to keep us safe. You must be worth every penny of your salary. I bet the powers that be are well happy with you and your team, mate. I'm glad you don't work for me. Do you have me down as an establishment man, Mr. Butler, or have you overlooked my background?" asked Dell, beginning to get a little bored with the situation. Dell thought about Lightfoot's situation and could really do with Butler shutting up so he could alert him or one of the boys to the problem they now faced.

"No, no, Joe, I would never underestimate you, mate, my friend, but please will you let me explain? I'm sorry about the events at Dover earlier, but we had to act on information received."

"Information received! From who? Someone's pullin' your pisser, Mr. Butler," said Dell, trying to deflect the unwanted attention. *Bloody hell, who the f**k spilled the beans here?* thought Dell, but he never let it show. He kept a poker face that gave absolutely nothing away.

Amazingly, at this stage Butler had yet to manage to get out what he'd come to say. Eventually he did finally get Dell's full attention. As Butler explained the program, Dell's mind started to wander again. Right now, his main priority was to let Lightfoot know the move had to be aborted.

Dell listened for a while longer and then knew he had to cut the conversation short. This would have to wait for another day. He wasn't going to let this lot hold him over a barrel. If he was ever going to join forces with them, he was going to make sure he had his arse and those of the rest of the boys covered. Anyway, by now Butler had said enough and Dell had gathered enough information for his own purposes. The pair cut the meeting off, but not before they had arranged another confab in the next day or two so Dell had time to consider the proposition.

Butler sighed as he was shown the door, but as the proposed target hadn't yet been revealed, he felt confident he could win Dell and his boys round. How right he would be, but as of now, Dell needed to get hold of Funnel and let him know what Butler had revealed about Lightfoot and Sweden. This was an urgent matter. People needed to be told of the situation and quickly.

Dell waited for Butler to vacate the premises before he left his apartment and set out to get hold of the other two. He didn't feel safe to call from his place just in case it could now be bugged. He headed straight for Big Burt's to let him know no cash transactions were permitted from the prearranged account and to get hold of Funnel. Lightfoot was hopefully not too far into Europe yet and they'd be able to stop him. Dell knew this would cost them a few quid, but that was better than losing a few good men.

Burt got hold of Funnel easily enough and then he, Dell, and Richards met on the shop floor at Burt's. It was there that Funnel had to notify Lightfoot to either turn his trip into a break or turn round and get back on English soil, and to ditch their non contract phones and purchase some more and regroup.

Obviously, Dell had to tell the boys of Butler's proposal and how he didn't have time to hear him out to the full because of Lightfoot's position, but he noticed their change of expression. They looked like a pair of hyenas about to scavenge for their first meal in weeks. The three of them sat in the bookie's shop and contemplated their futures and the futures of many others around them.

CHAPTER 32

Strangely enough, they weren't the only ones considering their future right then. Dick Durley suddenly got struck with a bout of reality, like someone had hit him with a brick. This could well be the first time in his miserable little life this had happened to the man. He sat alone, thinking about the position he and his son were now in. Things couldn't get any worse, he thought, contemplating spending the autumn days of his life in prison. He took to drink, gulping back bottles of gin, and serious depression quickly engulfed him.

The devious self-centred Bart wasn't going to help matters either. He was looking to put the blame on his dad in any way he could and considering their ages, the old man was pretty much going to have to bear the brunt of it by himself. Although the pair were only in prison a week or so, Dick knew he didn't want any more of it. Bart didn't fancy going back either. But even in his short time there, he had managed to become another man's bitch. So, in a way, it wouldn't be too bad. Being no stranger to those situations, at least he could cuddle up with someone!

Gerry was happy for the time being, given what he looked at as a license to kill. He carried on business as usual and kept the money flowing into the

DSTC's coffers. This arrangement delighted Butler as it was playing the terror mob right into his hands as planned. The only end that hadn't been tied up properly was the Dell part of the operation.

As Butler mulled over this rather large problem, Dell put through another call to Ronnie Slaughter from his new number to ask more about the in-laws' arrangements for Armistice Sunday and to talk to him about the situation in London.

"Still, they're comin' at me, Ron, different names, same old faces!" moaned Dell.

"Told ya, didn't I?" came Ron's terse reply.

Dell asked whether Ron had heard any more about his son coming over with his mum and her parents. Ron confirmed he had and they were. This was great news for Dell. He could now make firm plans to meet his son. However, Dell wasn't the only one with a trick or two up his sleeve, as listening in on the conversation were Wilson and an MI5 agent. Butler received a transcript almost as soon as Dell put the phone down.

Dell may have changed his phone and gotten a new number, but that didn't matter. MI5 naturally had the most sophisticated listening equipment and they'd caught Dell on a voice recognition device. Butler was ecstatic. He now knew that the only bit of family Dell had was coming over for Remembrance Sunday and were going to be at the targeted Legion at the intended time of impact.

"Perfect, bloody perfect!" rejoiced Butler as all three agents high-fived each other. Now they didn't need to try and get mud on Dell. They'd use his son as a lure. He'd become a sort of hostage and Dell would become the hero who rescued him.

Later that day, Dell and the boys ended up huddled around a table in the pub discussing what they should do about Butler's proposition. All three were quite excited by it all, but they needed to know more. They would want some proof for starters, guarantees and assurances that this was government work and that Butler wasn't setting them up. Also, they weren't going to show their hand. Dell would remain poker-faced and try to drag as big a bounty out of it as possible.

Although he wasn't quite as keen as the others, Dell was happy for a second chat with Butler. He would apply the same tactics as last time, but this time, Dell might be a little more attentive. Butler was eager to cut a deal with Dell. The clock was running down and Dell was aware up to a point of Butler's desperation, but of course unaware of what Butler now knew. The second meeting took place the day after the first, but this time the pair met at a local church where they wouldn't be bothered by anyone.

Butler arrived early and sat in a pew at the back of the church, waiting patiently for Dell, who arrived on time. A couple of old ladies fussed around flower arranging, but did not bother the pair.

"Morning, Mr. Butler," said Dell quietly.

"Morning, Joe."

"Bit of an ironic venue for a meeting, don't you think?"

"Not really, Joe. We're on neutral turf but common ground, and besides that, he's on our side," replied Butler as he looked up.

"Ha ha, yeah, I s'pose he is," chuckled Dell.

Butler knew he'd divided Dell's attention last time by trying to frighten him about Lightfoot. This time, he'd go about it the right way. He should have known scare tactics would not work on Dell. They made a little light conversation before getting down to business. Butler had made a good choice of venue; no one would suspect them of anything. They had both dressed smartly, Dell sporting his poppy on the lapel of his two-piece suit, no tie and his shirt unbuttoned at the neck. Butler was similarly dressed, but with a tie and no poppy. They looked like a pair of city gents coming in to pay their respects to the big man upstairs. In a way, they were doing his work one way or the other, at least Butler was.

Dell listened properly this time as nothing was here to distract him, although he wasn't entirely comfortable talking about something of this nature in a church. Butler, however, was a lot more at ease than yesterday and after eavesdropping on Dell's conversation, didn't think it was necessary to try and win him over. But he had to make it look and sound good. Dell felt there were other mobs in London better equipped for the job, but Butler was having none of that.

"Joe, if you were writing out ya team sheet for a London Eleven, you three would be the first names on it. You lot have been together for a long time now, apart from the odd vacation. Together you're a force to be feared and certainly respected. Forget the East End and that mob over South. You and your boys are the ones. No one else has your experience. You were born for this and this is your calling. You could look at ya'self as a sort of underworld civil servant."

"Yeah, exactly. A servant. You said it. I ain't about to become your slave, Mr. Butler," said Dell, wanting to swear but thinking that was inappropriate in a church.

"It's not like that, Joe. It would be a one-off job with a nice few quid on the table."

"Hmm, you'll have to do better than that," said Dell.

Butler knew he could do better than that, much better. He paused for a moment as he looked Dell straight in the eyes and then dropped the bombshell. He lit the fuse and sat back and watched.

Dell's face was a picture. He actually looked like he was about to explode, but managed to contain himself.

"Let's go outside for a walk," suggested Dell, as he needed some air.

They walked around the peaceful grounds of the churchyard, hands in their pockets, only taking them out to gesture as both men asked questions or made their point. Butler knew this would work and really felt God was on his side as he said to Dell, "I like to think that my enemy's enemy is my friend. Don't you, Joe?"

"Depends who it is and what they've done or intend to do. But in this case, you're spot on," said Dell.

The two men spent all morning together, going through all kinds of details. A strange bond was formed. But would it be for one night only?

Eventually the pair adjourned their meeting. Dell was going out for a late lunch, but didn't want to be seen in Butler's company. His head was spinning. He was experiencing all kinds of emotions. Butler on the other hand was simply a very happy man and felt victorious. He'd finally got his man.

CHAPTER 33

Rita had got her man too and she also felt elated. But for her husband, life was quite the opposite. Two weeks is a long time, and how things can change. One thing that didn't change, though, were the panic attacks father and son kept experiencing as they both started to face up to their current predicament. It had been good fun at the time, but it wasn't at all funny now. Rita was well rid of him, or so she thought. She and Ifty carried on as usual and she felt no need to hide it. She hadn't done anything wrong, after all. They went for a drink later that afternoon and showed their faces down at the pub as usual.

As they showed their faces, two other now-familiar figures also showed theirs. Badini and Dasti turned up awaiting Gerry's arrival. As they had arrived early, they took the opportunity for a quiet word with Ifty. They were after a stolen car, one that had to be taken to order in the next week or so, one that wouldn't stand out too much and that was not from anywhere near here. This was very important to them, as they had a very important use for it. Ifty knew what sort of thing they were after, but he had no idea what they wanted it for and he certainly wouldn't ask. But they had asked the right man. He could sort that out for them, no problem. They shook hands and left the details with Ifty.

Butler reported back to his superiors with the good news and had visions of promotion or even early retirement. Dell called his lieutenants and arranged a meeting in the pub as he felt a chat over a drink was appropriate for what they were going to discuss.

Cairo meanwhile was getting herself ready for another visit to the Legion while The Ayatollah was putting the final touches on his battle plan. The poor Durleys were having to prepare themselves for yet another quiet night home on tag.

That wasn't an option for Dell and the boys; he'd called it and now they needed to get busy. He explained the deal. It wasn't exactly new territory, but it was certainly a new contract and a new client. As Sweden had gone wrong, a new source of income would be very welcome indeed.

Secrecy was the order of the day and compliance with Scotland Yard, Butler, and MI5 was now very much at the top of the agenda. Sweden was as good as forgotten about as a lot had to be discussed on this latest issue. All were in agreement that it had to be dealt with, but a lot of questions needed answering first. Top of everyone's list was payment. How much? This issue would have to be taken up with Butler and nothing would be guaranteed until they'd all agreed on a price. After all, they would be putting their lives at risk.

During this one-off court meeting, they returned to the subject of Dell's quieter family life. Although he'd been out of prison only for all of about five minutes, one man had already lost his life and several others were about to be put in front of a firing line in order to fulfil a government contract. So how quiet did he want it?

One thing was certain, though. All three were willing to meet with Butler and his men and to get things moving along quickly as they didn't have loads of time left. But then again, would they really need it? There couldn't be that much to sort out. Killing for a living wasn't exactly new to any one of them.

"Let's stop messing about, then, and get on with it!" said Dell.

"Okay, let's do it," the pair replied.

Over at the other end of the pub, Gerry's eyes told another story. They were scanning the pub, working overtime. He was nervous and looking everywhere for unwanted faces as he prayed to God none of Butler's mob would turn up. That incident had shaken him up, but he had to carry on with his work. As he sat with his two Asian mates, it was a scary position for him to be in and he didn't like it one bit. The only people he overlooked were the pair of undercover cops who had been using the pub for so long now they'd almost become part of the furniture. He'd taken them as a young courting couple and was completely unaware *he* was the reason for them lingering so long in the pub.

As Ifty and Rita sat at the bar, Ifty's mind drifted, thinking of what sort of car the two Asians would be happy with and what they'd want to pay. After a while, he went over and had a quiet word with one of them the word "inconspicuous" was used. "Inconspicuous" ran through Ifty's head for a while and slowly he got a picture in his mind of the type of motor that would suit them. As Ifty knew dodgy types of people of all colour and creed, he knew he would have no problem delivering what was required when it was required.

Dell's firm were all agreed. They'd meet Butler the next day and would most likely engage with his project. They were angered by what had been said, but they were also quite excited by the offer, so they'd tie up the loose ends and get involved. They had a few more beers and then joined Burt and Mickey at the bar. Not a word was mentioned of Butler and his scheme and it would only ever be spoken about amongst the three of them.

It's funny how things happen. Once upon a time, if you were a member of the police force, or for that matter, any person in authority, the Country was a very hostile establishment to enter, but all of a sudden the police were welcomed with open arms. The English, when pushed, will unite in the face of a common enemy. Some of the strangest liaisons occurred that way. Dell's firm was no exception. They loved their country and its way of life, the same as everybody else. And it now looked like the bad boys and the good were going to join forces. It was therefore hoped that everyone present at this meeting would be satisfied with what was on offer and they could get on with Operation Desert Storm.

A restaurant in the Buckinghamshire town of Beaconsfield was chosen as the venue for a table for five. A short journey up the M40, out of West London, it was calculated to be just far enough away from the prying eyes of the big city for the men to merge into the scenery and talk the whole thing out unnoticed. It was a good choice as the restaurant was spacious and a table reserved in the very back would be perfect. They could conduct business without any unnecessary interruptions.

*   *   *

Dick Durley had had an exceptionally bad night descending into even deeper, darker depression, home alone, with no wife or son for company. Dick bombarded Rita with calls and texts, which all fell on deaf ears. She couldn't sympathise with her husband whatsoever and felt very strongly that his current predicament was all of his own making. She was just happy to be away from him. He used to drive her mad before all this. What did he expect? *Get on with it* was her attitude. Bart on the other hand wasn't quite as bad because he felt he had a chance and in his selfish little mind would let the old man become the fall guy, panic attacks or not.

The Ayatollah, by contrast, had had an exceptionally good night. He was very happy with his troops and the way his plan was unfolding, particularly the way Cairo was gaining the confidence of the RBL members, enabling her to relay in great detail the full program for the one-hundred-year memorial service. The boys too were doing a magnificent job fundraising for the cause and they now had a vehicle on order. With less than three weeks left until the big day, nothing could possibly go wrong.

Apart from recruitment and giving orders, The Ayatollah had also managed to secure for his team a small unit big enough to work on a single car on a local industrial site, where they could also store all their vital equipment and weapons. This was going to be his 9/11 and it would make 7/7 look like a nonevent.

CHAPTER 34

Butler greeted Dell and his two henchmen as if they were leaders of a big corporate business and, to be honest, they were all dressed as if they were. Any curious onlookers wouldn't have known any different. Two old couples were there in perfect disguise as a normal foursome out for a bit of lunch, who were in fact there to ascertain what the government was going to get for its money and it would actually be them who said yes or no.

Butler was in the chair today and as if to impress his possible contractors, took care of all the hospitality arrangements as instructed. The boys were impressed and quickly realised he meant business, so took full advantage of what was on offer. The group retreated from the bar to the reserved table well out of earshot of the general public. It obviously didn't matter about the dithering old couples situated pretty close by.

Butler started. "Right, gentlemen. We all know why we're here. I won't bore you with the details as Joey here tells me you have been briefed on our goal. I would just like you all to know, we want the hatchet buried regarding any old cases and to let you know that, with your cooperation, there will be no present or potential past cases involving any of the three of you that we would wish to review again."

The boys glanced at each other briefly and let Butler deliver what was to be a very rousing speech indeed. As chairman, he was very impressive and professional at delivering his talk and even his government eavesdroppers noted this. He came across as a team leader on an incentive drive with his employees. He mentioned nothing about terrorism or ISIS or bombs, nothing at all. But, by the way he spoke, everyone around the table fully understood what he was saying. Had this been with a different clientele, he would have received a round of applause when he finished, and he was right—he hadn't bored anyone. After he had finished, he told the boys to take full advantage of the á la carte menu and if they wanted to ask him anything, to feel free, but to be discreet. He even announced they would be more than compensated for the loss of the Swedish contract that had left such a bitter taste. In truth, all they knew about that was what Gerry had told them and when Lightfoot's car was clean, they thought they'd been double- crossed. Gerry was a small cog in the machine, but these boys were going to be the engine. Butler felt happy so far with the way he'd oiled it and would fight to maintain it.

There is nothing like a nice meal washed down with expensive wine to put minds at ease, and this unlikely gathering was starting to feel a bit more comfortable in each other's company. Dell sat back in his chair, straightening up his poppy as he did so, and looked around the table at the gathered faces. This whole thing intrigued him and gave him much food for thought, but he kept his feelings to himself for now.

The quintet enjoyed a delicious lunch before Butler turned to Dell and said, "What are you boys saying then, Joe?"

"Well, Mr. Butler," began Dell, but Butler stopped him.

"Please stop calling me that—just Tom or Tommy will do."

"Okay, Tom, well, I'll have to talk to the boys once we've left. They just wanted to hear it from the horse's mouth, so to speak, before making a decision. They actually thought I was on a wind up."

"Wind up, eh? I'm just the go-between. This thing isn't my idea. It's been commissioned by the government," said Butler a little heatedly.

"Yeah, so you say, but we don't know that, do we?"

"Do you think I would have wasted my time and money coming out here, and gone out of my way to find you and try to get you on board?" responded Butler.

"No disrespect, Tom, but you have to see it from our point of view. What you're asking is no mean feat. We could be being set up. Besides, you always had it in for me when I was young," protested Dell.

"Don't be silly, Joe. We've both come a long way since those days. Look, you've got a tight little firm here and I know there's plenty more where these two came from and men like you in these unpredictable times are of great value to our country," pleaded Butler.

"Well, let me talk it over with them and I'll be in touch later or at latest in the morning. Anyway, you keep saying we'll be looked after financially. You haven't mentioned a figure. Also, we could end up dead ourselves. There's a lot for us to consider and a lot more proof will be needed before we form an alliance," said Dell.

"Okay, I understand," replied Butler, calming down. The pair stared each other out for a few seconds and then shook hands.

Dell wasn't about to jump in with both feet and neither were the other two, but they were interested in the offer and they wanted to let Butler sweat on it for a while. Dell also wanted to speak to his old confidant, Burt, about this, as he'd been there for him most of his life and Dell respected his opinion. After a pleasant lunch, the group got up and shook hands. Dell's lot left the other two behind to settle the bill as they headed back up the M40 to London.

As he sat in the back seat alone, Dell asked the other two what they reckoned.

"We can't just sit back and let these scumbags blow up the Legion. My mum and dad go there," said Funnel.

"Yeah, and my old man gets in there too," said Richards.

"Well, I spoke to Butler at the table and I didn't show our hand and I told him we want a bit more evidence and not just his word. I totally agree with you boys. I know what it's like to lose family and I wouldn't want you two to go through any of that. Anyway, Chrissie and my Harry are going to be there that day too and I ain't letting anything happen to them. Fuck it, we'll play him along a bit, but I still don't trust the cunt. Anyway, it'll give us something to do. We've been a bit quiet of late," he continued tongue in cheek.

"Yeah, sod it. Let's go along with it for now. We can always change our minds and just warn 'em at the Legion," said Funnel.

"Let's fuckin' waste the dogs!" said Richards in his succinct way.

"Well, I wanna run it by Albert and see what he thinks," said Dell. The other two nodded in agreement. They all looked at Burt as the fourth member of the inner sanctum and they respected his opinion. But when Richards said what he'd just said, Dell knew the death knell had started to toll. Richards was a bloodthirsty type and that was his way of settling matters. They continued talking it over as they headed up the A40 to Big Burt's.

As they all walked in, Burt knew something was not right. They looked like a mafia hit squad with faces to match.

"Alright, boys?" said Burt. "You look dressed to kill. What's up?"

"Nothing, mate, we just need one of our chats if you've got a minute," said Dell.

"Yeah, 'course, we'll go upstairs. Sharon, you alright for a bit?" Burt asked.

"Yeah, sure, Burt," replied his assistant.

The four went upstairs to the office and Burt sat at his desk as he looked up at the three.

"It's Butler, innit?" said Burt.

"Yeah! How did you know?" asked Dell.

"Because I had that bad feeling, remember? And now it's come back again."

"Bloody 'ell, premonitions are rife round here," said Dell, then continued to tell Burt the situation with Butler and supposedly MI5, with the other two putting their bit in every now and again. When Dell finished, Burt sat back in his chair and said, "Fuckin' 'ell! I told you something was going to happen, but I never imagined anything like this. What are you gonna do then?"

"Well, a part of me wants to go ahead with it, but I don't trust Butler. I know him of old. These two are pretty much in. They fancy it," said Dell, motioning toward Funnel and Richards, who nodded in agreement.

"Erm, well, this one has surprised me, Joe. But let me think on it and I'll talk to you about it later. Is that alright? By the way, what are you boys doing now?" asked Burt.

"Well, not much, why?" asked Dell, looking at the other two.

"I need a few quid picked up from old Wisey's place in Chiswick. There's a grand in it for ya, if you fancy it. Seeing as you lot are looking like the mafia out on a hit," joked Burt.

"Yeah, we'll do that for ya, Burt. Where we going? To his shop on the high road?"

"Yeah, he said he's got it, but if he ain't, he'll soon get it when you lot walk in," said Burt with a grin. "Anyway, if I go over there, he'll make up some excuse to short-change me or get me punting with him so he gets it back."

Dell laughed and then said, "Yeah, he's a slippery cunt like that."

"Thanks, Joe. Tell ya what, I'll see you boys in about an hour in the Country and we'll have a chat. That alright?" asked Burt.

"Yeah, we'll shoot over there now and get your dough and we'll see you there," replied Dell, shaking Burt's hand, as did the other two.

When the three of them entered Wisey's shop, "Bet the Wise Way," Wisey looked up and said, "Can I help you, gentlemen?"

"Yeah, hello, Don," said Dell, as he knew he hadn't recognised him. Don Wise looked at Dell for a moment, then the penny dropped.

"Fuckin' hell, it's Joey Dell. What are you doing here?" he asked nervously, expecting the worst.

"I've come to pick up the scratch for Big Burt," said Dell.

"Oh, right, why didn't Burt come himself? There was no need to send in the heavy mob."

"Don't panic, Don. He's busy and we're all going out soon, so he asked us to come over," replied Dell. "You got it or what?"

"Yeah, yeah, 'course I have," said Wise, shaking as he went to his safe to fetch it.

Dell turned to the others with a smile, then winked and turned back to face Wise as he handed over a package containing fifteen grand in cash. He hated parting with this sort of money, but he knew this time he wasn't going to be able to pull a stroke on Burt.

"There you go, Joe," said Wise, as he begrudgingly handed over the case.

"Thank you, Mr. Wise, I'll see that Burt gets it. I assume you don't want a receipt? Now have a nice day," said Dell, smiling as they left.

"You too," replied Wise, but without a smile.

As they drove away, Dell said, "That was nice and easy. Mind you, he hated parting up with it, didn't he?"

"Yeah, not much, it was painful," said Richards.

"He's alright, Wisey, really, but I don't think he liked us turning up," replied Dell. "Come on, let's go and see Albert."

They headed back to base, where Dell was doubly keen to see Big Burt and talk things over. He felt there was a lot to go through and there was too. This was a completely new situation for all of them and they were all going to need Burt's expert opinion.

The boys got back to the pub before Burt arrived and immediately took the corner table, where they could chat without unwanted ears. Burt joined them as soon as he walked in and took his payment after dishing out the grand as promised. On being asked his opinion, Burt gave them a little speech.

"I must admit, I didn't expect this, but what I will say, is knowing you boys as I do, in this world, you're either in or you're out and some people are neither in nor out, but you lot are definitely in. So I think it doesn't matter what I say, I know where you lot are gonna go, and I think this situation is out of my hands already. Otherwise, you'd have told Butler to fuck off already. But, boys, all I can say is, be very careful and make sure at the end of the day you're in control, because if not, you'll be in trouble and you, of all people, don't need me to tell you that."

They were only doing what they thought was right. But Burt was also right in what he had just said and every one of them knew they were heading into a very short-fused powder keg.

"I think you're walkin' into a very dark place this time," said Burt.

"Well, you could be right, but like everyone else, we're fed up with the state of our country and if we can't help out in some way, then who can? Something has to be done and quick. The target is where their dads and mums go for a Sunday drink for Christ's sake, and my little Harry is expected to be there, Burt. And I ain't havin' that. No fuckin' way!" Dell said, slamming his hand down on the table.

"Nah, I understand where this is all comin' from. I just ... well, you know, I don't want anything to happen to any of ya. This reminds me of something years ago in the States involving the CIA and the mafia. It had something to do with Castro, the new Cuban leader at the time, and I'm sure it all went wrong for many of them. Even the president copped it and I'm sure it was all linked somewhere along the line," said Burt, with a look that said he was trying to recall something he wasn't too sure of.

"Yeah, but this lot are just two-bob terrorists and they're right on our bleedin' doorstep," piped up Funnel.

"I know that, but even two-bob terrorists will have links to others like them, won't they? I just think you're going into very murky waters if you go ahead," replied Burt.

"Well, we're gonna go to the next level and see what happens from there," said Dell.

It was a possible Pandora's box, but they couldn't resist a peep inside. Much to Butler's delight, another meeting was set up, but this time with people much higher up the food chain than Butler. Problem? Maybe, but although the boys had each spent a bit of time at Her Majesty's pleasure, they all felt an allegiance to the Queen, and especially the country. Not one of them had a job, but they were certainly paid and now they all felt it was time to give something back. Despite Burt's words, they were going to make sure England wasn't going to be just another country. They were *in*.

CHAPTER 35

Rita meanwhile continued to enjoy her time away from her husband and her son. Both had disgraced the family name and at that moment in her life, she really didn't care about them. Dick was becoming a real pain. Having had a small taste of prison, he knew that life wasn't for him and now he didn't have the support of his wife or his son. He had no one to talk to about it. All Bart was thinking about was himself and what he could possibly inherit from his father's demise. His mother, having defected as well, just made him even more self-centred and depressed. The Durley family looked set to implode.

While they were enjoying a night out, Ifty made a mistake. He was about to implicate Rita by saying too much in front of the wrong people. The residential undercover couple wearing their usual matching North Face jackets hadn't been clocked by Ifty. He sauntered over to Gerry and said, "Alright, Gerry? Where are the boys tonight?"

"Yeah, fine. What boys?" asked Gerry, looking up from his phone, more interested in that than talking to Ifty, who had clearly had a few.

"The two Asian guys I put you in touch with. Only they asked me for a motor and I've got one sorted for them."

"Dunno, mate. I didn't know they were after one," replied Gerry.

"Yeah, they wanted something inconspicuous, so I got a sixteen-plate black Astra lined up for them, You see it's just that me and Rita can drop it off to 'em when they're ready."

"I don't know anythin' about it, Ifty. Give 'em a bell," said Gerry.

"I have, but no answer," said Ifty.

"Okay. If I see 'em, I'll tell 'em," said Gerry, getting back to his phone.

This was precisely why Gerry had been released. He was a priceless source of information even if he didn't realise it. So now Butler's team had gotten a bit more information to hand over and a Durley was now involved, and although she would be involved unwittingly, the surveillance team weren't to know that.

The following day Bart rang Gerry for some cocaine. His father's persistent moaning was affecting him. Bart fancied getting on it and getting some light relief from the local escort agency. He was no stranger to these places and in fact was very well known amongst the local call girls, although more as a disappointment than an hour's excitement, but no one ever told him. This was probably why his wife sought the company of other men, as Bart was apparently notoriously underdeveloped in the male regions. If he didn't earn half-decent money, he would probably still be a virgin.

CHAPTER 36

Dell and Butler's meeting with the big boys was arranged for the next day, which gave them a bit of time to talk it over amongst themselves and that included the apprehensive Burt. He thought the whole thing stank and just couldn't see it ending well for any of them as he constantly reminded them.

The trio were picked up by Butler and Wilson and then whisked off in a people carrier with blacked-out windows to the same location on the South Bank of the Thames where Butler had had several meetings with the MI5 team. They had been closely monitored as they approached the building and each man had been secretly identified before they even reached the entrance. They went up to the second floor and were shown into a room where they were greeted by two men. One of them opened the meeting.

"Morning, gentlemen. Please take the seats with your nameplate and thank you for attending this meeting concerning a matter of national security. Now, you all know why you're here and Mr. Butler, I'm sure, has kept you all well informed as to what we are looking to achieve with our program that has been termed Operation Desert Storm. Oh, excuse me, I don't think I have introduced myself yet. I'm Mr. Brown and my colleague here is Mr. Green. As you have probably gathered by now, we are the agents heading said operation. This is a trial, very much an ideology in its infancy, and I am very pleased to have you on board as the pioneers of this very important test. If successful, this could be the start of things to come and the birth of a new no-nonsense approach to terrorism on our soil.

"As you have most probably seen in the media of late, Islamic State are very much on the brink of defeat in the Middle East, with many of its 'brave' soldiers fleeing and trying to return to their countries of birth. Not only men, but women too, and pregnant ones at that, looking to give birth to future terrorists back here in the UK. Well, we've got news for them—they're not wanted and they're not welcome.

"This brings me to the subject of Operation Desert Storm, ODS for short. The cell which we've had under surveillance for a long time consists of two IS fighters who returned here in early 2017, a mad mullah type that we suspect sneaked into the country on a false passport from Iran, not one hundred percent sure when, and a female convert. White English, no less." Brown looked around as everyone, including Green, shook their heads in disapproval.

"Now, before I go any further, have you all signed the Official Secrets Act document concerning this matter?" he asked.

"No, they haven't," said Butler before anyone else had a chance to answer.

"Okay, that's not a problem. If any of you do not wish to sign this document, I must ask you to leave right now," said Brown, continuing to look at his subjects.

"No, I'll sign," said Dell readily and the others agreed they would too.

The signing ceremony took a while, as one or two other bits needed to be signed as well. When all finished, more information could be divulged and the rest of the day would be a real eye-opener. The amount of intelligence gathered on the cell was frightening and it certainly made the others wonder what the government knew about them. After a couple of hours, the subject changed slightly. This time, the subject was the real IRA.

"Now, we know you are no stranger to Irish paramilitaries, Mr. Dell, and we'd like to show you a short clip of where they stand on the subject of Islamic extremists in their country," said Green, as Dell sat shocked.

They were all treated to a press release video from the Irish, all wearing balaclavas and camouflage jackets, sporting rifles across their chests. The footage was short but powerful and they made no bones about what they would do if Islamists tried anything on their soil or even plotted anything from their soil. They finished with, "There's only room for one fuckin' mob on this island!"

Green said, "We can all learn from that clip and that's just the sort of attitude we expect our mob to take." They all nodded their approval and couldn't help but admire the Irish attitude.

Now came the moment they'd all been waiting for. How much were they going to receive for their services? When they were told, the trio sat expressionless, not wanting to show any elation, but it was a jaw-dropping amount. At last the cream of West London's underworld were about to earn a bounty worthy of their reputation.

This time, it was Brown's turn to get up and ask, "Is everybody happy with what you've heard?"

"Yeah, yeah," they all replied.

"Is there anything you'd like to ask before we hand you over to Mr. Butler here? He'll be the go-between for us and you and you'll have no need to return here, as all information will be passed down to him, as will the money," explained Brown.

"Do we get money up front, or is it all paid on performance?" asked Dell.

"All will be taken care of in a fair and business-like manner and when you've completed your mission, we'll exchange what belongs to us for what belongs to you," replied Brown.

"I think we'd all feel a lot happier about the situation if you could put some sort of deposit down for our services as a sort of goodwill gesture," said Dell.

"Okay, we'll arrange an interim payment via Mr. Butler here," replied Brown.

"Thank you."

They all shook hands, wished each other luck, and bid their farewells. They all felt as though they'd achieved a lot.

As they drove back to West London, Butler commented, "I see you didn't wear your poppy today, Joe."

"Ah yeah, I must've forgotten," lied Dell.

Changing the subject, Dell said, "So now that is falling apart, we can expect a lot more of this sort of thing on our doorstep, can't we?"

"Yeah," said Butler. "And that misfit they call The Ayatollah knows everyone in that game, not just here, but all over Europe. If he don't know 'em, they ain't worth knowing."

"Well, he'll fuckin' know us soon!" said a sneering Richards.

"That reminds me. You're going to need to see the surveillance pictures of this mob."

"Yeah, that would be interesting," replied Dell, who then asked, "When do we start our training?"

"It'll be this week, 'cause we haven't got long to go now, not that you lot need much teaching," said Butler, casting them a funny look.

"Ha ha, very funny," retorted Dell.

"Where do you boys want dropping, or is that a stupid question?"

"Could just do with a pint as it happens," said Dell, looking at his watch.

By this time, Ifty had managed to get in touch with his terror pals and they had arranged to meet in the Country to discuss the delivery of the car he'd gotten for them. A strange scenario was unfolding in the pub and neither group knew there was any sort of connection between them at this point. As they passed each other, they would acknowledge each other, a pretence that would have to be kept up right until the big day.

They knew it would be stupid to talk about the day's events, but Dell had to ring his trusted friend Burt and get him out for a chat and to brief him on the meeting. Burt arrived as soon as he could and was dying to hear how it went. In the usual hushed manner, Burt said, "Has it not occurred to you lot that you're the most unlikely mob to be selected as saviours of the people, heroes? I don't see it somehow and if I were you lot, I'd fuck off somewhere until they solve the issue themselves." Burt was still far from convinced, even after hearing what they had to say.

"You worry too much, mate. Anyway someone's gotta do it, and we start our training this week," said Dell, leaning in even closer.

"Training, for what? You lot could most probably train them better than they could train you," said Burt, trying to get through to them.

"Don't worry, Burt. I've taken out some insurance even these two don't know about."

"For fuck's sake! Well, you're gonna need it, that's all I can say," replied Burt.

Over at the other end of the bar, arrangements were being made for the delivery and the payment of the car requested by the pair of ex-ISIS fighters. Rita, who was not present today, was given the unenviable job of driving said car, while Ifty was to follow behind. The delivery of the potential car bomb was to take place that coming weekend to an address Ifty would receive on the day. Car bomb making was the expertise of Dasti and Badini, a skill they'd picked up in Syria that was now second nature to them. Only a week and a half left before they could reap their reward of chaos and death. They had agreed to a brand new strategy, one that was actually the brainchild of a female whose roots were deeply implanted in the UK and West London especially. Her forefathers would be turning in their graves.

As the clock counted down, Dell's firm embarked on a crash course of special training provided by the best, the sort of training that would excite even the most casual of Bond fans. The very best of British intelligence was going to take this semi-organised underworld trio and turn them into a new breed of British criminal—a combat force to be reckoned with, not just in the shadows of Britain's underworld, but a force that would have the potential to be the envy of criminals and noncriminals the world over. Look out any would-be terrorist, the UK has under its wing a new weapon you would have never seen coming in a million years. But if it becomes the success its aiming to be, the world of the sitting duck civilian was about to sprout some very big muscles indeed and would certainly change the face of counterterrorism and terrorism the world over. Britain was about to give something to the world once again. No longer would the country's back be up against the wall on its own streets. The tide was turning and not before time either. As the almost completely defeated IS men and women tried to limp back into the UK, thinking they'd just returned from a package holiday in the Middle East and expecting to carry on their life of destruction, they would face a new enemy that would play them at their own game.

Butler watched, delighted, as his first choice of recruits filed in and reported for training. This was surely a major lift for him in his desire to get the promotion he felt he thoroughly deserved. Out of earshot of the Dell firm, he spoke with total conviction about the latest addition to the government's new idea.

"Look what I got for you," he muttered to himself with pride as Dell, Richards, and Funnel arrived.

"This is London's A Team," he told one of the men assigned to train them. "Not the reserves. These boys are Premier League and they are no strangers to death. No! They're lethal, so make sure you treat 'em with respect."

"Oh yeah?" replied the instructor. "Who are they then?"

"That's Flowery Dell and his right-hand men," replied Butler, puffing out his chest as if he had really achieved something.

"Yeah, well he might be a pansy, but we'll make a man of him," was the instructor's reply. Butler looked at him as if he'd gone bonkers and then muttered, "You prick!" He continued, "Just make sure they come out the right end and, as I say, treat 'em with respect. Handle with care, if you know what I mean."

The man nodded, totally unimpressed. Butler may have puffed them up unnecessarily, but he was pleased to have them on his side. *London's calling and it's time for everyone to sit up and listen*, thought Butler as he went over to greet his team. Now that he was in charge of the situation as MI5 had handed over the baton of command to him, he felt unstoppable. Now he could make things happen and as they didn't have loads of time on their hands, they quickly got down to the training. Actually, the timescale was perfect as he didn't want time for idle chatter that could let the cat out of the bag, and because of that so far there he had heard no rumours floating around London's underworld grapevine about this newly formed association.

Of course all three of the new recruits were well used to the tools offered to them. Practice was easy and they actually surprised their trainers, if not themselves. Progress was made and made fast. The first day's training brought smiles and happiness all round. Everyone involved quickly realised no time had been wasted on no-hopers and another day's teaching and learning lay ahead the day after next. No dust gathering here, just pure concentration and absolute cooperation between men who all believed in each other. If you fancied causing an upset, then good luck, because this was England, not a messed-up city in the desert, and it wasn't about to become one either.

As Dell's firm settled easily into their role as accomplices to the government, there were no laddish bets flying around the building as to whether they'd cut the mustard. That was very much apparent from the off. The most enthusiastic of them all was Tommy Butler. This thing wasn't his idea in the first place, but it had certainly become his baby and he felt honoured to have been selected as the man in charge on the street level of Operation Desert Storm.

A very excited Butler arrived at the school of training to see how his protégés were getting on. It was all good news. It was day two and massive progress had been made as the whole team involved were more than satisfied with Butler's men. They were glad to inform him it looked like he *had* made the right choice. But as he went to join his in-training team for lunch in the canteen, he got a bit of a shock.

"Alright, chaps?" he asked with a grin like a Cheshire cat. He just couldn't hide his joy. "Mind if I join you? All good news so I hear," he continued.

"Yeah, go on, sit down. What did you expect? That's why you got us involved in the first place wan it?" said Dell, now getting a bit bored with the training program. It was so repetitive. They'd proved their skills and were now fed up with it.

"You don't sound too happy, Joe. What's up?" asked Butler.

"Look, mate, with all due respect, we've proved we're up to the job. Two f**kin' days solid doing the same thing all the f**kin' time. We've had enough now. This operation of yours, are you really serious? Because we thought you were just pullin' our pissers," moaned Dell.

"Pullin' your pissers. Are you pullin' mine? After all this and what we've been through, you thought we were takin' the fuckin' piss?" asked an astonished Butler. The smile had been completely erased from his face.

"Yeah," said Dell, as he tucked into his lunch.

"Ah, don't tell me you're havin' second thoughts. For God's sake, you can't pull out now, they'll kill me. In fact, they'll kill all of us," panicked Butler.

"Well, we've had enough of all this old bollocks, ain't we boys?" said Dell as the other two nodded in agreement.

"Fuckin' 'ell!" exclaimed Butler. "I thought you were bang up for this one, Joe. Doing what you do best, but this time for the good of the country."

"Yeah, we are, but this is getting right on our nerves and that pompous little instructor might end up with one in him if he keeps on," said Dell with attitude.

"Well, they're more than happy with you lot," retorted Butler.

"Do us a favour, then, and see if we can fuck off after lunch. We don't need any more bloody training. It's like a refresher course for us," said Dell.

"Okay, leave it with me. But promise me you ain't havin' second thoughts, please!"

Dell looked at Richards and Funnel and he knew they were all equally keen to see it through, but just felt that the afternoon session was a pointless exercise. Butler went off to find someone to talk to quickly. He didn't want his men upset and pulling out over something so trivial. So he would bend over backward to keep his men happy. They had so far proven a good choice and at this stage he couldn't afford any trouble.

Butler came back all smiles once more and this time he had a pretty fair compromise. "Right," he said. "You two can sign out whenever you like. They're done with you both," he said, pointing at Dell and Richards. "But Tel, they just want to go through a bit more with you. It won't take longer than an hour and then you're free to go. That alright?"

"Yeah," sighed Funnel. "I s'pose it'll have to be, won't it?"

They were happy enough with that and, on reflection, it wasn't all that bad and they had actually learned a thing or two. They had brushed up on one or two self-taught skills and if they were deadly before, they were now lethal.

Butler wasn't the only person this side of the Thames feeling that way. The Ayatollah felt exactly the same about himself and his team. After he'd completed this atrocity, he would escape to France, where he had good connections in the Paris ghettos, and start all over again. He was a man on a mission and when he finally got to meet up with Allah and all those virgins, they would receive him with much fondness. He may even be looked upon like the martyrs who had gone before him. 9/11, 7/7, and now 11/11 was rapidly approaching. 11/11 had a great ring to it and he would get the credit for another job well done.

CHAPTER 37

With Dick constantly threatening suicide, his smarmy son Bart chose the comfort of the local whores instead of offering comfort to his father. He also had a solicitor's letter sent to his mother's lover. He thought that should the old man carry out his suicide threat, he'd be entitled to all his father owned. Bart was typical of a boy who had been spoiled and abused, who had now grown into a man. He was as messed up as his father, but greed was now his motivator. Not really having any real friends, he only ever thought of himself. He had become a vindictive person who felt betrayed by his parents, and the only way to get recompense was to try and seize everything possibly on offer. He had become a little Hitler, much to the disgust of his mother. Even his one-time and possibly only mate and sexual partner, Gerry, wasn't on hand as a shoulder to cry on. They both had their problems and neither was sure how to deal with them.

The only people at this particular time in the pub who knew how to deal with their problems were the members of Dell's firm and they didn't look at their predicament as a problem. To them it was a challenge and a challenge they would see through to the end, the words of the Irish paramilitaries still ringing in their heads.

Ifty was right on the case of sorting out the car for his two Asian pals and it would be delivered as required. Rita, bless her, was going to be party to a crime she thought was going to be an innocent delivery of a car on behalf of her lover that would earn her a few quid. The Durleys couldn't resist the chance of a pound note in their pockets, any one of them. Ifty had made the appropriate arrangements to drop the car off at an address he would only know at the very last minute. He didn't think anything of it as a lot of people want to keep the location secret when receiving stolen goods so as to avoid being set up. Even when Rita was behind the wheel and on the move, they still didn't know exactly where they were going. They were just told to head toward such and such.

Rita had no idea what she was actually getting herself into and neither did Ifty. Rita didn't even know the car was stolen. She just thought she was helping out. Obviously neither one of them knew they were being watched by several undercover Met Police officers in various motors strewn along their route. Due to intelligence, they knew exactly where the car was being taken. Ifty on the other hand was receiving instructions over the phone through Bluetooth from Badini and every now and then, he had to relay them to Rita, who said, "Why all the secret stuff? Can't they just tell us where to go?"

"I don't bloody know," said Ifty.

Eventually they arrived at the destination, dropped the car off, and collected the money. It was a garage unit on the Park Royal industrial estate in a quiet corner just big enough to garage one car at a time. It had a little reception area to the side with a door and once inside you could walk into the workshop area, which had rolling doors to get your vehicle in. For the next week, this was to be the DSTC's headquarters, and they were of the opinion that while they were there, they were pretty much out of sight of the general public. They had a car to work on, which was nothing unusual in this environment, and at the same time they could finalise their plans for 11/11.

Ifty took the cash and said his goodbyes. He and Rita left the scene, thinking no more of it as they headed back to Ifty's place, where once indoors they planned on getting cleaned up and going out for lunch. They would soon find out this was not to be. As they drove onto Ifty's street, they suddenly found themselves surrounded by unmarked police cars with flashing blue lights coming out of the front grills. The pair were completely taken aback and their first reaction was that there must be some sort of mistake. Armed officers sprang from the cars, pointing their weapons at the pair and making them get out of their vehicle with their hands in the air and lie face down in the road.

Rita thought to herself, *This is a bit much for having a pedophile husband*, but this of course had nothing to do with Dick whatsoever. Rita and Ifty were arrested on the spot and bundled into a van, having endured the usual search procedures. Both were taken to the Paddington Green police station of all places, and this came as an even bigger shock because this was where terrorists were taken. It didn't make any sense to either of them. They weren't terrorists and didn't even know any, or so they thought. In fact, Ifty couldn't even spell the word. But they soon came to realise that, for whatever reason, they were in deep trouble. Rita had gone from being the wife of a nonce to the top of the terror list in less than a month. Now that takes some doing by any standards.

The pair were grilled for hours on end, but neither could offer anything because neither of them knew anything. So nothing could be leaked back to the real terrorists, neither would get bail and the pair would be remanded in jail once they'd been to court. Operation Desert Storm was in full cry now and nothing was going to halt it.

Bart Durley was totally unaware of his mum's situation and, as laughable as it was, Ifty hadn't received any solicitor's letter. Even if he had, it wouldn't have made any difference to him in his current predicament. Bart stupidly had always thought any type of threat to him could be resolved by a solicitor's letter. What he hadn't taken into consideration after living like that for years was the fact that some people didn't give a damn about a soppy letter. They were just waiting for Bart to turn up in the wrong place at the right time, and Bart was about to do just that.

His lust for cocaine fuelled romps with prostitutes or brasses, as they were more commonly known, were getting out of hand. The more his personal problems grew, so did his desire for escapism. Little did he know an old friend from his childhood days had been waiting many years for Bart's appearance and would have a permanent cure for his desire.

This man was one of three brothers with a reputation of their own. They were also on very good terms with Dell's firm, but were unaware Durley had been using Dell's headquarters, the Country, for a while. Anyway, that didn't matter, as coked out of his tiny brain, Durley was about to present himself to the Yerby brothers on a plate like a stuffed turkey at Christmas.

They'd all grown up in the same street as kids and the middle brother, Jimmy, was more Bart's friend than the other two. In fact, the other two couldn't stand Bart, but Jimmy had taken pity on Bart back then and although he knew Bart was a compulsive liar and a proper little sissy, it amused him really. He even went on to be Bart's best man when he married Sebrina.

Then, a few years later, Bart, being Bart, offered to help Jimmy out with a business deal but couldn't help himself. He embezzled twenty grand out of the unsuspecting Jimmy. When Jimmy discovered what he'd done, never thinking for one minute Bart would do such a thing to him, he confronted him. Bart promptly went to his solicitor and then the police with tales of blackmail and extortion, which came to nothing. But the mandatory letter from Bart's legal advisor dropped through Jimmy's door, which left his hands somewhat tied. The whole episode was never forgotten by the Yerbys, especially Jimmy, and they decided to bide their time and give Bart his punishment when the opportunity presented itself. Today was that day.

The Yerby boys owned a sauna room and tanning shop that offered the added extras for dirty little pervs like Durley and just as the youngest brother,

Rodney, was having a fag outside the bookie's, he watched Durley park right by the saunas, get out of his car, and head for the door. There was no mistaking it being Bart, as he had the private plates on his car he'd had for years: BND 118.

Rodney couldn't believe what he was seeing and as neither of his two brothers was on the premises at that particular moment, he quickly got on the phone to tell them what he'd just witnessed. Bart obviously didn't know who owned the place he'd just entered, or if he did, he was too out of it to realise. Tony and Jimmy were there in minutes and joined Rodney at the bookie's opposite. They rang reception to inquire about the man who'd entered the building about ten minutes earlier wearing a red jumper. Sure enough, the reception informed the brothers the man had booked a sauna and massage with all the extras and was planning on staying a while.

"Beautiful," was Jimmy's answer.

"Get the tools. He's getting the full treatment, but we'll make sure he's paid up first!" said Tony, the eldest brother.

The girls were instructed to keep an eye on Bart and keep him occupied for as long as they could. They needed a bit of time to get the torture room ready and as it soon became clear Bart was holding a sizeable amount of a Class A drug on his person, things just got better. The torture room was just that. It was full of whips, handcuffs, masks, ropes, and other little items of pain, which was a further service the establishment offered.

Jimmy had an idea and ran it past the other two, who agreed it was a better move than using tools. Anyway, they didn't need to use tools on a prick like him, although they all would have liked to. Jimmy was more than capable of dishing up a bashing to Bart and could probably do it with one hand tied behind his back. So the brothers waited for Bart to spend a bit of cash in their establishment and when he was all finished, one of the girls was to bring him to them.

While they waited for Bart, they exchanged reminiscences about him. One story in particular that Jimmy always laughed about was when they used to go to Stamford Bridge together to watch Chelsea play. It involved a punch-up outside the stadium, as it often did, during a midweek cup tie against Man United. Bart was always telling people what a football thug he was and how he was always fighting opposing fans. This couldn't be further from reality, as he was frightened of his own shadow, but it was amusing to listen to because those who knew him knew different. Jimmy took the story up:

"So, there was about six of us on the Fulham Road, just outside the West Stand when about the same number of Mancs came across the road shouting to us, 'Who are ya? Who are ya?' So, without saying anything, we just let 'em 'ave it, except for Durley, of course, he ran off straightaway and just as I'm weighing up this northern monkey, I looked up and saw him dodging his way through the crowds, trying his hardest to get away. What a cunt, eh? And I got nicked for it! God knows what stories he told people after that one. I never did forgive him for that. I mean, why pretend you're something you're not? People just used to laugh at him. He was a fuckin' embarrassment. Anyway, it's payback time for the smarmy cunt and I'm doing it, boys, if you don't mind."

"No, no, not at all. You've got more reason than any of us to do it," said Tony.

Bart seemed to be taking his time and the boys were getting impatient. He was doing a lot of talking as usual, but the use of drugs made him worse and his stories more exaggerated. The brothers actually felt sorry for the poor girl who had the misfortune of entertaining him.

"How long's 'e gonna be, the prick?" asked Rodney.

"Don't worry about that. Every hour he's in there, it's costin' 'im," was Tony's reply.

"Well, I was thinkin' we might 'ave to push a pair of waders through the door, 'cause the bullshit must be really thick in there by now," laughed Rodney.

"You ain't wrong there, Rodders," said Jimmy, who couldn't wait to get his hands on Bart.

"Ain't 'e the idiot that used to call his missus Sexy Sebs?" asked Tony.

"Yeah, that's 'im," said Jimmy.

"Well, she looks like a little boy, what I remember of her," he replied.

"Yeah, well, that would explain a few things, wouldn't it?" said Jimmy. "And she's got a nose like a dog sniffin a shitty arse," he continued.

As the brothers sat around laughing at Bart's expense, the door opened and in bowled Bart, thinking one of the other girls wanted to see him and that she'd got the hots for him. Well, that's what he'd been told. The atmosphere changed in that room instantly and so did the colour of Bart's face. He stood there shaking like a jelly on a tumble dryer when he saw all three stony-faced Yerby brothers staring back at him.

"Hello Jimmy, how are you, mate?" he blurted out, as if nothing had ever happened between them.

"Well, fancy seeing you here," started Jimmy. "Still got a taste for the brasses, I see. Oh dear, and what would that sexy wife of yours say if she found out?"

"Ah, she wouldn't mind. Anyway, she knows what I get up to. We don't keep secrets," lied Bart.

"No, 'course not, mate. Anyway, seeing as you've just invited yourself in, I think we have a few things to talk about, don't you?"

"Look, if you touch me, my mate Joey Dell will sort you all out," said Bart, thinking he'd just issued a threat to the brothers.

"Will he now? Well, if you don't mind, I'll give him a quick ring and let him know you've burst into our meeting, uninvited, throwing his name about," said Jimmy as he went through his phone contacts looking for Dell's number.

"Yeah, you do that," said Bart, all cocky.

Bart was quick to jump on the fact that he may be harmed by the Yerbys, but at this point, they hadn't issued any threats whatsoever. They were quick to seize the chance to test his alleged friendship with Dell. They knew Dell well enough to know Durley was never his type of associate.

Dell's phone rang and he answered to Jimmy. "Hello," said Dell.

"Alright, Joe, how are ya?" asked Jimmy.

"Alright, thanks. Who's this?"

"It's Jim, Jimmy Yerby."

"Hello, Jimmy, how are ya? I ain't seen you for ages, mate. What can I do for ya?"

"Well, Joe, me and my brothers were in our office havin' a chat when a supposed mate of yours let himself in and very rudely interrupted our conversation."

"How rude of him. Who was it?" asked Dell curiously.

Jimmy looked straight at Bart as he paused for a second or two and while looking him up and down said with a grin, "Bart Durley."

"Who?" exclaimed Dell.

"Bart Durley."

"Bart Durley?" Dell repeated down the phone, trying to get his head around it.

"Yeah, thinks he's one of the boys, full of shit, and he reckons he's a good mate of yours," said Jimmy, trying to jog Dell's memory.

"Ah, fuckin' 'ell. I know the idiot and he ain't no mate of mine, Jim. In fact, I'm not sure if I've ever spoken to him. Ah, yeah, I did go somewhere once and he was there, but trust me, he ain't no friend of mine," assured Dell.

"I didn't think he'd be your cup of tea, Joe. I'm sorry to trouble you with such trivialities. We'll have to have a beer sometime," said Jimmy apologetically.

"Yeah, tell ya what, Jim. I'm in the Country over Ladbroke Grove most evenings. If you fancy a pint, it'd be nice to see ya," said Dell.

"You know what, Joe? Me and my brothers might pop over later if you're there. It would be nice to get together for a beer with you and the boys," said Jimmy happily.

"Yeah, come over. It'd be nice to see you lot too," said Dell.

They said their goodbyes and hung up as Jimmy turned back to Bart Durley, who was doing all his usual panic stuff by now, trying to gain a bit of sympathy.

"Well, Bart, looks like you been telling lies again, my son, 'cause Mr. Dell reckons you ain't no friend of his," said Jimmy, turning a bit nasty.

"He's lying, not me. I ... I ... I ... don't tell lies," stuttered Bart as he stood there white as a ghost, shaking like a leaf, and hyperventilating.

"See, there you go again. You just can't help ya'self, can you?" said Jimmy, as he walked toward Bart and then WHACK! He smashed him straight on the chin with a right hand that would have made Mike Tyson proud. Bart hit the deck like a sack of spuds, out before he even hit the floor. Then Jimmy carried on kicking the shit out of him as he lay there unconscious. Screaming all kinds of obscenities at him, through gritted teeth, Jimmy concentrated on doing Bart's ribs in with his boot. Tony and Rodney had to stop him before he killed him, then the boys served up the coup de grace.

Jimmy stopped, grateful to his brothers. As Bart lay motionless on the floor, the brothers went through his pockets, knowing full well he had a decent-sized package of cocaine on him. After they had found it, they got on with their plan and took about an ounce of the drug from Bart's person. They weighed out about a dozen grams of it, put it all in the usual paper wraps, then returned it to Bart's pocket. Then, with the rest of the bag, they wiped some around his nostrils and over his top lip, so whoever found him would know straightaway what he'd been up to. Then, with surgical gloves, Tony tied up the bag, gave it a good wipe, and placed it back in Bart's other pocket.

Bart was also holding a fair bit of cash on him, so they begrudgingly left that on him and dragged him out the back and dumped him on the pavement before ringing the police. They'd stitched Bart up good and proper and as the police were told of a disturbance involving drugs, they were quick to turn up on the scene.

Tony and Jimmy left as Jimmy needed to get out a bit lively and Rodney stayed behind in case he needed to deal with the police. They'd arranged the perfect story and Bart was back in the shit once more. The Durley family now looked like public enemies in the eyes of the law. Things can change pretty fast when you don't want them to.

When the police arrived, they found Bart on the pavement starting to come around, holding his head and trying to sit up.

"Afternoon, Sir, are you alright?" asked an officer.

"Ooorrrrh," groaned Bart. He was far from alright. He was suffering properly. Apart from a concussion, he had several broken ribs, and when he was out cold on the floor, Jimmy couldn't resist kicking him right where it hurts. Bart had spent most of his life avoiding a good beating and it had finally caught up with him. In fact, he had actually gotten off lightly because the Yerbys had wanted to go to town on him for old time's sake. When Jimmy came up with the idea of setting him up for a conspiracy to supply charge, they thought they'd take the best of both worlds.

As Bart laid on the pavement moaning and groaning, not knowing what day of the week it was, both officers noticed the residue around his nasal area and as he wasn't outside a bakery, they realised it wouldn't be flour that was over half of his face. Rodney Yerby went out the back to investigate the situation and told the police of Bart's obnoxious behaviour inside his sauna and how he'd been upsetting customers and staff all afternoon and that he'd been told to leave. It was no surprise to find him in this condition as someone was bound to hit him sooner or later.

The police, however, were more concerned with searching Bart for drugs and on learning his name was Bart Durley, a name very familiar to law enforcement, they were doubly keen on nicking him. And after finding a considerable amount of Class A drugs on him, they decided to call an ambulance as he was in no fit state to be taken to the station. He needed treatment.

The Yerby brothers decided to take Dell up on his invitation for a drink and arranged to go over and have a couple with him in the Country. They wanted to tell Dell firsthand about Bart Durley and they knew he'd enjoy the story. What they didn't know was that if they hadn't gone to see him then, within the next day or two they may never had gotten to share a drink with him ever again. Nonetheless, he and Big Burt were there to meet all three brothers and a good laugh and a catchup was had by all and they particularly liked the Bart story. Mickey liked it the best out of all of them, as he loved the way Jimmy told a story. When backed up with a couple of pints, his stories always sounded even better.

CHAPTER 38

Now that Rita was behind bars and Bart was hospitalised with new charges to face, Dick's despair spiralled out of control. He was totally alone. He had no one he could turn to for support. Dick sank deeper and deeper into a black hole from which he would never extract himself. Suicide now figured heavily on his mind. The drink wasn't helping and neither were his constant visits to Father O'Reilly. His whole world was falling apart and everyone in it seemed to have turned their backs on him. He couldn't take any more and the fact that he was facing a very long time in prison and would probably die there meant he started to plot his own death. If Bart thought things were bad now, they certainly weren't going to improve any time soon.

The final straw for Dick was when a group of local kids who'd found out about his exploits knocked on his door and then ran off and hid behind Dick's hedge, only for him to find a burning package on the doorstep. Dick fell for it and immediately started to stamp the fire out while the group looked on in amusement, shouting obscenities at him as he frantically tried to extinguish the burning package wearing only his slippers. It only took a couple of seconds, but it was too late. The damage had been done. The paper bag set alight on his doorstep contained dog shit. An old prank, but a funny one nonetheless for those behind the hedge watching as this disgusting man walked back indoors, not realising he was covered in it all up his jogging bottoms and obviously all over his slippers. Dick walked it all through the house as he returned to the living room to carry on drowning his sorrows in gin. He hadn't smelt the unbelievable stench of the dog muck. All he could smell was smoke and he wouldn't realise the full extent of the prank until much later, after he'd woken up from his drunken stupor, by which time it would be far too late. When he did finally wake, the stench was so much that he was sick. It was everywhere. This was more than he could take.

Dick looked at the mess and the smell that now filled his once spotless abode, then looked at his watch. It was nine twenty in the evening. He ran back into the bathroom and was violently sick again. The tag around his ankle felt like a shackle never to be removed. His house stank, his life stank, he'd been hung out to dry by his wife and son and he could not face up to prison life for the crimes he'd committed all those years ago. Still half-drunk, he went to the drink cabinet to see what was left. A half-started bottle of Scotch would do. He kept hold of it as he looked for his car keys and grabbed his coat. This was it. Dick's darkest hour had arrived and he'd made up his mind. Still clutching the Scotch, he staggered outside, got in his car, and drove to a quiet, dead-end road about a mile away from his house. He parked in a cul-de-sac and sat in his car swigging from the bottle with tears streaming down his face. His world had fallen apart in a very short time and he no longer wanted any part of it.

The drunken Dick Durley finally got out of his Jaguar and walked into a dark wooded area that had a pedestrian path that crossed a railway line. He leaned on the gate for a while, crying and gulping at his bottle, which he clutched for comfort. He watched a train rattle past him. He felt freedom would be the next passing train as he battled to keep himself upright and then, as he stood there, engulfed in the silence, he heard a train approaching down the line. He paused for a moment or two as the noise grew louder. This was it, the grand finale.

He could now see the train as he staggered out of the darkness and into its path. With a sickening thud, the train sent him spinning into a million different bits. Dick was gone—dead! He'd squeaked his last and now out of his suffering, he'd passed the pain of his last couple of weeks on to the poor train driver, who at the point of impact had hit the brakes and pulled the emergency lever. Although it was pitch black, the driver just caught sight of Dick's face as he splattered up the front of his train, a sight that would haunt the driver forever and consequently also ruin his life forever. Dick had ruined so many lives when alive and he had now managed to achieve the same in death.

CHAPTER 39

The following day, as the news broke about the train jumper and who it was, the Flowery firm members were falling in with Butler in order to make their final preparations for Operation Desert Storm. They, like the DSTC, were about to disappear from public view until their mission was accomplished.

But before anything happened, Dell had put into action his back-up plan, a plan he'd come up with right from the very start of Butler's reappearance, one he had devised with Burt during their discussions of what Butler might want and why he might be hanging around. It was a plan that if things should go wrong at any time for Dell or any of his firm that they'd have a bit of life insurance. Dell was obviously dubious of Butler's intentions and planned to protect himself and his boys. This was precisely the sort of thinking that set him apart. These things made him numero uno and once he was satisfied everything was in place, he packed his bags and met up with Richards and Funnel, making sure they'd got all their essentials, the ones Dell had instructed them to take, and off they went to meet up with Butler's men and form that team of special men Butler had so proudly put together. They were so special even Butler would never have guessed in the end just how special they would turn out to be.

* * *

While everyone was making plans to change the world around them, Bart's world had already changed, and he didn't even know it. By the time he came out of his induced coma, which his one-time and only friend had helped put him in, Bart's life would be unrecognisable. With his dad having taken his own life and his mum incarcerated on terrorism-related charges, Bart would wake to a living nightmare. The life he knew before was forever destroyed.

* * *

Richards drove to pick Dell up from his apartment with Funnel alongside him, the pair buzzing with excitement. They loved adventure coupled with action, as did Dell.

"Alright, boys?" inquired Dell. "You got everything I told ya to bring?" assuming his role of boss.

"Yes, Joe, of course," was the reply.

Dell sat in the back and took his bag off his shoulder and placed it on the other side of him as he sat down.

"What's in that bag?" asked Funnel.

"That, my son, is insurance," said Dell with a smug little grin on his face.

"Ah, looks like some sort of PC to me," replied Funnel.

"Yeah, it is actually the very latest in modern technology, that is, my son," said Dell as he patted it gently. Reality had already hit Dell and he was under no illusion as to what was around the corner for them. Dell, the new James Bond? He didn't think so. Once he'd patted his iPad again, he said to the other two, "This, boys, is our lifeline." Then he quickly changed the subject as he wanted to keep his cards close to his chest.

"Go to the Country. We gotta follow Butler and he's meeting us out front."

"Where are we going?" asked Funnel.

"Dunno, but wherever it is, that's where we're stayin' until the big day," responded Dell, making himself comfortable in the back.

Richards did as Dell said and when they got there, Butler was waiting with Wilson. They headed off toward the A40 once more and made their way out of London.

Dell, sitting quietly in the back, thought about what the next few days held. They were entering new territory and what else? God only knew, but one thing he was sure of was once all this was over, he would be reunited with his son. This was the most important thing for him, but first he had to carry out his duty, and if his instincts served him well, the whole thing would go without incident.

They went over the Greenford flyover on their way out of town, where just below them on their left was the DSTC's intended target, the Royal British Legion. They carried on out, past Northolt Airfield, and as before got off at the Beaconsfield junction, only this time, they turned left and headed toward Slough before turning off to the right and into Burnham Beeches, a very large Area of Outstanding Natural Beauty. The winding country roads took them through confusing miles of woods and finally to a very large country hotel just outside the picturesque town of Slough. They weren't a million miles from home, but they could've been absolutely anywhere for all anyone knew.

They pulled up alongside Butler in the car park and everyone got out and looked around at their peaceful and tranquil surroundings.

"This looks alright," commented Dell, taking in the scene.

"Glad you like it. This is where we'll all be staying until the job's complete," replied Butler. "Come on, we'll go and check in."

Butler looked at his watch. It was almost five in the evening on November 7, 2018. Just over four days remained until the terrorist plot that would shock their community, their country and the world was due to be enacted and here he stood in a hotel lobby with a carefully picked team that was going to prevent the atrocious act. Butler checked them all in under false names, using the equally false company name of Lewis and Co., and when they got their room keys, suggested that they meet in the bar in half an hour for a few drinks, paid for of course by the company. This suited everyone and off they went to drop their bags. They still had a few details to discuss and had yet to see any pictures of the terrorists and that was certainly going to throw up one or two surprises!

The mood in the bar was relaxed with no signs of any last-minute nerves. This of course was to be expected as this lot weren't known for being bottle merchants and they were looking forward to the task that lay ahead. The pretence of being corporate businessmen was to be played out right until they checked out and when Butler announced he'd booked the conference room for just after breakfast the next morning, everything looked and sounded just as it should.

After a couple of hours in the bar, they all went into dinner and then Dell retired to his room for an early night in front of the TV, as did Butler and Wilson, while the other two had a couple more drinks.

The next morning, they were all up for breakfast and then headed for the meeting, where they were joined by another member of Butler's team, a man known only as Mullins. During this meeting, locations were discussed, as were the finer details of the forthcoming events, and a series of the all-important surveillance photos was seen.

Mullins took to the stage and the others were mesmerised by him as he appeared to know everything you could possibly want to know about the terrorists. Every little move, planned times, places, you name it, Mullins knew about it, and this left a big impression on Dell and the others, including Butler.

The atmosphere in the room took on a more sinister feel as they listened to the plans of the DSTC and their IS ideologues. The plans had to be stopped and this team were more determined now than ever before. Mullins revealed much that morning that nobody else had known before. He got the room outraged and fired up as never before. Then he pulled out of his briefcase the surveillance photos of those intent on making this whole horror story a reality.

Before the pictures were passed around, they were warned they may see people in these pictures that they knew or might recognise, as some of the pictures were taken in places they all frequented. Shock was an understatement. Some of these photos had been taken in the Country and they recognised all four terror suspects. Two of them had been in the pub on more than one occasion and the other two they'd seen on the streets on their patch. This was frighteningly close to home and no one was happy with what they saw, especially Terry Funnel. There were several pictures of his brother, Gerry, fraternising with two of the fundraisers. Also in their company were Ifty and of course Rita. Terry felt embarrassed and angry about what he saw, not to mention a raft of many other emotions as he stared at the photos.

"What the fuckin' 'ell is 'e playin' at?" he said in disbelief.

"Don't worry Terry. Gerry didn't know their political leanings. He was only trying to earn out of them. Anyway, he has been of great help to us in this operation without even realising it," said Mullins.

"And what the hell is Rita Durley's part in all this?" asked Dell, trying to divert the attention from Terry.

"Well, she drove a car the terrorists intend to use as a car bomb and dropped it to their workshop with her lover, Ifty Khan," replied Mullins.

"So now there's a Durley involved, is there?" asked an angry Dell. "Those cunts can't keep their fuckin' noses out of anything, can they?"

"Well, Rita and Ifty are safely under lock and key and will be dealt with at an appropriate time," said Mullins as he handed round more photographs.

"Good!" replied Dell as he studied the images of The Ayatollah and Cairo. "And we've seen these two about on several occasions," he spat out.

"Yeah, well, you'd notice them two with your eyes shut," chipped in Butler.

As they all had a good look at the photos, Richards sat poker-faced as usual and hardly said a word. He just looked at them with complete and utter contempt and, being a man of few words, certainly wasn't going to waste breath on these people. He was itching to get on with it.

"Which one of you is planning on doing the driving on the day?" asked Mullins.

Richards volunteered and Mullins said he'd have to take him on a reconnaissance mission later on. Richards was more than happy to go along, as he knew he'd be shown where the terror cell was working from, which was obviously of interest to all. Also it would keep him occupied. They were asked if they would like to keep any of the images, but no one thought it necessary.

It was Thursday, November 8, and it was getting closer to the big day. Dell's mob were expected on Friday the 9th. That was their D-Day and they were getting very excited at the prospect. No one was nervous at all, but they could smell blood. They were fast becoming thirsty men. The Godfather of West London didn't mind getting his hands dirty from time to time and he looked upon his part as a service to Queen and country.

Once the meeting in the conference room was over, Richards took off with Mullins. They made their way back into London and to the small unit being rented out on the Park Royal Industrial Estate. Mullins soon became aware that Richards was no conversationalist, but he noticed an immediate change in his attitude when he drove slowly past the terrorists' lair and saw them working on the Astra that Ifty had supplied. This excited Richards as this was something concrete. They could see two men obviously hard at work on the car and they'd learned via the eavesdropping surveillance that the process of turning the vehicle into a deadly car bomb was well underway. This meant the likelihood of events taking place tomorrow looked pretty certain and as Richards sensed the others were keen to get to work too, this made him a very happy man indeed.

Mullins drove past the unit and turned the car round further up the road and then drove past once more without being noticed. They then made their way to what was to be the final rendezvous point. This was on the same industrial estate, but quite a way from the unit the DSTC were using. Mullins made sure Richards was happy with the directions even though all the coordinates would be in the SatNav of the car they would be using on the day, which would be supplied to them by the Met Police. It was an unassuming vehicle that would never get pulled over by the police as it was exempt from such things.

Richards was more than happy with the setup and started to be a little more chatty toward Mullins, which in turn made Mullins a happier man. The two men headed back to the hotel, both satisfied with the morning's work. They would know later that day if the job was definitely on for the next day.

* * *

Rita Durley was languishing in HMP Downview, a women's prison in Surrey, regretting her love affairs with cab drivers, when she received the news of her husband's suicide. She was devastated and broke down uncontrollably. She blamed herself entirely and was inconsolable. She was left alone in her cell with nothing but her thoughts of what a mess she'd landed herself in, not to mention the mess Bart was faced with. She and Bart were never that close. He never forgave her for leaving him and his dad for a cab driver when he was a kid, but Dick was never an easy man to live with at the best of times. She felt you couldn't really blame her. But right now, Rita didn't see it like that and she wanted Bart to come and see her, but he was still in a coma and still didn't know anything about his dad, or his mum for that matter. Rita cried all day long. If only she hadn't met Ifty, none of this would have happened. She cried herself to sleep and was kept under constant watch before being taken to the prison hospital, where she was sedated for her own safety. Rita and Bart, now, strangely enough, were in very similar positions and only time could be the healer.

*　*　*

On the drive back, Mullins explained to Richards that the pair working on the car in the workshop were more than likely Dasti and Badini. The pair had learned how to convert a vehicle into a potential lethal weapon in Syria while fighting for ISIS and had become experts in this type of terrorism. If they ever got the chance to detonate that car, the damage it would cause would be phenomenal and the death and mutilation would be unbelievable.

"Bastards!" muttered Richards after listening to Mullins.

When the pair arrived back at the hotel in time for lunch, they all sat down together and discussed what they had been up to. Richards said he knew the workshop area well as his dad had worked in the same road a few doors down for years. Finding the place wasn't going to be a problem at all.

All they were waiting on now was confirmation that the next day was the day. They were all hoping very much it would be, as they wanted to see the job done and to get on with their lives. But no one wanted it more than Dell. He had other plans he needed to confirm and he would welcome the go-ahead sooner rather than later. He knew things weren't going to be as straightforward as they were being led to believe.

Mullins' phone buzzed and he disappeared for a few minutes. The surveillance team had intercepted a call to Gerry Funnel's phone. Dasti had ordered an ounce of crack to be dropped at the unit in Park Royal at two thirty the next afternoon, Friday the 9th. This was the news they'd been waiting for as Gerry's information was vital to Butler's team's plans. It was on for tomorrow. Mullins returned to the room, all smiles. He announced to the table the job was on for tomorrow. There were smiles all round and a sense of relief amongst the team members. Butler stood up and proposed a toast and when all their wine glasses were filled he said, "To tomorrow!" and raised his glass. The rest of the table stood and repeated, "To tomorrow." They then all sat around chatting excitedly. Dell excused himself and quickly headed up to his own room. He had unfinished business and now was the time to finalise it.

Inside the militant Islamic camp, the atmosphere was a little different. Three members of the group were planning on being reunited with the creator himself and they weren't planning on doing it on a clear head. Crack cocaine was going to be their flying carpet and who better to serve it up to them than Gerry Funnel?

Gerry had become a major player in this business and the poor bloke didn't have a clue. All he thought he was doing was earning himself a few quid, but he was right in the thick of things and playing a great game as far as Tommy Butler was concerned. Gerry didn't get released for nothing. Butler couldn't have written the script better if he'd tried. Gerry was going to be there to the death, as he was going to take a left turn instead of a right in the very near future. Nonetheless, he was still going to be the asset Butler intended him to be.

Dell had had plenty of time that afternoon to get his house in order and now felt comfortable enough to join the others for a relaxing drink in full knowledge he couldn't do any more than he'd done to keep himself and his trusted firm safe from harm and to make sure they collected their reward.

The DSTC on the other hand believed they were totally untouchable and had the freedom of West London to carry out their evil plan unhindered and undetected. They certainly did not suspect they could well be about to be upstaged by the Godfather of West London and his cohorts. Who would be first to the punch? Only time would tell and that was fast running out for all sides.

"Fail to prepare or prepare to fail" was the appropriate saying in this particular situation. Mullins' superiors thought he'd prepared well enough and told him to rejoin surveillance, where his experience would be better used in the final preparations for the showdown. He would relay details of movements, times, and the whereabouts of the DSTC.

Mullins therefore said his goodbyes and left Butler and the others socialising in the bar. Dell could have left with his two henchmen if he felt like it, as there was nothing to stop them sneaking off at any chosen time, but once he'd committed, that was it. He'd see the job through.

So they looked forward to evening and to dinner and as the food was first class, they couldn't wait. A sort of last supper was looming. No one knew one hundred percent how this would all end exactly. The boys intended to enjoy what potentially could be their last meal, and that's exactly what they did before turning in early so each man could make his final preparations.

Mentally, they were three very strong men who knew mental preparation was just as important as anything else and each individual achieved this in his own preferred way. But one thing you could guarantee was all three of them would be playing tomorrow's events over and over in their heads, each one playing out his role and using his training and his own experience to achieve what he would consider perfection.

Were any of the trio worried about what lay ahead of them? Very doubtful, considering their history and that each one knew the element of surprise was always a surefire winner. Were the opposition nervous? That too was doubtful, as they were going to be doing God's work and as that particular job wasn't until Sunday, they were very relaxed.

Dell was checking and rechecking that he'd prepared properly. The right people had the right information, which included his old mate Albert

Kinsley and his trusted brief, Petey Doyle. But there was another man that was probably the most important at the moment and that was Paul the pilot. He was vital to Dell's last-minute arrangements and once he was satisfied all was in place, he could rest easy. This was one job they couldn't get nicked for, but on the other hand there was a possibility they could all die. Dell felt that he'd got that covered too.

Tommy Butler experienced a sleepless night. It seemed his conscience was now getting the better of him as from the very start he'd opted to betray Dell and the others. But as they'd started to work well together and he had spent so much time with his old adversary, he was now very much regretting his suggestion of putting the case to bed on completion once and for all. Butler had wrongly assumed that Dell had had something to do with the death of a colleague of his back in the late nineties. At the time Butler couldn't prove Dell even knew the culprit, yet he'd had a bee in his bonnet about that case ever since. Now he was starting to grow a little bit fond of Dell as a person and as Dell and his team were good to work with, Butler was wondering if he could somehow reverse the finale, although it must surely be too late for that now.

Dell may of course have saved Butler his sleepless night if everything went according to his plan and as he was always an early riser, he'd arranged to meet Richards and Funnel for breakfast.

CHAPTER 40

"Morning, boys. Sleep well?" asked Dell.

"Yeah, alright, thanks. You?" was the general reply.

Dell rubbed his hands together with excitement. "Big day today, boys. Get this out the way and we can get on with the rest of our lives."

"Do you think we're sailing a bit close to the wind?" asked Funnel in concern.

"No, why do you say that? You're not having second thoughts, are you, Tel?" asked Dell.

"No, no. It's just ... well, I've never had anything to do with terrorists before."

Dell looked at Richards and the pair exchanged a look of disappointment.

"This is just like any other job we've done, only this one is almost fool proof," explained Dell.

"Are you not a little bit concerned about the outcome, Joe?" asked Funnel.

"Not where the terrorists are concerned, I'm not. As I've said before, it's the other lot that concern me more," said Dell.

"What, Butler's mob?" asked Funnel.

"Yeah, and MI5, but like I said, I've got our insurance sorted out. So don't worry," retorted Dell, patting the iPad that was hanging across his shoulder and had been more or less all the time since they'd been at the hotel. In fact, you could say it had become part of his dress code, as had been the poppy a couple of weeks back.

"Now, let's enjoy our breakfast. We need to keep our strength up," said Dell as he grabbed the menu from their table.

Butler may have had trouble sleeping and it certainly showed, but two people definitely sleeping well were the two remaining Durleys. Bart was still in his coma and Rita was still under sedation. It can be great to be in your own little world without having to face up to reality.

"Morning, Tommy. Rough night, was it?" quipped Dell.

"You could say that. You lot look like you slept well. What you having for breakfast?"

"We've already eaten, mate. Got a long day in front of us," Dell replied.

"Yeah, you can say that again. Nothing seems to bother you lot too much, does it?"

"Not really. Just another day at the office. Don't tell me your bottle's gone, Mr. Butler," said Dell, giving him a friendly nudge.

"Don't be daft, Joe. Just can't get on with that bed. Plays my back up."

"As long as that's all it is, mate."

"By the way, that Dick Durley topped himself the other day," said Butler, trying to change the subject.

"Cor, that's a big loss to the world," said Dell sarcastically.

"Yeah, well I think the Force are getting a bit sick of that lot. They've made themselves very busy of late and all in the wrong way, I might add."

"Yeah, you're not wrong. I s'pose they'll be flying that stupid flag outside his house at half mast," joked Funnel.

"I wouldn't put it past 'em."

Butler ordered a pot of coffee in an attempt to pick himself up a bit as he looked at his recruits in amazement at how relaxed and unworried they looked. "Hope you lot are up for it later. You look like you've just had relaxation therapy," commented Butler.

"May I remind you, Tommy, my old mate, we ain't up for anything until we have seen the dough," reminded Dell.

"Yes, I know that, Joe, and everything will be taken care of this morning, when you will get everything you need for your meeting. And that includes the money," explained a weary Butler.

"Good! Anyway, where's your oppo this morning?" inquired Dell.

"He thinks he's on bleedin' holiday. Sleep for England," replied Butler, sipping his coffee.

Wilson hadn't been told the full story. He knew only the basics and didn't know all the ins and outs like Butler did. He had nothing to keep him up at night and right now Butler wished he didn't either. Taking another gulp of coffee, Butler swallowed and then said to Dell and the others who were all sitting at the table next to him, "And we should know the time of your meeting by midday."

"Well, as long as the money's all there, there won't be any problems, will there? 'Cause it's nothin' personal with us lot, it's business," explained Dell.

"I know that. You're good boys," said Butler, now unable to look them in the eye. How he wished he hadn't suggested the double-cross. It was too late. The plan was already in place. He'd started to think he'd messed up. He wasn't to know one man had outthought him. It's the same old story, over and over. Fail to prepare or prepare to fail. Only one man had done the latter. To be fair, Butler was as good as his word. When he said everything would be in place by midmorning it was. Other than that, he looked very dispirited as he knew he had made a wrong move. He started to worry about himself and his family. Maybe he should have turned left instead of right.

As promised, four men arrived at just after eleven. They were all armed and they also came bearing gifts. The money was all there and was placed in the boot of Richards' car, all £1 million of it, as an armed man stood guard over it. This pleased Dell and his firm as they knew now it was game on. The given time for the big meet was two thirty precisely and final details were discussed out there in the car park. Every man was very clear on his role. Dell's mob didn't know if these men were police or MI5, but it didn't matter. All they knew was they'd delivered the goods and dished out information and orders.

Gerry Funnel had also arranged a meeting at two thirty, at the headquarters of the DSTC, and this was the very reason Dell's firm had been told to go there at that time. Gerry was vital to the plan, although neither he nor Dell's lot knew it. He was the reason the eavesdropping team couldn't give an exact time until they knew when Gerry was due to arrive with his package of drugs.

Dell kept his iPad over his shoulder as he would for the rest of the mission and when asked why, he would simply answer, "Insurance." They were all set and ready. It was just a matter of waiting, which sounds easier than it actually was. Everyone was raring to go and couldn't wait to get the job started and finished, for that matter.

At the lockup in Park Royal, Badini and Dasti had arrived to put the finishing touches on the Astra Ifty and Rita had so kindly dropped to them. When they'd finished that, they were going to have a look for a bag for Cairo, which would also be converted into an explosive device. Not too long now before London's streets were paved with the blood of infidels.

Two armed officers were to drive Richards' vehicle, loaded with the cash, back into London to the rendezvous point, while Dell's firm drove the undercover police car with a virtual police escort almost to the door of the terrorists' lair. Dell's thoughts kept drifting between the job at hand and the safety of his son, who he knew was due in London at some point that day with his mum and grandparents. They'd certainly change their opinion of him if they were ever to learn what he and his pals had done to make sure their precious memorial service went off without problems.

News came through from the surveillance team that all four terrorists were at the lockup in Park Royal and that it was time to hit the road. The three-car convoy headed into London with Butler and Wilson having left earlier. Excitement was high in their vehicle as Dell delivered his "England expects every man to do his duty" speech. They were loving every minute of this and they were on schedule for a two thirty arrival.

Gerry Funnel had also hit the road and he too was on time.

Dell's firm's move wasn't a comeback job. Theirs was a prevention move and prevention was the intention. No one was going to get one over on Dell's firm. "Fuck 'em" was the attitude.

Gerry, much to his obvious annoyance, was pulled over by an unmarked police car. They'd told him the reason for the pull was that he was driving an uninsured vehicle, which of course he wasn't. His car was perfectly legal in every way, but the police insisted it came up on their system that the car had no insurance whatsoever. It didn't matter how much he protested, the police were having none of it. Gerry was forced to abandon the car by the side of the road and told to pick it up from the compound at a later date when the matter had been sorted out.

This whole charade of course was to delay Gerry from making his appointment. He would have to walk the rest of the way, which would make him about twenty-five minutes late. This was enough time for Dell's firm to pay their visit and make their exit. The whole thing had worked like a dream.

As the three-car escort drove into the industrial estate, the first car turned off to the left with the car in the middle carrying on straight and the third car taking the same left turn as the first. Those two cars headed for the empty warehouse Butler and Wilson had unlocked a while earlier. This was where they had arranged to do the swap once the mission had been accomplished.

A few minutes before Dell's firm's arrival, the phone Butler had given him for this job rang. Butler informed him the gang were all there and that there was definitely firearms on the premises, but most probably hidden in a safe place and it was highly unlikely they would actually be armed. After all, it was Friday and they liked to say a prayer or two on a Friday and God knows, they were going to need one.

Butler's last words to Dell were: "Don't leave any man, or woman for that matter, alive. Make sure you take them all, the bastards! You have enough ammunition, make sure you use it. Good luck and we'll see you at the other place. Remember, you're doing your country a service."

Dell looked at the phone and said, "Don't worry, we don't intend to."

The mood quickly turned very serious as they approached their target and adrenaline started to pump. In front of the unit, they saw the Astra. Richards pulled their motor around the side, out of sight from the unit, and parked.

Terry Funnel was wearing a baseball cap identical to one his brother often wore and also sported a rugged, unshaven look as Gerry often did. To the untrained eye, this could be Gerry as Terry hadn't added the usual gel to his hair that day. All three men put on latex gloves and Dell handed out the police issue black 9 mm semiautomatic pistols, each holding fifteen rounds in the magazine. Each man had a couple of spare ones just in case they needed more bullets.

This trio was in fully trained assassin mode as they got out of the car and walked the short distance to the terrorists' lair. Each man completely focused on what they had to do. Dell and Richards held back a bit, just enough to keep out of sight from whoever was going to answer the door to who was expected to be, Gerry Funnel.

Terry approached the door that led to the small reception area and then into the main workshop. He paused for a short moment as he reassuringly felt the gun tucked into the back of his jeans. He then gave the door a good knock. This was it. There was no turning back, and in a few short moments the whole assignment would all be over—with a bit of luck, of course.

Hussain Dasti heard the knock, but he'd been expecting Gerry anyway. He stood behind the door and asked, "Who is it?"

"Gerry," replied Terry.

"Password, Gerry," said Dasti as a precaution before he opened up.

Terry swallowed hard as nervous tension started to grip him.

"Three-legged dog," said Terry, prepared for action. To his surprise, Dasti opened the door just enough to catch a glimpse of him and satisfied with what he'd seen, walked away, leaving Terry to let himself and the other two in. This seemed too easy. Had they no idea whatsoever that their world was about to come crashing down? Obviously not.

The three assassins walked into the reception area and encountered no opposition whatsoever. They followed the now out of sight Dasti into the workshop area, where they could hear voices talking. The information they'd received from surveillance so far was pretty good. Surely it couldn't be this easy. Dell and Richards followed a few paces behind Terry as he turned left into the main part of the unit. Sure enough, the four militants were all there and none seemed bothered at Terry's presence.

Dasti then pulled an envelope from his back pocket and threw it on to a worktop. He said to Terry, "Have you got it?"

Terry couldn't believe it. No one else bothered to look up at him. They remained seated, talking to each other, and there wasn't a firearm in sight. But this was their cue. Terry reached for the gun tucked in his waistband as he said, "Yeah, I got it, you cunt!"

At this point, the other two burst into the room with guns drawn. Terry fired the first shot, hitting Dasti straight in the middle of his head. It exploded like a melon, brain matter and blood flying everywhere. The other two simultaneously opened fire as the three remaining terrorists jumped out of their chairs with horrified looks, and gunfire exploded all around them. They'd been caught totally unawares and were like sacrificial lambs being led to slaughter.

Badini tried to lunge forward toward the gunmen, but he was cut down by a volley of shots fired by both Dell and Richards as they moved around in silence, hitting their targets in exactly the places they'd been trained to hit. The power of the gunshots blew Badini backward and he flew into chairs just behind him. Dasti had been killed with the first bullet, but Richards pumped three more into his chest, just to make sure, Dell and Funnel did the same to Badini.

Cairo got a single shot right between the eyes and slumped back into her chair. She also received more shots to the chest for good measure. The back of her head had also been blown away, her brains splattered up the closed shutter doors, steam rising from her demolished skull.

This left The Ayatollah. He hadn't been shot at yet, but the naked fear was clear for all to see. He tried in vain to reach for one of the guns tucked away on a shelf behind him, but it was no good. The three assassins rounded on him like a pack of hungry wolves with a taste for blood. They'd agreed that if possible, they'd leave him last.

"Don't you fuckin' dare!" snarled Dell as all three of them had their guns trained on him.

He froze, powerless. With three guns pointing at him, he promptly messed himself. He'd been caught and for him the chase was over. This was the last mission he was ever going to take part in. The smell of gun smoke filled the air as The Ayatollah stared helplessly down the barrels of three guns. Who would deliver the coup de grace? As it happened, all three opened up on him at pretty much the same time. The only one who bothered to waste any words on this despicable man was Richards. "Die, you fuckin' dog!" he eloquently commanded.

The Ayatollah died in a non-heroic fashion in a dirty old lockup in West London, left in a bloody crumpled heap on an oily concrete floor in his own excrement. As all three assassins had emptied their weapons into various parts of his body, he was guaranteed a quick passage to the seventy-five virgins, if they would have him.

"Let's get the fuck out of here," said Dell as he turned and made his way to the exit. No one bothered to look back at the damage they'd done. Mission accomplished. It was time to meet up with Butler and the others at the arranged venue. They walked purposely to the car without breaking into a trot and then Richards drove away in an orderly manner. They'd been in and out in less than two minutes and in that time had eradicated an entire terror cell.

This operation had been successful and could pave the way for others like it, but it couldn't be celebrated. It had to remain a top secret mission with only those directly involved allowed to know about it, so a smokescreen was going to have to be created. The public, or anyone else for that matter, was never to get wind of what happened on November 9, 2018.

Terry broke the silence as they made their way through the Friday afternoon traffic. "Well, they certainly thought I was Gerry, didn't they?"

"Yeah, they did. I can't believe we didn't face any resistance," said Richards with real surprise in his voice.

"Well, that was always the plan. Catch them unawares—the element of surprise. But, boys, I have a horrible feeling that was the easy part of our mission. This next bit is going to be the hard bit. You watch," said Dell. He felt pretty sure he could trust his sixth sense in this case.

Gerry Funnel meanwhile was making his way on foot to the fateful unit. He was running late after the incident with the law, so he decided to give his friends a call to let them know the situation. He first rang Badini's phone but got no answer. That wasn't unusual, so he tried Dasti's number and he didn't answer either. This didn't worry Gerry too much as he thought they were both probably busy. It had happened before. Anyway, he'd be there in about ten minutes or so, so it wouldn't be an issue. By the time Gerry got to the unit, he was almost half an hour late. As he approached, he saw the Astra parked in front of the doors, but no sign of anyone, so he knocked on the door a couple of times. Again, no answer. They'd arranged a meeting and now it seemed no one was here. Gerry wasn't very happy. He rang both phones again. He could hear them ringing in the workshop but no one was answering. *Odd*, he thought. He knocked on the door to the reception area once more before he tried the door handle. It was unlocked, which was again strange as they had never left the unit unlocked, even if they were inside. Gerry took the liberty of letting himself in. The keys to the Astra were on the small reception desk. That was the first thing he noticed as he headed to the door that led into the main workshop, which.

Gerry froze. He stopped as though he'd just walked into a brick wall. Nothing on this planet could have prepared him for the scene laid out in front of him. He'd just come face to face with a St. Valentine's Day massacre here in West London on an ordinary Friday afternoon in November. This was pure carnage. Four slaughtered bodies strewn all over the place. The smell of blood and death was mixed with the smell of cordite and shit.

Gerry glanced around the room in total and utter disbelief. He struggled to take in what he was looking at and promptly threw up. He couldn't stop it, it just kept coming. This was one of the most sickening sights anyone could witness. But the scene this lot were plotting in a couple of days would have been a lot worse. He wiped his mouth as he panicked. As he started to back himself out of the door, he happened to look down at the workbench to his left and saw a white envelope sitting there with a few spots of blood on it. Gerry put his hand out and grabbed it, as he knew it contained money and at the end of the day, it was this bit of money he'd gone there for in the first place.

He'd never imagined in his wildest dreams that he'd be confronted with such a sight. He also didn't know he was a key but minor player in this act, a bit part performer in a very big West End show. But no one could have worked out the significance of their roles in this performance other than Joey Dell, and he'd already summed up the whole situation. He'd learned from previous mistakes and had never been convicted for murder although he was a gun for hire.

Gerry scurried away with a couple of grand in his pocket and also the goods, but he was now damaged for life. What he'd seen was unbelievable and was never ever going to be erased from his mind. Blood, guts, and human tissue spread everywhere was just too much for Gerry. He ran out of the unit and as he had no car, he grabbed the keys for the Astra parked out the front. What was a man supposed to do now? What was he supposed to think after being confronted with that?

CHAPTER 41

Big Burt finished up work and went to the Country for a drink. He noticed the place was unusually quiet. He knew something was happening, but didn't know what exactly. But knowing Dell as he did, he knew it was going to be complicated. He was extremely worried about his mate. He knew he was up for pretty much anything if the money was right, but maybe this was one step too far.

He'd warned him about Butler, not that he needed a warning in the first place. He was only doing what he felt was his duty. Dell was no mug. He knew what he would and wouldn't do and no matter what anyone else said, he'd always do what he felt like doing. Although he did respect Big Burt's opinion.

Butler waited for his chosen few to return. When they turned up it was with the job done!

Gerry was in a different position. He had to think fast, something he didn't have the capacity for, although he had had the foresight to take the money and the keys to get himself away from the nightmare scene. Under the circumstances, Gerry had done well. If he'd known his twin brother was party to what he'd seen, and if he'd known he was the doppelgänger that was his twin brother, he might have felt differently about the situation, but that was very doubtful indeed.

He got in the Astra and got out of there as quickly as possible. He'd got two grand in cash and two grand worth of crack. That was good enough for him as he made his getaway from the crime scene. He of course had no way of knowing the car was a ticking time bomb. Not wasting any time, he booted it away from the unit and to a place where he could gather his thoughts and plan his next move. This was a serious situation and he needed to think it out.

He was understandably shaken. He still felt physically sick by what he'd seen, his mind flashing back to the young woman in the chair with a bullet hole in her forehead. She looked so peaceful. But the worst sight of all was her associate Dasti with half of his head blown off. Who could have done such a thing?

This whole scenario would effect Gerry for the rest of his life and he would never be the same again. He made his way out of the industrial estate in a blind panic, unable to think straight and with the vision of death firmly imprinted on his mind. He made his way on to the A40 and headed out of London to a place he remembered he used to go fishing with some mates a few years ago. He remembered it being just outside West Drayton and he was desperately trying to remember the way.

In the boot of the car was a great amount of explosives that could be detonated by pressing the stereo ON/OFF button, or by a mobile phone, which had fortunately been left behind at the crime scene. So the only way this car could blow up would be if Gerry inadvertently pressed the detonator switch as he moved through the slow moving traffic that was now building due to school closing time. In fact he'd only just realised the radio was on. His head was so scrambled he hadn't heard it.

He was desperate to find the fishing spot that had a nice parking area surrounded by trees with the canal on one side and the River Colne on the other, but the school traffic was holding him up. He became more and more distressed and he found himself checking the rearview mirror every two minutes. He was sweating like a Durley on a rape charge.

Just as he was beginning to make a bit of progress, out stepped a lollypop lady outside an infant school, which stopped Gerry in his tracks. She gave him a dirty look, suggesting he slow down in the built-up area by a school. Gerry waited impatiently as queues of school kids with their mums and dads spilled onto the road. Gerry could see he was going to be a while and started to change channels on the car radio very aggressively. He was not happy. He was turning the volume up and down, then tapping the steering wheel as he watched the constant flow of people passing in front of him and there didn't look to be any end to it either. He couldn't have come at a worse time.

"Come on, come on. Hurry up," he shouted in frustration, banging on the steering wheel. He continued channel hopping and played with the volume. "Come on, will ya!" he said as he sat there in his bomb. Finally, the lollypop lady, seeing the aggravated look on Gerry's face, decided to stop the flow of kids crossing the road and let the traffic that was starting to build pass through, much to Gerry's relief. He put his foot down and headed for the fisheries to try and get his head together.

Eventually, after what seemed a lifetime, he reached his destination and instantly panic was replaced by calm as he inhaled the smoke of the very latest super skunk weed. He was parked well out of harm's way by the canal, puffing away like a steam train as the painful memory of that afternoon's horrific sights were replaced by beautiful mellow thoughts of peace and tranquility. He lay back in the car seat and relaxed as he enjoyed this new calmness. He listened to Smooth FM on the radio. But as he tried to cope with the day's stress, he was starkly brought back to reality by a tap on the window. Peering at him was a dirty, scruffy-looking old man who, when Gerry opened his window, appeared to be drunk and stank of stale alcohol and many other things nasty.

He didn't mean any harm, as Gerry could see. Gerry was in fact happy he had been brought out of his drug stupor.

Gerry let his window down to see what the poor old chap wanted. Unable to understand his drunken speech, Gerry asked him to repeat what he'd just said. The man only wanted a cigarette, but Gerry was unable to hear him properly. He pressed the OFF button on the radio to get a better listen. Boom! The homeless man was no longer homeless and all of Gerry's problems disappeared in an instant. The pair of them were scattered into millions of pieces, destined only for crows, foxes, and rats.

So the DSTC had finally managed to score a couple of strikes, although it wouldn't have been the sort of score they would have been happy with, but if Gerry had pressed the button earlier, things would have been a hell of a lot worse. When Gerry exited the planet, he'd probably done himself a favour because for one, he'd have been mentally damaged by what he'd seen, and two, Butler had planned to set him up for the murder of the four would-be terrorists, claiming he was supplying them with drugs to fund the operation. Then he found out what they were up to and he was so incensed he killed them in a fit of rage. This would be supported by surveillance pictures of him meeting two members in the pub taken by the two undercover lovers and with guns and ammunition planted in his car, not to mention his fingerprints being at the scene of the crime.

Butler's scheme was already falling apart. Another thing he hadn't bargained on was the local police being called, as someone had heard what they thought were gunshots. Now they were swarming all over the place and someone had also contacted the media, obviously for financial gain, and they were all over it too. This didn't please Tommy Butler, but he was over the moon with his trio when they turned up at the rendezvous as arranged and started to reveal details of the assassination.

Butler had been starting to get a little bit worried when the boys had taken so long to arrive. That was because Dell had gotten Richards to pull over, as he thought he should explain everything to the other two, just in case his hunch was right. Dell always trusted his sixth sense and wanted to prepare the others because he had a plan. He didn't want to say anything before because he didn't want to put them off in any way.

Another reason for Butler's momentary panic was he'd puffed Dell's firm up so much. It was, after all, he who had put them forward for this covert operation in the first place and he certainly didn't want to end up with any egg on his face that might jeopardise his future in the Force. When Butler saw them pull into the warehouse, he couldn't hide his happiness and he started to feel a great sense of pride. His boys had returned safe and sound and not a blemish on any of them.

Dell was most surprised to see just the two officers standing there. He actually expected more, but then he was pretty more were on their way. The three men stepped out of the car, which had been parked next to Richard's vehicle. Dell, wearing his bag over his shoulder, told Richards to check the boot of his car to make sure the cash was still there, as a beaming Butler asked how it went.

"Good," replied Dell cagily.

"Good! Hand the guns over please, boys, then you can tell me all about it."

Dell turned to Funnel and motioned with his head for him to do as Butler said. Richards took his head out of the boot of the car and shouted over, "It's still there, Joe."

"Good," he replied. "Now, what do you wanna know then, Tom?" he asked.

"What happened, of course," said Butler.

"What happened was exactly what you asked for. Oh yeah, and we left the fella with the funny name for last, just to make him suffer a bit. Know what I mean?"

"Good boys. I knew you'd pull it off," said Butler, getting anxious again.

"Yeah, and he squeaked and squealed and made funny noises before we even put one in him. He made sounds like that mate of yours Durley used to make when he was in the pub."

As he was explaining what happened, a vehicle sped into the warehouse with lights on full, followed by a minibus-type motor with blacked-out windows, all with lights on full, temporarily blinding everyone for a moment. The cavalry had arrived as expected. Dell and Co. hadn't spotted the van parked among other vehicles in another warehouse car park, hidden out of view. But this was something more like what Dell had expected in the first place. Although they had been physically disarmed, he felt that mentally he was fully armed and had told Richards and Fennel such earlier.

Butler looked at the entourage that had now invaded the place and regret and embarrassment embraced him like a poison. Although he'd gone along with the plan from the off, he now felt so proud of his team he wanted the ground to open up and swallow him. The look on his face was one of deep regret. Why hadn't he tipped them off toward the end? Butler couldn't say, but he sincerely hoped they'd walk away from this situation alive.

But he and everyone else had overlooked the cunning of Dell, the very cunning and foresight that made him who and what he was. He didn't need a tipoff from Tommy Butler. He'd already thought the whole thing out himself. He'd already positions himself right in between Butler and Wilson for safekeeping. Dell looked at the SWAT team and said to Butler, "Oh yeah. So what do they fuckin' want?"

"I, I don't know, Joe."

"Not much, you fuckin' don't. You set us up, you dirty cunt," spat Dell.

"No, no I didn't, Joe. You got it wrong."

"Yeah, I did, didn't I? You must think I'm some sort of idiot. You'd better call that lot off, mate. 'Cause I got somethin' here you all might wanna take a look at," said Dell as he and his boys now faced a potential firing squad.

Butler had set them up, but he now found himself between a rock and a hard place. His feelings were very much divided and he knew he should never have tried to pit his wits against Dell. He never failed to surprise and today was not going to be any different.

They faced too many guns to count, but Dell's nerve held firm, even if Richards and Funnel's flapped a bit. Could Dell save them? They surely hoped so as they'd been so loyal and put their trust in him. After all, it was Dell that had gotten them in this position in the first place, although it hadn't take too much arm-twisting to be honest. If Big Burt could see the scene here now and how cool and calm his mate Dell was, he'd place every penny on his old mate walking away unscathed.

As Butler tried to sidle away from Dell, Dell moved along with him, using him as a human shield. He wasn't going to let him leave him a sitting duck. But, privately, Butler wanted Dell to prove him right and pull something extraordinary out of the hat. He was secretly in awe of him, which was out of character for a man who'd been in the police force so long.

Wilson on the other hand was the least informed man there and didn't have a clue what was going on. He was only there to make the numbers up and to give Butler backup, a sort of ventriloquist's dummy. Dell, now looking around at the situation, judged it was the right moment to exercise his authoritative position and told Butler as he held on to him with a vice-like grip, "Right. I'm in the driving seat now, so get them to lower their weapons while I demonstrate something."

Butler did as he was told and shouted over to the SWAT team to lower their guns.

"Okay, boys, lower the guns for a moment, please. Let him have his moment if you don't mind," said a nervous Butler, worried he was about to be at the business end of a police marksman's bullet. The team did as they were told. The situation was very tense for everyone, except, it appeared a very confident Dell, who slipped off his shoulder bag and pushed Butler toward the car bonnet of the vehicle provided to his team. Butler moved slowly and Dell kept pushing him. All eyes in the building were on the Swat Team. Dell wasn't going to take any chances. He wanted to protect himself and his loyal companions. Dell held out the bag for everyone to see.

No one in this company had ever been in a situation like this before, but Dell took control as if it was second nature to him. The foe that surrounded him had been trained for such circumstances, but what training had he had? Only the instinct to survive and lots of time to think out his future while on lockdown in prison and his absolute certainty he would never return.

While holding on to Butler with one hand, he slowly with the other pulled out his iPad.

"Watch this, you fuckin' maggot," demanded Dell as his eyes warily scanned the warehouse.

"Don't worry, Joe, mate, I'm all eyes," said a very nervous Butler.

"Don't call me, mate, you fuckin' toe rag," said Dell, pressing the play button. Butler stood wide-eyed and watched what unfolded before him. How could he have been so naïve to fall for such a stroke? This was a schoolboy error, but fair play to Dell whose video revealed every meeting he and Butler had ever had. Every conversation and all the details of Operation Desert Storm were on view, as clear as day, right there on Dell's screen. "Like what you see, Mr. Butler? I've made several copies and they've been distributed to various people in professional positions in my trust. All sealed on the instructions not to open, UNLESS ANYTHING HAPPENS TO ME OR MY PALS. Do

I make myself clear? Neither you nor anyone else, would want this exposé revealed, would you?"

Butler was silent as he watched his dream of promotion or early retirement disappear.

"Would you?" repeated Dell as he yanked Butler up to prompt an answer, his eyes blazing. Butler stood grim-faced as he thought for a moment, the SWAT team awaiting his command. Dell sure hoped this was enough to set them free.

After watching the damning footage, Butler knew it was over and Dell had won. Butler looked up at him with a slight hint of a smile and admiration on his face and nodded in Dell's direction. He then turned toward the team awaiting his command.

"Abort. Abort!" he shouted across the warehouse.

"What?" someone shouted back in disbelief.

"You heard me. It's over, done. He's got me hands down. Mission over. Put your weapons away and get out of here," instructed Butler. This was as much a relief to him as it was to Dell's mob. Butler had been shown up for his incompetence by a common criminal in front of many colleagues, but you had to hand it to Dell for his forward thinking and his cunning.

"How did you do it?" asked Butler.

"Remember that poppy I used to wear? It was camera'd," said Dell as a big smile appeared on his face.

"Bloody hell," replied Butler.

Richards and Funnel, who were both standing by the motor with all the cash in it, watched in semi-amazement as the people carrier and the unmarked car pulled back out of the warehouse and left.

"Thank Christ for that," said Funnel to Richards.

"You're not wrong," he replied. "I thought we were fucked."

Dell, reinforcing his grip on Butler, looked at him and said, "And I wanna fuckin' word with you."

"Look, Joe, it's not how it looks. Is it, Wilson?" he said, turning to his sidekick for support. Wilson pulled a face and shrugged. He didn't know anything.

"Don't give me that old bollocks. Right now, I want you to do me a favour," said Dell sternly.

"'Course, whatever you want," replied Butler.

"Get your slimy little arse down to that Legion we just saved from being destroyed and go and speak to my son's granddad and tell him about the threat they were under. Then tell him how helpful my two friends and I were in diffusing the whole thing. Alright? And don't give him none of your old flannel," said Dell.

"Of course I will, Joe. What's his name again?" asked Butler.

"John Hathaway. He's the club chairman or president or something. But make sure he gets the message. You understand?" said Dell, letting go of Butler.

"Consider it done, mate," said a relieved Butler.

"I told you earlier about calling me mate," said Dell, pointing his finger at him.

Dell turned to the others. "Come on, let's get out of here." They all jumped into the motor. They pulled away, leaving Butler and Wilson standing, watching them go.

"Win some, lose some. But it weren't that bad. I'm glad they got away. It was a dirty stroke, thinking of killing 'em off after all they'd done," said Butler to a completely bewildered Wilson. He'd have some serious explaining to do, but at least Dell had given him a copy of the video as proof of how he was completely outwitted by a very clever criminal indeed. Butler and Wilson watched as they sped out of sight, soon to be swallowed up in the Friday afternoon traffic leaving London en masse.

"Go on boys, go and enjoy yourselves," said Butler, with a hint of emotion in his voice. "You deserve it." He turned to Wilson and said, "I hope there's no hard feelings. I've grown to like that mob over the past few weeks. Anyway, there never was any proof of Dell being involved in the killing of that PC all them years ago."

"Eh?" said Wilson, even more dumfounded than before. This was all Chinese to him. He didn't have a clue what his superior was talking about.

Richards inevitably hit the traffic and the tension in the car started to ease up a bit and heart rates slowed. Funnel turned from the passenger seat to Dell, who had resumed his position in the back and said, "Fuckin' hell, Joe, that was a fuckin' close one."

"Yeah, it was a bit. But you boys had faith in me, didn't ya? I told you numerous times that I'd got us some insurance, didn't I?" said Dell, a huge grin spreading across his face.

"Yeah, you did. 'Course we had faith in you, mate." They all started laughing and the tension lifted even more. When the laughter stopped, Dell asked, "We have got the dough, haven't we, boys?"

"'Course we fuckin' have," said a very serious Richards. "A million quid in cold hard cash."

"Good! Right, I'm gonna ring Paul the pilot and tell him we're on our way. We're going on a well-earned holiday," said Dell, grinning from ear to ear. He had arranged for them to be smuggled out of the country by a friend of his who flew rich businessmen to Europe on a regular basis. Today, he was going to Spain.

"Ronnie Slaughter, here we come!" announced Dell.

"Yeah, and get them Viagras out!" chipped in Richards, who was actually smiling.

Dell sat back in the comfort of Richards' motor after he'd spoken to the pilot, feeling quite rightly very pleased with himself.

CHAPTER 42

The Met Police and the TV cameras were all over the murder scene and it looked very much to be just what it was, a gangland slaying on a rather large scale. Butler was ordered over there as Scotland Yard were about to retake control and create some fake news to cover their tracks. This was going to be made easier by the news of a car exploding on the very edge of London that had been seen leaving the scene at about the time of the massacre. Things started to look up again for Butler as the day's events unfolded.

"Thank you, God," said Butler at one point, looking to the sky.

In the Country during the late afternoon–early evening session, Big Burt and Mucky Mickey stood at the bar chatting. Mickey was saying what a strange occurrence the Durley thing had been and how you never know what skeletons people had in their closets. Burt listened and chipped in every now and again, but he was more interested in getting news on his mate Dell, when who should appear on the TV screen but Tommy Butler.

"Quick, turn it up," said Burt, pointing to the large flat screen TV on the wall by the bar. The pair listened intently as Butler told of a suspected terror cell being wiped out in a West London garage, and then going on to talk about a car bomb going off on the edge of the City and how it appeared they were connected.

Burt knew Dell was involved in all this, but he wasn't sure if Mickey knew or suspected anything. They both stood in complete silence as they stared at the screen. Mickey said in disbelief, "Bloody hell, a terror cell wiped out and a car bomb going off all on the same day. I don't fuckin' believe it."

Burt turned to him and said in his familiar rough deep voice for all to hear, "*WHAT A COUNTRY!*"